THE SNOW GLOBE AFFAIR

A CHRISTMAS COZY MYSTERY

ANA T. DREW

Editor: Janine Savage

This is a work of fiction.

Names, characters, places and incidents are the product of the author's imagination or are used fictitiously. Any resemblance to actual events, locales, or persons, living or dead, is purely coincidental.

CONTENTS

FREE BOOKS

Join my sporadic newsletter for new release and deal alerts, juicy anecdotes, deleted scenes, and subscriber-only giveaways! As a welcome gift, you'll receive a **hilarious novella** titled "The Canceled Christmas," and **a dessert cookbook.**

The quick and easy gluten-free recipes in it include:

- macarons, cookies, brownies
- tiramisu, fritters, puddings
- and more!

Sign up here:
ana-drew.com / free-books.

My newsletter is a spam-free zone.

ABOUT THE AUTHOR

Ana T. Drew is the evil mastermind behind the recent series of murders in the fictional French town of Beldoc. A first place winner of the Chanticleer MYSTERY & MAYHEM Book Awards, she is published in several languages, both independently and traditionally (with HarperCollins France and Straarup & Co).

When not writing cozy mysteries, she can be found perfecting her low-carb cookies or watching *The Rookie* to cope with the void left by *Castle*.

Ana lives in Paris with her husband and their dog, but her heart resides in Provence.

Website: ana-drew.com

amazon.com/author/ana-drew
x.com/AnaTDrew
facebook.com/AnaDrewAuthor
tiktok.com/@ana.t.drew
bookbub.com/authors/ana-t-drew
goodreads.com/anadrew

CHAPTER 1

Catherine "Cat" Cavallo hurries through the corridors of the *métro*, her gaze darting from banner to banner. Half of them are selling dreams, urging passersby to grab the perfect gift. Others rave about Christmas films, musicals, and delicacies. And then there are a few unclassifiable ones like this:

A thrilling scavenger hunt, the likes of which Paris has never seen!
For adults. The chance of a lifetime!

Her interest piqued, Cat slows down to read the fine print and see what it's all about. But then she decides not to stop. There's no time. She took her morning off to get a specific task done—not to loiter around métro billboards. If she can finish her Christmas shopping by noon, she can be back in time to have lunch with her shop neighbor and friend Dalila before her client arrives at two-thirty.

As Cat emerges from the mouth of the métro, the cold nips at her like a cheeky pigeon on a piece of croissant. Pulling her wool cap down over her ears, she quickens her pace toward the entrance to the Tuileries Garden.

The next couple of hours are going to be a pain.

She makes her way through the boisterous crowd of people shopping at the brightly lit stalls of the Christmas market. It's a quarter to ten on a gray Monday morning. Christmas is still almost a month away. But none of those facts have deterred the market goers.

In the background, la Grande Roue—Paris's Ferris wheel—looms large, its silhouette a funky contrast to the historic buildings lining the edge of the garden. The tantalizing aromas of street vendor food fill the air, tempting Cat. If she were here for leisure, she'd be indulging in gooey raclette or roasted chestnuts, washing it all down with fragrant mulled wine. But this isn't that kind of visit, and she has no time to indulge.

She pushes past the booths, through the crowds of delighted children, doting grandparents, and hand-holding couples. With each step, her unease swells in silent rebellion against the enchantment of the park.

Cat lets out a heavy breath.

No doubt, those who know her well would point out that she feels this way because someone tried to kill her this time last year. That may well be the case. But there's another, more trivial reason for her current anxiety—Christmas presents.

In a sane universe, gift shopping would be a breeze for a professional clairvoyant. But our world being the mess that it is, Cat's psychic powers are useless when it comes to her family and herself. That unfortunate blind spot includes never having a clue what to get her loved ones for Christmas or any other gift-giving occasion. She may be able to glimpse a stranger's future, but she has difficulty predicting if her twin sister will enjoy a book, or if Grandma will like a necklace. To say that Cat's track record in that department is spotty would be a sympathetic euphemism. The honest way to look at it is to admit that she's consistently off the mark.

Forget the sixth sense, girl, and pretend you have some common sense! Can you do that?

Her jaw set, Cat zooms past the stalls of glittery, colorful baubles that, under other circumstances, would have caught her attention. But today she's more interested in the practical than the pretty. Cat has no illusions that she'll ever be able to pick out the perfect gift for her doting father, her adoring grandmother, her three sisters and their partners, or her niece, Rania, whom she loves to death. But she's hell-bent on making sure her choices this Yule will at least be of some use to her relatives.

As she dodges a pair of overexcited kids, a vendor waves a hand with practiced cheerfulness. "Mademoiselle! A special charm for the holiday?"

He holds up a snow globe. Designed for tourists, it has the requisite flakes of glitter swirling around a quaint little house next to a snow-covered fir tree against the backdrop of the shimmery Eiffel Tower.

"No thanks," Cat mumbles, barely slowing her pace.

But then she takes another look at the globe—and stops. Inside the glass sphere, the snowy wonderland fades into the background, making way for something unexpected and completely out of place. It's an eerily realistic male figure, its presence vivid, almost tangible within the snow globe.

Dumbfounded, Cat gawks at the tall, brown-haired man, dressed in a bottle green wool turtleneck and beige tailored chinos. Midthirties, lovely jawline, broad shoulders. His heavy, black-rimmed glasses cut his hot allure with a dash of geekiness as he stares back at Cat.

She takes a step closer, unable to tear her eyes away from the mesmerizing figure, half expecting him to speak to her. But when she blinks, he's gone, leaving only the tacky winter scene in his wake.

"Are you all right?" the vendor's voice cuts through her confusion.

"Huh?" She looks up at him before rubbing her eyes. "Yes, I'm fine, thank you."

He chuckles. "Seemed like you saw a ghost."

Cat gives him a tight smile, her gaze drifting back once again to the banal snow globe. There was only one other time in her life when a vision had hit her in a way just as sudden and unbidden as this. It was during that indelible rough patch last year shortly after the worst breakup in her measly love life when an assassin had her in his crosshairs.

She reaches out, fingers trembling as they close around the glass. "How much?"

"For you? Twenty euros. A steal for such a unique snow globe!"

Unique, my foot!

Then again, it kind of is, isn't it?

She hands over the money.

The seller passes her the globe, wrapped in protective paper. "Take care of yourself. And, Merry Christmas!"

She wishes him the same, tucks the globe safely into her backpack, and wobbles away.

What the deuce just happened?

CHAPTER 2

At last! In her shop on Quai de Valmy, Cat takes her coat off. She heads straight to her séance room and lights some sandalwood incense. Its scent never fails to calm her. The indigo of the wallpaper, which shrouds the room in a mystical hue, and the deep red of the Persian rug on the couch have a similar effect. Surrounded by these carefully chosen elements here in her sanctuary, Cat always feels the weight of the outside world dissolve. That allows her senses to sharpen and her mind to prepare for the visions that await.

Speaking of visions.

She picks up the snow globe and turns it over and over in her hands, watching the snow settle inside the glass ball. The handsome stranger remains conspicuously absent.

It's just a silly trinket!

The weird vision that struck her at the Christmas market was no doubt a fluke—or, rather, a dud caused by the stress of gift shopping. After buying the snow globe, she somehow managed to compose herself and complete her shopping within the allotted time. Her bamboozlement returned with a vengeance on her trip back to the office when she forgot to pick up the pizza for her and Dalila's lunch. She remembered on her doorstep and dashed out of the building, cursing herself. Fortunately, the line at the pizza place was short, and Cat was back—with the pizza—by one.

Phew.

The door to the adjacent shop swings open with a flourish, and Dalila bursts in with a laptop under one arm. Instantly, her bubbling energy fills the space. She's gone full Oriental today. Her eyes are heavily lined with kohl and her long, dark hair cascades in loose waves over her shoulders. Her fashionably folksy kaftan, a riot of bold red and black patterns, sways as she moves. Her eyes sparkle with excitement as she walks over to the round table draped with an Indian motif tablecloth, sets her laptop down, and pulls up a chair.

Assuming she's excited about the pizza, Cat serves her a slice. "I got your favorite, prosciutto and arugula."

"Great, thanks," Dalila mutters, opening her laptop. "You have to see this!"

Cat scoots closer and looks at her screen. It's flashing with the bold colors of a promotional poster, announcing an "unforgettable, epoch-making scavenger hunt."

Could be the one I glimpsed in the métro… "I saw something similar on a poster this morning," she offers.

Dalila squints at her. "Did you read the small print?"

"No."

"You should have!" Dalila's fingers dance across the keyboard as she pulls up a website. "People are freaking out on every psychic, clairvoyant, and medium discussion board I checked today."

Cat knits her eyebrows. "Why?"

"The organizers are looking for teams made up of a mathematician and a psychic. The prize is a hundred grand each for the winning team. I already signed up!"

"You mean… a hundred thousand euros each?"

"Yes!"

"That's a lot of money," Cat admits. "But I'm swamped this month."

Dalila hikes an eyebrow. "You're always *swamped*. When was the last time you had a date?"

"I'm not ready."

"It's been a year, Cat! Get over yourself, already! It's not like he died on you like your mom, is it? He dumped you."

Her words recall the last time Cat saw her mother alive. She was holding onto Cat's youngest sister Flo, then seven, to protect her from falling debris.

Dalila clamps her hand over her mouth. "I'm so sorry, hon! I didn't mean... That was a most unfortunate turn of phrase."

Cat waves it off. "No biggie. What are the odds of winning this contest?"

"That's beside the point, dum-dum! You've been holed up here, withering away, for much too long. All work and no play. You need this."

"No, I don't."

Dalila rolls her eyes. "Oh, come on! This could be a blast, a real adventure! And who knows? Maybe even lucrative."

Cat's skepticism lingers as she looks at the colorful display on the screen. The idea of scrambling around Paris in the freezing cold and chasing whatever wild goose the game master lines up, seems daunting.

"Come on," Dalila presses. "When was the last time you did something just for the thrill of it? It will be a fun distraction if nothing else."

"I might've considered it, if you and I could do a psychic-psychic duo..."

"No exceptions," Dalila says. "Every duo must have a psychic and a math head."

"You sure?"

"Let's hear it from the horse's mouth!" Dalila clicks the Play button in the center of a video frame embedded in the web page.

The image of an impeccably dressed sixty-something man with a neat little beard, a bow tie, and piercing blue eyes, comes to life. A female journalist's voice outside the frame introduces him as Damien Wiet, a business mogul, philanthropist, patron of the arts, and mastermind behind the scavenger hunt.

The interviewer holds the mic up to him. "Please, tell us why this Christmas hunt is so special."

"Because it's so much more than a game!" Wiet exclaims. "It's an unforgettable adventure into the world of art, mystery, and the spirit of Christmas."

The journalist leans in. "Can you tell us more about the prize?"

"I'm glad you asked!"

Wiet brings a framed painting into view. The style is as poetic as it is recognizable, even to someone whose art education amounts to tidbits shared by her sister the gallerist and an odd visit to a museum.

It's a Chagall.

The painting is vibrant with color and whimsy. It depicts Santa Claus soaring through an orange sky on a white horse holding a Christmas tree—the horse does the holding, to be clear. Below, a woman cradles an infant, much like the Madonna and Child. Their faces are turned upward in wonder. In the distant background, a village nestles in the green.

"*Father Christmas* by Marc Chagall," Wiet says. "This particular Santa was painted in 1952."

"Are there others?" The reporter's voice is tinged with surprise. "I had no idea Chagall had Christmas-themed paintings!"

"Oh, he has a few," Wiet answers. "If you ask me, the best is the 1938 gem, *Christmas Fantasy*. But most of his Noël-themed works are watercolors and gouaches depicting Santa Claus. Hence the name of my scavenger hunt, Looking for *Father Christmas*!"

"Very apt," the journalist comments.

"I'm hardly exaggerating when I tell you that in the 1950s, Chagall painted one Santa Claus a year," Wiet says. "He was in a good place once again, happily remarried, healing from all the suffering he'd endured during the war. And his paintings show it."

The video continues, and Wiet talks about Luc Stratte, the con artist who had stolen the painting from Chagall's widow back in 1990.

"Stratte was a high school dropout who worked as a mole catcher," Wiet says. "But he was gutsy and charismatic. He also had a knack for solving puzzles."

"You're using the past tense..."

"He's dead now," Wiet clarifies. "He did get caught before he died, though."

The reporter's finger appears in the frame. "So, this *Father Christmas* is the painting he'd stolen?"

"This is but one of the thirty or so paintings he'd pilfered from Valentina Chagall."

"When did the police recover it?"

"This one?" Wiet smiles enigmatically. "Never."

"Then who found it?"

"I did."

After a stunned second, the journalist demands, "How? Were you able to persuade Luc Stratte to reveal where he'd hidden whatever the police hadn't found?"

"Unfortunately, I learned about Stratte only recently when I returned to France after three decades in Australia. Stratte was dead by then."

The reporter listens without interrupting.

Wiet goes on, "My fondness for math and cryptograms, much like Stratte's, plus some help from a clairvoyant led me to the painting."

"Extraordinary!" the reporter enthuses. "Bravo, Monsieur Wiet! Is this painting now part of your art collection?"

"Oh no, I returned it to its rightful owners, the heirs of Marc Chagall."

"Of course, you did." The reporter coughs, clearly embarrassed she hadn't assumed he would.

"That said, I'll be happy to buy it at market value if they decide to sell it to me," Wiet adds.

"What's its market value?"

"Three hundred thousand euros, I'd say." Wiet shrugs. "It's gouache and ink on paper. We're a long way from the thirty million that Chagall's oil painting *Les Amoureux* fetched at Sotheby's a few years back."

"Thirty million!"

"As I said, not the same category."

"Was it your experience tracking it down that inspired you to organize this scavenger hunt?" the reporter asks.

"Indeed, it was. I thought, why not let others experience that thrill?"

"How thoughtful and generous of you!"

Damien Wiet nods. "To make it even more fun, I threw in some puzzles and ciphers of my own creation. Consider it my Christmas present to the psychics and math buffs of this town!"

"And the general public," the journalist interjects.

"Yes, of course," Wiet agrees. "It's a pleasure to be able to share my love of art and fascination with ciphers with everyone."

"What if one of the competing psychics *sees* where you hid the prize from the get-go?" the journalist inquires. "That would ruin your game, wouldn't it?"

Wiet shakes his head. "Not going to happen."

"Why not?"

"The clairvoyant who helped me find *Father Christmas* is one of a kind, the best living psychic in the world. No one comes close, believe me."

He puffs out his chest as if the abilities of the clairvoyant he just praised to the skies had rubbed off on him. Then he continues, "But even so, her gift only did so much. My skills and determination did the rest."

"Who is that exceptional clairvoyant, if I may ask?"

"She doesn't wish to be named," Wiet replies.

"Jacqueline!" Cat and Dalila cry at the same time.

"Can't see who else it could be," Dalila adds. "The woman is a living legend."

They fall silent for a brief moment, gazing at the web page.

"Are you feeling the thrill yet?" Dalila asks Cat, her expression playful. "Me, I can barely wait for the kickoff!"

There's no denying the spark of excitement that Wiet's pitch and Dalila's pep have lit in Cat's heart.

What if Dalila is right? Could this adventure be just what Cat needs right now?

The front door buzzer interrupts her introspection. It's two-thirty already, and her Wednesday afternoon client is as punctual today as she's been every week since her first visit.

Dammit!

CHAPTER 3

Zack stands by the panoramic window of his QuantumTech Cybernetics' office in La Défense. The modern glass façades of the neighboring skyscrapers gleam in the afternoon sun, casting sharp reflections. Next to him is Damien Wiet, a potential investor, who seems impressed by the view.

Wiet gestures toward the skyscrapers outside. "This district with its futuristic architecture that's such a contrast to the rest of Paris, is a uniquely fitting backdrop for your company."

"The thought has occurred to me too," Zack turns away from the window, a slight smile playing on his lips.

With a congenial nod, he leads the way to the conference table in the center of the spacious, minimalist office. The room is a blend of function and elegance with interactive screens and digital interfaces seamlessly integrated into the clean lines of the furniture.

They sit across from each other at the tempered glass table. For a moment, Zack listens to the hum of the city, muffled by the high-end windows that create a bubble of tranquility. He clasps his hands, ready to dive into the specifics of his business.

"I'm all ears," Wiet says.

"Great," Zack begins. "Let me give you a deeper insight into our operations and how your investment could accelerate our growth."

"Before you do that, can I ask you something?"

Zack gestures with an open palm. "Please do."

"Why do you want to accelerate growth? You've done pretty well for a new company." Wiet narrows his eyes. "Why this hunger to grow fast?"

Zack hesitates before answering. "I know I'm expected to blather on about my ambition to become an industry leader…"

"But you won't?"

"Don't get me wrong, I do have that ambition," Zack says, hastening to reassure his would-be investor. "But that's not why I'm looking for capital."

"Then why?"

"Because I'm responsible for six people, and I need to bring on three more to meet our goals," Zack replies. "Considering that the cost of labor in this country is—"

"Absurd," Wiet interjects.

"I was going to say 'prohibitive,' but I like your term better."

"Thank you."

Zack leans back in his seat. "What I want, Monsieur Wiet, is to ensure that my employees and their families are financially secure for the next decade."

"Are you telling me that's your main motivation?"

"It's the truth," Zack admits.

"You didn't have to answer truthfully."

"What can I say? I'm a truthful guy." Zack smiles. "Which is why I never liked playing poker, but I do love protecting our clients' digital assets."

Wiet laughs. "Is this your first company?"

"Yes."

"Thought so." Wiet stares Zack in the eye. "May I speak as frankly as you did, Monsieur Rigaud?"

"Of course."

Wiet strokes his tie. "Your only fiduciary duty is to your shareholders, not to your employees."

"I am aware of that, and I take my obligations to our investors very seriously."

"Good." Wiet nods. "And a word of advice. Remind yourself from time to time that your employees aren't your family."

You just wasted some valuable advice, sir.

Zack needs no such reminders. He's the only child of a couple consisting of a now-dead narcissist and an irresponsible jerk. For him, being on his own is a blessing—and he prefers to keep it that way. No, the reason he's so keen to do right by his employees has nothing to do with likening them to family.

The reason is gratitude.

His team has worked their tails off for the past two years to help him build the company. They took a huge risk when they chose to join a start-up over an established high-tech giant. Zack knows his luck. He's been able to attract some of the best software engineers in the country, especially Greg, his lead developer. And he couldn't have gotten where he is without his assistant, Letitia, who keeps him organized and on track.

"You don't owe your employees anything," Wiet dishes out more unsolicited advice. "You know that, right? Unless you used blackmail, they came to work for you because they smelled potential. They saw promise."

"And I have to deliver on it."

"Very well, Monsieur Rigaud." Wiet pulls a digital tablet from his briefcase. "What can you promise *me*? I'm particularly interested in how you integrate cryptography with cybersecurity."

Enthusiastically, Zack presses a button that causes a screen to rise smoothly from the table. "We use cryptography to develop secure communication protocols for our clients."

Wiet nods.

"We encrypt data and protect against breaches and hacks," Zack continues. "We also provide services such as secure email encryption, VPNs for Internet access, and secure cloud storage solutions."

"What about AI? There's great potential there I am told."

"Not great—tremendous!"

Zack outlines QuantumTech's AI-enhanced innovative approaches to cybersecurity, illustrating his points with graphs and data on the screen. The presentation is slick, mirroring the technological prowess of their surroundings.

Wiet tilts his head to the side. "And how is the market responding to your products?"

"We have a small but loyal and growing customer base," Zack replies. "And we're already profitable—only two years in! Imagine what we could do with some serious capital..."

He leaves the sentence hanging.

Wiet leans back. "You're hoping to take your company to the next level."

"My ambition isn't just to keep up, Monsieur Wiet. I want to set the pace. I want QuantumTech Cybernetics to innovate, expand, and drive the industry forward."

"Are you a cryptographer yourself?" Wiet asks, his gaze sharp.

"I started with a bachelor's in mathematics, then specialized in computer science and cryptography."

"Excellent, excellent."

"We've grown over the last two years, but I'm still deeply involved in every project," Zack adds.

"Very good!" The sincere approval in Wiet's tone is as telling as the smile that tugs at the corners of his mouth.

Zack smiles back. Potential investors tend to find it

reassuring when the CEO is intimately familiar with the subject matter.

Zack crosses his arms over his chest. He's done talking for now. The ball is in Wiet's court.

The investor glances around the minimalist office, then back at Zack. "Your passion is clear. And passion coupled with expertise is a winning formula."

"I couldn't agree more."

Wiet watches him intently. "Do you like solving puzzles?"

"You mean, for fun?"

"Yes."

"I used to, but I haven't had time lately."

Wiet slides a glossy flyer across the sleek table toward Zack. It's bright and festive with details about a scavenger hunt splashed across it in bold colors.

"You should sign up for this," Wiet suggests. "There's a 100,000-euro prize for every member of the winning team."

Zack glances at the flyer, then back at Wiet. "I'm sure it'll be fun, but between running a company and looking for venture capital, my schedule is full."

"Something tells me you love a challenge, Monsieur Rigaud."

"Who doesn't?"

Wiet arches an eyebrow. "You'd be surprised how many people don't. Anyway, I've designed several ciphers for this hunt that I'm certain you'll find stimulating."

"You're behind this hunt?"

Wiet points to a website URL on the flyer. "Would you like to watch the interview I gave last week to explain the why and the how? It's very brief."

Zack types in the web address and plays the interview on the retractable screen.

When it's over, he glances at Wiet. "Psychics? Really?"

"You may think they're all frauds, but the fact is, one of them helped me find *Father Christmas.*"

Zack harrumphs. "Just a lucky break."

"The poet Guillaume Apollinaire called Chagall's work supernatural," Wiet asserts, as if it's pertinent.

"I'm afraid I'm the wrong person to bait with a supernatural challenge."

Unperturbed, Wiet rises to his feet, adjusts his suit, and plays another card. "How about I bait you with being a Good Samaritan during the holidays?"

"Meaning?" Zack stands up as well.

"Meaning, you have a chance to make a difference," Wiet replies. "If a team finds the painting, not only will they win big, but I'll donate 100K to the Chagall Museum in Nice, another 100K to the Louvre, and 100K to promote math in schools."

Zack makes a suitably impressed face.

Wiet studies Zack's reaction before concluding, "If no one finds it, there will be no donations."

Why does he care so much that I take part in this?

As if reading Zack's mind, Wiet adds, "You're hoping to raise at least five million from me, right? Consider this a test to help me make up my mind."

"Understood." Zack disapproves of the mogul's approach to decision-making, but he wisely keeps any signs of his displeasure from showing on his face.

Wiet extends his hand. "Don't disappoint me, Monsieur Rigaud."

They shake hands, and Zack walks Wiet to the exit. After the door clicks shut behind Wiet, Zack returns to the window. The light has shifted, bathing the room in golden hues. He picks up the flyer, pondering his would-be investor's unconventional ways, but more pressing matters take center stage in his mind.

In five minutes, he has a back-to-back marathon that could put the Olympics to shame. First, a powwow with Greg to dissect and evaluate his product developers' latest brainchild. Next, Zack will dial into a high-stakes conference call that could make or break his relationship with a key customer.

Then, it's strategy time with his marketing guru to map out their next big campaign. And just when he'd be desperate to catch his breath, he's scheduled for some number crunching with his accountant to navigate the treacherous waters of taxes.

But the ultimate challenge?

Once all the spreadsheets and strategy decks are put to bed, he'll be off to his home base in the 9th arrondissement where the real battleground awaits. There at eight in the evening, Zack must tackle the most daunting task of his day—a meeting of his building's Christmas Planning Committee.

CHAPTER 4

Zack throttles his Yamaha to life and moments later, the world around him becomes a dynamic canvas. He navigates the congested cityscape toward his building on rue du Faubourg Montmartre, delighting in the fast, fluid motion on his scooter.

As he rides, his thoughts turn to Damien Wiet's visit this afternoon. The idea of joining the hunt tickles his competitive spirit. The experience could be a fun diversion, but also an opportunity to exercise his puzzle-solving muscles, show Wiet what Zack is made of, and convince him to invest in QuantumTech Cybernetics.

He swerves to avoid a cyclist.

Who knows, this departure from his usual routine might even spark fresh ideas for his work…

Should I make time for this? Pondering the question, Zack glides his Yamaha into the garage box he rents in a modern building a few blocks from his own. With a smooth maneuver, he parks the scooter, secures it, and makes his way to his own building.

At the massive green gate of the nineteenth-century limestone, Zack punches in the code and enters a charming, cobbled courtyard. A cast-iron bench graces one end. Potted plants are artfully arranged along the walls and a large, sturdy magnolia tree takes pride of place in the center, towering over its potted courtiers. Though its branches are currently bare, there is a serene beauty to its starkness.

Zack likes the building and his apartment, but it was this courtyard that convinced him five years ago to take out a mortgage and buy a piece of this condo. Just before he enters the lobby, his private line rings. Zack glances at his screen, his mouth curling down. He declines the call and responds with a text message.

Busy. Is it urgent?

Dad's reply is instantaneous.

No. Call me when you get a chance.

Zack doesn't reply to that second message. He won't call back. Dad must've suspected as much. Well, now he knows it.

By the time Zack gets to his apartment, swaps his suit for a sweater and hurries down to the second floor. It's already a quarter past eight and he's late.

The president of the HOA board, Lucile Flores, opens the door. "You're late."

"I'm sorry."

She leads him into the snug confines of her living room festooned with garlands and string lights. Sitting around the coffee table, cluttered with teacups, cookies and catalogs, are Ajay Bhatt, the board's vice president, and Monica Pereira, the building's no-nonsense concierge.

Lucile, Ajay, and Monica are the permanent members of the building's ad hoc Christmas Planning Committee that pops up every November and disbands in early January. Every year since he moved in, the Unholy Trinity, as Zack has dubbed them, has tried to browbeat him into joining the committee, because he owns the largest share of the condo. Zack had been able to wiggle out of it in the past, but this year, they left him no choice.

He sits in a leather armchair and smiles, trying to look at ease.

Lucile pours him a cup of tea.

Zack sips it at once, willing himself to ignore its scalding temperature. *They can't expect me to talk while I'm drinking, can they?*

Leaving him be for now, the Unholy Trinity members pick up where they'd left off when Zack arrived. He drinks as slowly as he can while they bicker over decorations for the glass doors to the building's lobby.

Monica brandishes a catalog and points at a Christmas tree sticker. "That should be it!"

"But we're going to have an actual Christmas tree in the lobby," Lucile points out. "The sticker should be something else—Santa, Rudolph, elves…" She turns to Ajay for help.

Ajay, enchanted by everything Lucile says or does as always, spreads his arms helplessly. "I'm happy with whatever you choose, ladies."

The ladies glare at him, dissatisfied.

Ajay turns to Zack.

Monica and Lucile follow.

Zack sets his teacup down, mentally dons his captain-of-industry-leading-his-troops hat and picks up a catalog from the top of the stack. He flips through it, stopping on a page with a glittering winter forest scene.

That'll do. "How about this instead?"

To his surprise, nods go around the room, and Monica even throws in an enthusiastic, "That's actually perfect, Zack!"

With the doors debate unexpectedly settled, Zack braces for the next agenda item—the condo Christmas party. He winces in anticipation of the familiar dance of discomfort that's about to unfold. Lucile will suggest they hold the party in Zack's apartment, which is by far the biggest unit in the condo. Monica will heartily agree. Ajay will shift and look away. Zack will say he doesn't think it's a good idea. Awkwardness will ensue.

When Lucile opens her mouth, Zack jumps in with a distraction. He gestures toward the Nativity scene set up under Lucile's Christmas tree. "That's probably the cutest Christmas manger I've ever seen."

"Really?" Lucile glances at the clay figurines, her expression tinged with embarrassment. "It's been in my late husband's family for generations."

It looks old enough to have been at the actual Nativity.

"I know it's tacky," Lucile says, "but it has a lot of sentimental value, you see."

"I wouldn't call it tacky," Ajay protests. "The artistry is remarkable."

Lucile tucks a strand of gray hair behind her ear. "Well, it's a way to remember the reason for the season, isn't it?"

Zack, intent on keeping the spotlight off his apartment, prods shamelessly, "It must have some great stories to tell."

"Oh, it does!" Lucile's eyes turn misty.

Unfortunately, before she can start reminiscing, Monica looks up from her watch, impatience in her eyes. "About the Christmas party—"

Everyone turns back to Zack.

The room falls into another awkward silence. Then, there's a knock on the door. Lucile opens it. Monica's boys burst in as if they're reenacting a Viking raid.

"Mom!" the younger one bellows. "We can't find the ice cream!"

"Yeah, the freezer's just full of pathetic vegetables," the older one says, backing up his brother.

"It's too cold for ice cream," Monica counters. "Supply will resume in April."

The boys' protests erupt into cries of disbelief, betrayal, and human rights violations, but Monica just rolls her eyes.

With an I'm-raising-future-trade-unionists apology to the adults, she herds her sons out.

The siblings leave behind a blend of eau de candy and gym socks that sends Zack reeling down memory lane back to his days in Lille.

With his defenses down, Monica renews the assault, "So, Monsieur Rigaud, about the Christmas party. Your apartment has the space. It would be perfect."

"How about we rent a room?" Zack offers, thinking quickly. "Like at a community center or a bar? It would be fun and less... um, invasive."

The idea hangs in the air.

"I'll pay for it, of course," Zack hastens to add. "Consider it my Christmas gift to the building."

"I could get behind that, and I'll be happy to chip in," Ajay jumps in, bless his sensible soul.

As a recently retired software engineer who worked for industry giants, Ajay can certainly afford to chip in—unlike Monica for instance.

Zack nods his thanks, not so much for the offer of cosponsorship, but for respecting Zack's boundaries.

The men stare expectantly at the women.

The women stare at their hands.

Zack stands up. "Well, let me know once you've had time to think about it. And thanks for the tea, Lucile! It was delicious."

With that, he bids the Unholy Trinity good night and heads out.

CHAPTER 5

Cat sits across from her client in the dimly lit séance room, the air thick with the scent of lavender incense. The flickering candles cast shadows that dance across the walls. The tranquil ambiance created by the incense and candles helps her slip into a trance and connect with her client's physical and spiritual energy.

"What would you like to know?" Cat asks in a soft voice.

Isa, the client, shifts in her chair. "I need to know if I'm going to get back together with my ex."

Cat focuses on the nearest candlelight as she dives into Isa's aura, vibrant yet tangled with complex emotions. Images and sensations swirl in the space between them. Then, slowly, a vision forms.

"I see you in the arms of a man," Cat begins. "Medium height, athletic build, light brown hair, cropped short, receding hairline, blue eyes."

Isa interrupts hastily, "That's not him. My ex has dark hair and green eyes. Are you sure?"

Cat exhales slowly, meeting Isa's anxious gaze. "That's the man I see you with."

"Yes, fine, but will my ex grovel? Will he come back?" Isa persists, her voice tight with hope.

"I don't see that. Then again, I'm not in the business of scamming my clients by giving answers set in stone."

Isa blinks, confusion written all over her face. "I don't understand."

"Humans have free will," Cat explains. "We have the ability to change our future at any given time. What clairvoyants see are the options or potentials that present themselves at the time of the reading."

"The psychic I saw last week told me he was going to grovel..." Isa trails off, her brow furrowed.

Cat does her best to keep her composure. "May I ask why you're here, since you already had such a definitive answer?"

"I wanted a second opinion."

God give me patience!

Cat feels the energy drain from the room, the weight of Isa's ambivalence pulling at her. Clients such as her demand definitive answers. Funnily enough, they refuse to accept them if they don't like them. Even more ironically, they balk at nondeterministic readings that leave room for alternative paths. The truth is, they aren't ready to hear what the universe wants to whisper to them. That's not what they're looking for. They'll bounce from psychic to psychic until they stumble upon one that gives them the answer they were hoping for.

Readings like this one leave Cat tired for the rest of the day, if not longer. But there's something that makes Isa's case worse—her neediness. It reminds Cat painfully of her own.

When Cat's last relationship ended in the same way as the previous one and the one before that with the guy dumping her, Cat declared a unilateral moratorium on dating. She read a ton of self-help books and concluded that it was her needy, clingy side that was ruining her relationships. The books were unanimous. Don't even think about meeting someone new until you've fixed your problem and learned to be happy on your own.

Detoxing her system of this dependency has been Cat's goal in life for the last year. Since she's nowhere near the nirvana of self-sufficiency yet, she doesn't expect to be in another relationship anytime soon.

"If you can't give me a definitive answer," Isa interrupts Cat's gloomy thoughts, "can you at least put a percentage on the likelihood of my ex begging me to take him back?"

Cat forces a smile. "I haven't seen him on the current path of your future, so unless he or you do something drastic to change that path, I'd say it's a very small probability."

Isa asks another question. Cat summons all her willpower to concentrate enough to see through the fog in her mind. The session drags on with Cat meandering and Isa reluctantly nodding and scribbling down notes.

When she leaves, Cat's shoulders sag under the strain of the encounter. With a grunt she rises, blows out the candles, and opens the curtains. The snow globe on the shelf by the window—the one she bought at the Christmas market—catches her eye. Over the last week, Cat has stared at it quite a bit, but she never saw the bespectacled hottie again. It hadn't been a proper vision but a fluke, a glitch in her brain, likely triggered by the anxiety of gift shopping.

She's still staring at the globe when Dalila sweeps in, dressed in a gorgeous new Oriental kaftan and clutching a laptop.

"The deadline is tonight," Dalila announces.

"Please, not that scavenger hunt again! I already told you I'm not doing it."

With dramatic flair, Dalila flips open her laptop. A registration form appears on the screen.

Cat leans closer and inspects it. "Girl, what have you done?"

"I may have helped fate a bit by prefilling your details," Dalila admits.

With a brazen look on her face, she places the cursor over the Submit button—and hits Enter before Cat can formulate a protest.

Cat's mouth hangs open, the beginning of a "wait'" dying on her lips. A confirmation page loads, cheerful and final. Dalila throws her head back and lets out a mwa-ha-ha that would make the evilest of cartoon baddies proud.

"You're welcome," she says, when she's done laughing like a villain.

"You're insane."

Cat puts her hands on her hips and scowls. But she doubts Dalila will buy it, because she can already feel the corners of her own mouth twitching upward, and the anger that was boiling inside her a moment ago morphs into reluctant amusement.

Dalila's expression becomes serious. "Have you tried to induce a vision about this treasure hunt?"

Cat shakes her head. "Have you?"

"I read the dregs of the coffee I made for you after lunch."

Cat's eyes bulge. "Without my permission? You know I don't read my own future. I thought you respected that…"

"I do," Dalila assures her. "But when I asked Saint Charbel for guidance, he didn't forbid it."

"It's me you should've asked for guidance!" Cat exclaims in frustration.

"Anyway, the dregs were adamant that you do the hunt, so I signed you up."

"Adamant how? Did you see me find the Chagall and win the race?"

"We've been renting this place together for how long? Three years?" Dalila gives Cat a reproachful look. "You should know by now that coffee dregs can't be that specific. I just saw you having the adventure of your life."

"I already had the adventure of my life a year ago, dodging murderers."

Dalila cocks her head. "Was it fun?"

"No," Cat admits.

"This one will be, I promise!"

Aping her friend's head tilt, Cat says, "I believe you, but have you considered that since we can't be paired, we can't both be the first to find *Father Christmas*? If my duet wins, that means yours loses."

"That doesn't bother me." Dalila shuts her laptop. "We Maronites are a fair play bunch. If you best me, I'll be happy for you."

Cat gives her a squint-eyed stare and then rubs her temples, too exhausted to argue.

"Hey, cheer up and think of the good time that awaits," Dalila says, heading for the door. "Plus, the one hundred grand if you win!"

She stops in the doorway and turns around. "I hereby pledge that if I'm victorious, I'll use ten percent of my winnings to pay a year's rent for both of us, up front. Will you do the same?"

"Of course." Cat grins. "Now I see why you were so eager to sign me up."

"I've made sure we both have a blast, and I've doubled the chances we won't have to worry about rent for a year. Go, Dalila!"

With a proud toss of her head, she flings back her shiny mane and sashays out, her kaftan swaying prettily.

Cat sits down to let the reality of her new commitment sink in.

If I can have some fun, the hunt won't be a total waste of time, will it?

CHAPTER 6

Clad in a shimmery body-hugging gown with a long skirt that flares at the hem, Cat gazes at the magnificent interior of the chapel at Petits-Augustins. Dalila adjusts the strap of her glamorous number before covering her shoulders with her superb pashmina shawl.

Cat turns to her. "Did you know this place is part of the Beaux-Arts school?"

"I had no idea it even existed," Dalila replies. "But if I had to come up with a location to kick off the hunt, I couldn't've picked a better one."

Cat's gaze lingers on the intricate frescoes and murals, some of which look familiar. *Could they be replicas of Renaissance paintings?*

Actually, that would be quite appropriate, since copying the masters is how fine arts students learn to paint and sculpt.

Tilting her head upward, Cat takes in the vaulted ceiling that soars above. It's high, but not Gothic. Apparently, this chapel is only a few centuries old. Regardless, it's dripping with history.

Her gaze sweeps over the festive decorations. Garlands

twine around the columns, twinkling lights frame the archways and niches. Sconces add a touch of mystery to the festooned walls. Strategically placed, they illuminate the sculptures that stand, ride, sit, or lie about the room, their stone forms imbued with poise.

A majestic Christmas tree stands in the center with branches laden with colorful ornaments.

Dalila and Cat slalom through a hundred or so attendees toward the opposite end of the room. Cat surveys the crowd and realizes they are both overdressed. No tuxedos in sight. Quite a few of the women have turned up in colorful bohemian attire. A no-no on any other formal occasion, here it's professional apparel for half of the participants.

Reaching the end of the room, Cat and Dalila pause at an impressive mural which may be by Michelangelo. Trapped between the mural and a lectern is a striking statue of a knight in armor, mounted on a magnificent horse. It makes Cat think of the chivalric romances that once captured the hearts of maidens throughout Europe.

Who's the modern equivalent of a knight in shining armor? A fearless soldier in combat gear? A valorous firefighter? A medal-winning athlete? A charismatic movie star or singer? A visionary billionaire in a tailored suit?

As Cat ponders that existential question, a city hall official steps up to the lectern. "Welcome, seekers and solvers!"

The audience claps.

He introduces Damien Wiet. Holding Chagall's *Father Christmas* in his hands, Wiet takes the official's place at the lectern. He surveys the room.

"Good evening, everyone!" he begins. "Behind me, you can see a nineteenth-century copy of Michelangelo's *Last Judgment*. Such a fitting work, don't you think, given that this is the first day of judgment in our scavenger hunt?"

The room erupts in laughter and applause. Not that the joke was great, but the prize Damien Wiet is handing out definitely is.

"We've worked seventy-two hours straight, sifting through hundreds of applications," Wiet continues. "We've vetted only those psychics and mathematicians with undeniable skills. You are the cream of the crop!"

Delighted murmurs ripple through the chapel as Cat exchanges an amused look with Dalila.

"But rest assured," Wiet carries on, "the hunt I designed will be a real challenge even for the best of you. Are you ready?"

"Yes!" the room roars.

"The team that finds *Father Christmas* first will take home the prize and trigger my donations to schools and museums," Wiet reminds his audience. "Are you excited?"

"Yes!" the room roars again, the sound reverberating off the walls of the chapel.

"Monsieur Wiet!" someone calls out from the crowd. "How are you going to form the pairs?"

With an enigmatic smile, Wiet spreads his arms wide. "I am going to leave it to chance. Good luck, everyone!"

He steps away from the podium. His aides spring into action, directing all the psychics, including Dalila and Cat, to line up on one side of the room. Cat finds herself between Dalila to her left and Christelle Djossou to her right. Christelle, a fifty-something of Beninese descent, practices Fa divination rooted in voodoo. Gifted and astute, she's adapted her version of ancient rituals to modern sensibilities—and the French law.

Opposite her, the cryptographers shuffle into place, forming a neat line.

As they wait, Dalila leans toward Cat and Christelle, winking. "Notice how the stereotypes hold."

"You're right!" Christelle exclaims. "Most of the psychics in our line are women, and most of the mathematicians are men."

Cat follows her gaze. The mathematicians and cryptographers are indeed overwhelmingly male. Some are dressed in sharp business suits while others wear clothes that scream "tech casual." The dim lighting and Cat's nervous excitement make their faces blurry. Still, it's impossible to miss the amused curiosity with which they gaze at the far more picturesque bunch across the gap.

Wiet claps his hands to get everyone's attention. "When I drop this handkerchief"—he holds up a monogrammed white cloth—"the two groups will walk toward each other. The person you meet will be your partner for the contest."

"What, no Sorting Hat?" Dalila whispers to Cat and Christelle. "I am terribly disappointed!"

The three of them chuckle quietly.

With a flourish, Wiet drops his handkerchief. As it flutters to the ground, the two rows stir and begin to move slowly toward each other. Cat's steps are measured, and her narrowed eyes flicker over the approaching men, trying to gauge their trajectories and figure out who will be her partner. As the faces come into focus, she fixates on one man. The man she saw in the snow globe.

Cat's breath catches in her throat. *Impossible!*

Yet it's him. The resemblance is uncanny. Same build and height. Same hair. Dark green turtleneck, beige chinos, thick glasses, that angular, ruggedly handsome face…

He's going to bump into Christelle.

In an adrenaline-fueled move that surprises even herself, she leans toward Christelle, her whisper urgent. "Can we switch places?"

Christelle meets Cat's desperate gaze then flicks a glance at Monsieur Turtleneck. A mischievous grin spreads across her face.

"Going for the hottie, huh?" she teases, stepping back to let Cat slide into her place.

With a grateful nod to Christelle, Cat staggers forward, now directly facing the man from her vision. The switch has left her dazed. She's not usually one to disrupt the order of things or act on a whim—yet here she is.

As they come closer, Cat's heart pounds a staccato rhythm in her chest. She tries to steady her breathing, hoping to appear calm and collected. But that's easier said than done.

Monsieur Turtleneck looks at her with open curiosity. They stop, facing each other.

"Bonsoir," he says politely.

"*Salut,*" Cat manages in reply.

His eyes crinkling, he extends a hand. "I'm Zachary Rigaud, or Zack to my friends and"—he smiles, muddling her thoughts—"associates."

She slips her hand into his firm, warm grip. "Catherine Cavallo. But please, call me Cat."

As her initial shock wears off, a surge of curiosity and questions bubbles up inside her. She can barely keep herself from blurting them out, but before she does, Wiet taps the side of his glass with a knife.

Everyone turns and looks at Wiet, waiting for him to speak.

"Ladies and Gentlemen, I will reveal the first clue in one hour." Wiet points to the buffet tables. "In the meantime, please enjoy the refreshments!"

CHAPTER 7

Nibbling on a canapé, Cat leans against a column as Zack approaches with a glass in his hand.

"What kind of psychic work do you do, Cat?" he asks, his voice laced with curiosity.

"I practice what you might call 'pure' clairvoyance."

"How is that different from, um... the muddy kind?" He gives her an apologetic smile. "Sorry, I'm an alien in your world."

"It means I don't have to rely on props other than a candle to focus my energy."

Zack nods. "So, just you and your intuition?"

"I guess you could say that."

Cat gives up looking for an excuse for her questions and asks directly, "Were you by any chance in the Tuileries Garden last week?"

"No, I wasn't," he replies with a slight frown. "Why do you ask?"

She keeps at it. "Do you happen to know a vendor there? Someone who sells snow globes, perhaps?"

His surprise seems to grow with each question. "No, can't say I do."

"What about a snow globes manufacturer?" Cat ventures. "Any acquaintances there?"

Chuckling, he shakes his head. "Your questions are just as mysterious as I imagine your profession to be! Perhaps you could explain?"

I could, but I won't. It was simply to rule out any rational explanation for her unsolicited vision.

Before Cat can think of a funny quip to stand in for the truth, Christelle arrives, accompanied by a man about her age. His dress is bona fide casual, as opposed to the slick tech-casual style. Dressed in well-worn jeans and a red plaid flannel shirt, his white hair and beard give him a jovial presence enhanced by his rosy cheeks and well-padded belly.

He looks vaguely familiar, or rather, he reminds Cat of someone… *But of course, Santa!*

"This is Edgar, my partner for the hunt," Christelle introduces him.

Zack's face lights up with recognition. "Monsieur Jaume! I can't believe it's you!"

Edgar narrows his eyes at Zack. "Zachary? Zachary Rigaud? How you've grown!"

The men exchange a warm handshake.

"Monsieur Jaume was my math teacher in Lille," Zack says.

"Please, call me Edgar," the older man urges him.

With a nod, Zack carries on, "Edgar is responsible for the path I chose in life. He infected me with his passion for mathematics."

"You're both from Lille, then?" Cat looks from Zack to Edgar. "I'm not a native Parisian, either. I'm from Provence."

"And I'm all the way from Cotonou!" Christelle chimes in.

"I left Lille for Paris two years ago," Edgar says.

Zack's expression remains amiable, but Cat could swear that a tiny cloud snuck into the chapel, hovered in stealth mode under its vaults, and has now stopped over Zack.

He speaks in measured tones. "I was born in Paris."

"And then your family moved to Lille?" Christelle offers a guess.

Zack's upper lip twitches ever so slightly. "No, it did not."

Christelle blinks, taken aback by his brusque reply. Edgar's gray eyes fill with sympathy.

What's the story with Lille?

Just then, Dalila strides over with her own cryptographer in tow. He's a lanky fellow with an unruly mop of hair and round glasses perched precariously low on his nose.

"This is Cedric," she chirps. "He's a software developer who can't resist a good cipher."

Introductions are made.

"Cedric has programmed his coffee maker to start brewing exactly one minute before his alarm goes off," Dalila announces proudly.

After everyone compliments Cedric, the conversation turns to the scavenger hunt.

"I hate to be a spoilsport but we're competitors," Christelle cuts through the cheer. "You know that, right?"

Zack, his good mood restored, raises his glass. "I propose a truce for the next half hour, until Damien Wiet drops his first clue."

"I'll drink to that!" Cedric makes good on his promise by taking a sip from his glass.

Dalila holds her champagne flute up. "Me too, in the spirit of Christmas!"

"Oh, please!" Edgar blows out a breath that rattles his lips. "That famous spirit is just a bout of commercial frenzy, whipped up by manufacturers and glorified by marketers, so that people can buy lots of stuff guilt-free."

Ah, so the guy who looks like Santa is one of those anti-Christmas types…

"That's a very harsh take," Cat says.

"Yes," Edgar agrees unexpectedly, fixing his eyes on hers. "But is it untrue?"

Cat chews on her bottom lip, conflicted. She loves

Christmas. It's a huge deal in her family, a truly joyous moment. She knows it in her heart that Christmas is so much more than a commercial hustle. The problem is, she can't in all honesty deny that there's a truth to Edgar's words.

"Edgar's theory is sound," Zack backs his teacher.

Oh, great.

Cat almost growls at him. No doubt, he meant what he said, and it wasn't just to spite her. But the fact that he sided with his teacher, who's now his rival, against Cat—his partner—it feels like a micro-betrayal. Not on a personal level, of course, because there's nothing personal between Zack and her, and there never will be. But it doesn't bode well for the contest.

I knew the snow globe vision was a dud!

"Edgar's view has some merit," Christelle says. "But consider this: the shopping we do before Christmas isn't for ourselves. We buy *gifts* and gifts require giving. They entail coming together with our loved ones and spending time with them."

"Yes!" Cat exclaims. "Exactly!" *I could kiss you right now!*

Dalila rolls her eyes. "It's hilarious how you all discuss what Christmas is all about without ever mentioning it's our Lord's birthday."

"Your Lord's, sweetie," Christelle teases her. "I'm a pagan. Did you know that Yuletide was the celebration of the winter solstice throughout Europe before it became conflated with Christmas?"

"Many also consider the Christmas tree to be a pagan thing," Cedric adds.

"But most don't." Dalila points to the stand displaying *Father Christmas.* "See that picture?"

Everybody looks at the whimsical scene with Santa on a flying horse holding a Christmas tree and a woman with a baby in her arms below.

"Chagall clearly had Christ on his mind when he worked

on this," she claims. "Why else would he paint Mary and the baby Jesus?"

"Chagall was Jewish," Edgar informs her.

Christelle shrugs. "So is my husband and he just loooves Christmas!"

Dalila insists, "The bottom line is that Chagall painted Mary and Jesus."

"Can we agree that it's a mother and child," Zack offers, "and leave their identities up to personal interpretation?"

Before anyone can respond, a commotion at the statue has all heads turning in that direction. Wiet's assistants are moving the stand with *Father Christmas* and the lectern to the center of the hall. As soon as they're done, Wiet steps behind the lectern and beckons the crowd's attention with a sweeping gesture.

"Welcome to the official kickoff of our scavenger hunt!" he announces.

His aides wheel in a display cabinet. Six books are arranged on it, their covers emblazoned with artwork. Even from a distance, the vibrant colors, rounded shapes, and dreamlike floating figures on the dust jackets scream Chagall.

Wiet calls everyone to gather around. The duets form a semicircle, buzzing with anticipation. Cat and Zack are squeezed between Christelle and Edgar on one side and Dalila and Cedric on the other. They all lean forward, craning their necks to get a better view of the books.

"These are the six volumes of the catalogue raisonné of Chagall's lithographs, compiled by Mourlot and Sorlier," Wiet begins. "This first edition spans the sixties and early seventies."

A few hands go up, and voices ask what exactly *catalogue raisonné* and *lithograph* mean. Wiet begins by explaining the concept of a comprehensive, annotated inventory of an artist's body of work. He then delves into the specifics of lithography, a process for making high-quality limited-edition prints.

"Chagall began creating lithographs at Mourlot Studios in 1950," Wiet says. "He worked closely with the studio's master printers for thirty-five years, until his death in 1985 at the age of ninety-seven."

Cat leans toward Zack and whispers, "Almost a century!"

"I bet he had a lot of art left in him, even at ninety-seven," Zack says.

Cedric speculates, "Do you think Monsieur Wiet will ask us to interpret the symbolism of the lithographs?"

"As long as we don't have to reproduce them," Edgar mutters. "My drawing skills never progressed beyond stick figures."

Wiet's instructions cut through their banter. "Each psychic will be given a slip with their name and the titles of these six volumes. On my signal, you'll have five minutes to pick a volume. Trust your instincts."

Surprised gasps and whispers ripple through the crowd.

As the assistants pass out the slips of paper and pens, Cat's heart beats frantically. Her eyes sweep over the vibrant covers before her.

The task is simple yet daunting.

Wiet raises a hand and then drops it sharply. "Go!"

Cat's eyes shift from the books displayed to her wristwatch and back to the books. She tries to feel the energy emanating from each volume and finds it frustratingly uniform.

She focuses on the illustrations on the dust jackets. Is there a sign in their colors or themes? Nothing stands out or screams "Pick me." The esthetic appeal of volume 6 tempts her, but a little voice in her head tells her not to rely on esthetics.

There's got to be more to it!

She glances at her watch. Three minutes left. Three happens to be her favorite number. She's about to dismiss the thought as too trivial, when her gaze flickers to *Father*

Christmas on the stand next to the display cabinet. The painting has three human figures: mother, baby and Santa.

A coincidence? Maybe.

Cat shuts her eyes. The faces of her three sisters, Julie, Vero, and Flo, flash before her mind's eye.

Except, we're four *sisters, including me.*

Should she go for volume 4, then? Logic would dictate that she should.

But this isn't an exercise in logic.

The piece of paper crinkles under Cat's fingers as she draws a circle around volume 3.

CHAPTER 8

Zack watches Cat hesitate. Then she circles the title of volume 3 on her paper. If her guess is right, it will be up to him to pass the next challenge. But if she's wrong, this scavenger hunt will be over for him.

And would that be so bad?

He doesn't need the money—not as much as the others in the room, at any rate. Besides, he has far too much on his plate to engage in such unproductive pursuits. If Cat fails, it will knock him out of the running and send him back to square one, right where he was before Wiet's challenge.

Which is exactly where I wish to be!

All Zack wants is to get back to focusing on his company instead of chasing a Chagall painting around Paris.

He does some mental math. Statistically, there's an 83 percent chance that Cat will get the volume wrong. In that case, Damien Wiet will have to decide whether to invest in QuantumTech Cybernetics without first testing Zack's puzzle-solving skills. If he chooses not to invest, he won't be able to use Zack's potential failure to crack a cipher as an excuse.

Sounds like a great outcome, come to think of it!

If Zack were a religious or superstitious man, he'd be silently praying that Cat picks the volume wrong. But Zack isn't religious, so he isn't praying—he's just hoping Cat hits the jackpot.

What? Am I?

The blatant irrationality of that wish sends him into a momentary stupor. Why would he want Cat to win? Surely not because he finds the shapely brunette attractive. For all he knows, she already has a significant other in her life. The absence of a wedding band doesn't mean a person is single.

And even if Cat were single, Zack has no intention of asking her out. He could never date someone so irrational that she not only believes psychic powers exist, she's convinced she has them!

Zack's torpor is interrupted by Wiet's assistants, who go from psychic to psychic, collecting the notes. When they're done, they step aside and sort the papers into two piles.

The room watches them in tense silence.

The assistants hand the smaller pile to their boss.

Wiet counts the pieces of paper. "Fourteen of the fifty-four psychics gathered here got the volume right!"

Which volume was it?

The room erupts into muted murmurs. Without naming the volume, Wiet begins to read out the names, congratulating each team that made it to the next test.

Zack rubs his chin, his mind working.

Fourteen out of fifty-four? The math doesn't sit right. By the laws of probability, nine would've been a neat fit. Of course, the actual number could be a tad higher or lower due to the natural variance in random processes. But fourteen? That's an outlier.

Could the fourteen psychics' answers be more than just lucky guesses?

Zack shakes his head as if to dismiss that fanciful, unscientific idea. He should be ashamed of himself for even envisioning such heresy!

As Wiet reads out the names, the chapel fills with congratulations. Dalila's name is called, and those around her cheer. Cat and Christelle wrap her up in a jubilant hug. After a moment's hesitation, Dalila's teammate Cedric follows suit.

Wiet continues to announce names at a slow but steady pace.

Increasingly on edge, Zack tries to distract himself by doing a quick and dirty mental calculation to work out how likely it is that fourteen out of fifty-four psychics got the volume right. The probability should be... um... two percent, give or take. Not the most likely outcome, but still within the realm of possibility.

Christelle's name rings out, and again, the three women huddle in a joyous embrace.

Waiting for his turn to congratulate his partner, Edgar winks at Zack. "We got lucky, huh?"

"Yes, you did!" Zack manages to smile.

How many names has Wiet read so far? Ten? Twelve?

"Finally, the last name on my list..." Wiet pauses and surveys the crowd.

Zack holds his breath.

Wiet speaks again, "Our fourteenth and final winner is Catherine Cavallo. Congratulations!"

Zack blinks, processing. *Catherine...* It's only when Dalila jumps up with a cry of joy and pulls Cat into a victory hug that the penny drops. Catherine Cavallo is Cat. She guessed correctly...

"Well done!" he offers, coming closer to her.

Her face alight with excitement, she grins. "Thank you, partner!"

Something unreasonably warm unfurls in his chest.

Wiet picks up one of the books on the stand. "Volume 3 is an inventory of the lithographs Chagall made from 1962 to 1968. It also contains the next clue. You'll need to find it after a ten-minute break."

As Wiet walks away from the lectern, Edgar approaches

Zack. "Looks like your teammate has the magic, just like mine!"

If Zack didn't know him so well, he wouldn't have caught the hint of sarcasm in his teacher's voice.

"Magic is the only possible explanation, variance be damned!" he quips.

Feeling someone's eyes on him, Zack shifts his attention away from Edgar. Cat is staring at him. Her eyes tighten at the corners as if she can't figure out if his comment was a taunt. If her fading smile is any indication, then she's concluded that yes, it was.

Back at the podium, Wiet invites the fourteen victorious teams to come closer.

The prequalified pairs step forward. As they stand around Wiet, poised for the next test, a range of emotions ripples through Zack. There's excitement, anticipation, pride in Cat's success, and the pressure of his own upcoming test.

Wiet's voice cuts through his thoughts. "And now for something completely different, as the Monty Pythons would say. Are you ready for part 2 of today's test?"

Laughter tinged with nervous undertones babbles through the room. Zack straightens up, aware that Cat is watching him.

I can't screw this up!

Wiet picks up volume 3 of the catalog, its cover now familiar to Zack. "Inside this volume correctly identified by fourteen of the psychics present is your next clue. Mathematicians, your task is to find it!"

A male voice shouts from somewhere in the semicircle, "I don't have any extrasensory abilities, Monsieur Wiet! So, what am I supposed to do?"

The crowd laughs, a brief relief from the mounting tension.

"Don't worry," Wiet replies with a broad smile. "Clairvoyance is not expected of you. You must solve a cipher."

Assistants circulate among the fourteen teams, handing out slips of paper and pens to the mathematicians.

"Solving the cipher," Wiet continues, "will lead you to a lithograph in this volume, which is a key to unlocking the rest of the hunt." He winks. "But one step at a time!"

When Zack gets his note, he turns it over but finds only his name. No hints, no starters. Just a blank piece of paper.

Wiet's handkerchief twitches in his grip. "After I drop this, you'll have five minutes to solve a Fibonacci sequence cipher. I'm going to read it slowly, so you can take notes."

The mathematicians get their pens and papers ready.

"Multiply the twelfth Fibonacci number by the fifth," Wiet begins, "then add the product of the ninth and the seventh, and finally subtract the second Fibonacci number. What significant number do you get?"

The handkerchief flutters to the ground.

Time starts now.

Zack's mind kicks into overdrive. The Fibonacci sequence is straightforward—each number in it is the sum of the two before it. *Let's see…* He scribbles down a series of numbers, doing sums as he goes. Beside him, other mathematicians hunch over their papers, pens scratching in a frenzy.

Once he's worked out the sequence to the highest number that Wiet mentioned, Zack circles the twelfth, fifth, ninth, seventh and second numbers: 89, 3, 21, 8 and 1. Then he does the math.

Wiet's voice booms, "One minute left!"

The contestants scramble.

Zack double-checks his calculations, copies the result at the bottom of the page, and underlines it for good measure: 434.

As time runs out, Wiet's people collect the slips. Zack looks around. Mathematicians and psychics alike await the verdict, their expressions tense. Cat is biting her nails.

"Only eight mathematicians cracked the cipher," Wiet

announces a few minutes later. "It wasn't difficult, but nerves and time pressure got the better of six of you."

Am I among the eight that passed or the six that failed?

Zack exhales, preparing to find out.

"The correct answer is four hundred thirty-four!" Wiet declares.

Even before he reads out the names, Cat hugs Zack. "You did it! You got it right! I saw you write down that number."

Without thinking, Zack pulls her closer to his chest and wraps his arms around her, breathing in her perfume.

Then, his mental faculties snap back, and he lets go of her. "Thank you."

The names of the winners are read. Both Cedric and Edgar solved the cipher. Cat, Dalila, and Christelle congratulate them, then huddle together in jubilation. The men pat each other on the back. Eight mathematicians and eight psychics crowd around the lectern, while the unlucky teams are asked to step back.

Wiet opens up volume 3 and shows a colorful illustration. "For the remaining contestants, this is lithograph number four hundred thirty-four in Mourlot's catalogue raisonné."

Everyone steps closer to get a better look at the volume's frontispiece. Painted in vibrant greens and soft reds, it depicts musicians, ballet dancers, animals, and flowers. Zack spots a winged cellist whose instrument seems to merge with his body. There's a violinist in the lower left corner. A harpist higher up. A woman floats on her back with a swan… He snaps a picture with his phone.

"The title of this work is *Ceiling of the Paris Opera*." Wiet looks at the teams that have qualified. "And voilà, you have your next clue, my friends!"

CHAPTER 9

The morning air is as chilly as you'd expect for this time of year when Zack arrives at the Place de l'Opéra. He didn't take his scooter because it's only a short walk from where he lives, and he likes to walk.

It's ten in the morning. The city is fully awake, thrumming with energy and pulsating with the early December rush. Sunlight spills across the grand façade of the Palais Garnier opera house, highlighting its ornate carvings against the backdrop of a bustling Parisian crowd.

Around Zack, the scents of strong coffee and fresh croissants waft from Café de la Paix, inviting and warm. But he hasn't taken a day off work to linger in cafés, no matter how beguiling. He's here with a clear goal in mind.

Last night, Damien Wiet announced that the next clue was Palais Garnier, the older opera house with a concert hall ceiling painted by Chagall. It follows that said opera house is the next stop of the hunt.

And that, precisely, is Zack's mission. He's here to study Chagall's fresco up close, crack whatever cipher or puzzle he may discover, win the contest, and get Damien Wiet to invest 5 million in QuantumTech Cybernetics.

Zack peers at the stairs leading up from the mouth of the métro and spots Cat, ascending. A glance at his watch confirms that she's right on time. Zack didn't expect such punctuality from someone who tells fortunes for a living.

The other shocker is how hard it is not to ogle her. Dressed in jeans, a puffer jacket and a wool cap hiding her wavy bob, she's just as pretty as she was decked out in that formfitting evening gown that shimmered in the candlelight last night in the chapel.

A rebel strand of hair peeps out from under her hat. Zack has to shove his hands into his pockets to make sure he doesn't reach out, tuck it in, and brush his fingertips along the side of her face in the process.

What the hell?

For an awkward moment he wonders if he should go for a handshake, give her air-kisses on each cheek, or just greet her with a "Hello, partner!"

Cat extends a gloved hand. "Good morning, partner!"

"Good morning!"

A handshake it is, then.

Bypassing the main entrance, they skirt the magnificent building until they reach a side access on rue Scribe on the other side of the cast-iron fence. Here, a secondary ticket office welcomes those who wish to tour the opera house rather than attend a performance.

Cat and Zack join the end of a long line. They stand together, occasionally shuffling forward, surrounded by the murmur of eager tourists and the hum of traffic from the nearby boulevards.

Zack turns to Cat. "So, I did a bit of research last night after the gala in the chapel."

She gives him an encouraging look.

"Well, it's hard to know which tidbits will turn out to be relevant, but I'll give you a few, in increasing order of importance."

"Let's hear them."

He opens the notes app on his smartphone. "OK, here goes. Chagall hesitated before accepting Minister Malraux's commission for the fresco. In the end, he said yes, but he didn't accept any payment for his work."

He glances at Cat to see her reaction.

She nods and pulls a small notebook from her pocket. "It took him a year to create twelve panels and a round centerpiece. He finished in 1964."

"I see I wasn't the only one burning the midnight oil doing research!" he exclaims with a grin.

She smiles back. "As my grandmother would say, 'Great minds think alike.' "

"But you wouldn't?"

"Frankly, I suspect that every single one of last night's sixteen winners spent the night scouring the interwebs."

"Fair enough," Zack agrees. "What else did you dig up?"

Cat flips to the next page in her notebook. "The work is a two-hundred-twenty-square-meter canvas mounted on removable resin." She looks up. "It's huge. I wish Monsieur Wiet would tell us which part of it is the clue!"

They take a few steps forward as the line moves.

Zack glances around before whispering to Cat. "I have a theory."

"Do tell!"

"So, the Chagall fresco is like an inverted false bottom, right?"

Cat knits her eyebrows. "You mean, it covers the original nineteenth-century fresco?"

"The painter's name Jules Lenepveu," Zack says. "Chagall's work covers Lenepveu's without damaging it, thanks to the spacers that separate them. The two domes have coexisted, one on top of the other, for sixty years!"

Cat eyes him. "You think the clue might be hidden between them?"

"That's my current working theory for lack of a better one."

"It's good," Cat says. "There's just one teeny-weeny problem..."

Zack lets out a sigh. "You don't have to spare my pride. The problem is huge. No one's going to take down Chagall's fresco to let us take a look at Lenepveu's no matter how nicely we ask."

"Hey, Zack, Cat!" a voice calls from behind.

Zack turns to see Christelle and Edgar waving from the end of the line.

"Hope you're ready to lose today, my boy!" Edgar teases him, rubbing his hands.

"Nah, we're going to ace this one, sorry!" Zack replies to his former teacher.

Christelle seems to be searching for someone in the crowd, before she turns to Cat, "Where's your friend Dalila?"

"She had two regular clients this morning, impossible to reschedule," Cat explains. "She and Cedric will be here this afternoon."

As Cat and Zack approach the entrance to the ticket office, Zack spots a sign that stops him in his tracks. It's a simple laminated sheet of paper with a red *X* over a photograph of the auditorium. The sign confirms his sinking suspicion. The auditorium with its famous Chagall ceiling is currently off-limits due to an ongoing rehearsal.

Seriously?

Zack flags down a uniformed employee nearby. *"Bonjour, monsieur!* Is the auditorium really closed right now? When will it reopen?"

"Yes, it's closed," the employee says. "Please understand, this isn't a museum you're visiting but a living performance space. The dancers, singers, and musicians—they all need their rehearsal time."

Cat steps closer. "Any idea when they might be done for the day?"

The staffer shrugs. "Hard to say. They wrap up when the artistic director decides they're done. But if I had to guess, I'd say they'll go through lunch and probably finish around three."

"Thanks," Cat replies, her tone tinged with disappointment.

Zack feels the same way. Visiting the rest of the opera house, no matter how magnificent, is pointless. He might as well go home and get some work done.

Cat shoots him a comically sad look and heads to the end of the line, where she informs Christelle and Edgar of the setback. Zack joins her. The four huddle together weighing their options. Frustration hangs heavy in the air between them.

Edgar sticks his hands in his coat pockets. "What do we do?"

"We could brave the cold and wait around." Cat tucks her notebook away. "Or we could disperse and reconvene after lunch... Either way, I have to reschedule a client."

She fumbles in her purse for her phone.

Christelle pulls hers out. "I need to tell my husband about the change in plans."

While the ladies make calls, Zack phones his assistant and his lead developer. He's still discussing a stubborn little bug in a code with Greg when a completely unrelated idea pops into his head.

"How about we wait at my place?" he suggests as soon as he hangs up. "It's on rue du Faubourg Montmartre, just a fifteen-minute walk from here."

His suggestion is met with a mix of surprise and indecision.

"I have an amazing coffee maker," Zack argues. "It brews bistro-grade joe, I promise!"

Eyes light up.

To dispel any lingering doubts, he adds, "I also have a stash of artisanal pizzas in my freezer. We'll warm up, have some quality coffee, grab a bite, and be back here by three."

"If this coffee maker is as fantastic as you claim..." Christelle's voice trails off.

"Oh, it's a game changer, the Ferrari of coffee machines," Zack piles on. "Trust me, you haven't lived until you've tasted a cup from that beast."

Christelle laughs. "Who can say no to that?"

"I'm in," Edgar declares.

Cat meets Zack's gaze, a playful smile curling her lips. "Impress me, partner!"

CHAPTER 10

Zack strides ahead, his breath misting in the crisp air as the group turns onto Boulevard Haussmann. Here the displays of the Galeries Lafayette enliven the gray winter morning, each window a tableau of festive whimsy. They shimmer with snowy scenes illuminated by tiny lights that twinkle like stars against a night sky cut in blue velvet. Oversized animated toys—dancing reindeer, twirling ballerinas, and laughing jesters popping out of boxes—captivate onlookers. Including Cat.

Zack slows down, his gaze glued to the psychic. Mouth agape and eyes wide with childlike wonder, Cat comes to a halt in front of a particularly inspired scene. Christelle and Edgar backtrack to join her. Zack follows. A mad urge to grab Cat and hold her tight, lest she be sucked into the enchanted world on the other side of the glass, comes over him.

Being a gentleman, he channels his impulse into polite speech. "Those displays do make December more bearable, don't they?"

"Oh, yes!" Cat's voice melds with the strains of "Jingle Bells" that drift from hidden speakers.

"When my kids were younger," Christelle says, "I used to bring them here every year. It's like stepping into a fairy tale."

Edgar lowers his glasses and casts Christelle the same oh-please look he used to give his students twenty years back. "May I remind you that all this magic is far from altruistic?"

"I know, I know," Christelle says with an eye roll. "It's to entice passersby to come in and buy stuff."

Edgar pushes his glasses back up. "Exactly! Christmas is a worldwide shopping fest, an exacerbation of our consumerist culture, a cue to buy, eat, drink, and be merry. Nothing more."

His rant kills the mood, at least for Zack. Christelle's face lengthens. Even Cat shifts and turns away from the displays.

"*Maman, Maman!*" A tiny voice carries over the hum of traffic behind them. "Look there!"

Zack locates a little girl tugging on her mother's sleeve.

She points at Edgar.

"Look at monsieur over there! Is that Santa?"

Her mom studies the math teacher's Santa-like form, gives him a furtive wink of complicity, and turns to her daughter. "You're right! I think he is."

"Why isn't he wearing his red coat?" the girl asks. "Do you think he lost it?"

"No," the woman replies. "I think he's dressed like that on purpose."

The girl blinks. "Why?"

Her mother's eyes dart from side to side as she racks her brain for a good reason.

Edgar sighs and turns to the kid. "I'm in town incognito. Do you know what that means?"

The girl shakes her head.

Edgar explains, "It's when you disguise yourself to make sure no one recognizes you, like a fugitive or a plainclothes police officer."

The girl nods eagerly. "But why don't you want to be recognized?"

Her mom shoots Edgar an apologetic look. "She's in peak 'why' phase and it's... exhausting."

Edgar mutters, "Ah, the depths to which I'll stoop for the young 'uns!" before turning back to the girl. "Going incognito makes it easier to check that the kids have been good and deserve their Christmas gifts."

"I've been good!" The girl pulls on her mother's sleeve again, "Tell him, *M'man!*"

"She's been very good," the woman says.

"Duly noted." Edgar shifts his eyes to the little girl and then back to the woman. "You can't tell anyone about this conversation, understand?"

The woman beams and joins her hands in a thank-you. "I promise!"

"You can count on me, Santa!" the girl cries out, positively glowing, as her mother leads her away.

Zack and his companions move on. The *grands magasins* give way to apartment buildings. Soon enough, the mess of the big city overshadows any lingering charm of the Christmas displays.

Zack spots graffiti tags on a wall they pass. A traffic light bears the marks of repairs made too hastily and carelessly with brown duct tape holding the casings together. A patch of roadworks blocks the sidewalk, its rickety barriers enclosing a jumble of upturned cobblestones and scattered tools. The air is suddenly filled with the dull roar of jackhammers and the acrid smell of asphalt. Nearby, two drunken figures slump on a dirty mattress propped up against the wall. They say something to Zack, but their slurred words are unintelligible.

It saddens Zack that Paris seems to be losing its constant battle against chaos.

As they continue along the Boulevard Montmartre, snow begins to fall. Large, heavy flakes dance around streetlights and descend along the lamppost garlands. They settle on every available surface, including the shoulders of pedestrians. Within minutes, the old stones are covered in a lacy veil of snow that makes the buildings shimmer with an ethereal grace.

When they reach the iconic Passage des Panoramas, Zack can't resist sharing a bit of trivia about his neighborhood. "Did you know this was one of the first covered passages in Paris?"

Annoyingly, everybody replies that they did.

"It was built to protect the wealthy mademoiselles from the mud and dirt of the streets when they went shopping," Edgar says as professorial as ever.

Cat shakes the snow off her bobble hat. "I've lived in Paris since I was fifteen, but it never ceases to amaze me how every step you take here is a trip through history. I love this city!"

"Despite the rats?" Zack asks, cocking his head.

"Rats are the least of our problems," Edgar chimes in, shaking his head woefully. "The ever-increasing debt and shrinking public services will be the death of it."

"Paris will survive this," Christelle declares. "It's seen worse."

"Notre-Dame is already bouncing back like a phoenix rising from the ashes," Cat bubbles with enthusiasm. "We'll see the same spirit of rebirth in the rest of Paris before this decade is out. Mark my words!"

Zack's lips curl upward. There's no denying that her optimism, however irrational, is highly contagious. Even the chill in the air seems less biting, tempered by Cat's gusto and the promise of coffee mere moments ahead.

They turn onto the rue du Faubourg Montmartre.

At the gate to his building, Zack punches in the code and lets everyone into the cobbled courtyard. The massive wooden gate closes with a soft clang, insulating Zack and his companions against the hustle and bustle of the city.

As they cross the courtyard to the second entrance, Christelle gasps, "My goodness! What a hidden gem you have here!"

Cat takes in the setup with a look like the one she wore in

front of the department store's imaginative displays. Zack follows her gaze. The courtyard, blanketed in a thin layer of freshly fallen snow, sparkles in the morning light as the sun peeks through the clouds. Each cobblestone is outlined in white, turning the ground into a magical mosaic. The large clay pots holding a variety of plants—some green, some bare—shimmer with fairy dust that has fallen from the sky. The cast-iron bench, frosted with pristine snow, looks even prettier than when he left an hour ago.

Cat's amazement fills Zack with a renewed appreciation for his "hidden gem" of a courtyard. He's both grateful and proud that this charming secret garden in the heart of Paris is part of his daily life.

"You can tell that a lot of care has gone into maintaining this courtyard," Christelle remarks.

"Well, that's mostly the work of our HOA board president, Lucile, and Monica, our concierge," Zack says. "Me, I just cough up the dues and enjoy the scenery."

Christelle gives him a thumbs-up. "Lucky you!"

"This year, though, our Christmas Planning Committee wants more than just my money," Zack complains. "They're pushing me to host the condo's Christmas party."

Edgar grimaces. "Your building has a Christmas Planning Committee? You've got to be kidding me!"

"Are you going to host the party?" Cat asks.

"Not in this lifetime!" Zack's emphatic reply is accompanied by an exaggeratedly vehement facial expression.

Cat giggles, adding to the sparkling courtyard a layer of audio glitter. Zack almost giggles back but manages to stop himself in time. "Men don't giggle, and they don't cry" was the first of many life lessons the older boys at his boarding school in Lille taught him. The hard way.

He unlocks the glass door to the lobby, and ushers everyone inside. At the mailboxes, Ajay, wearing an old Free Assange sweater, fidgets with a stack of envelopes. He turns around. They exchange greetings. Ajay's is as friendly as ever, but his demeanor is jittery.

"Got a minute?" he asks Zack after a moment's hesitation.

Zack glances at his companions, who nod their permission.

He's going to bring up the Christmas party. "What's up, Ajay?"

Carefully, Ajay locks his mailbox, then shifts from foot to foot, eyes downcast. "You see, um, it's about Lucile's Nativity scene. Remember, the one we saw during the Christmas Committee meeting at her place?"

"I do." *You want to talk about a crèche?*

"It doesn't have a cow."

And that's a problem because…? "Okaaay."

"So, I, um, I thought maybe I could give her one for Christmas." Ajay finally lifts his eyes to Zack. "What do you think?"

"A real cow?" Zack inquires.

Ajay bursts out laughing. "Of course not! A figurine."

"Gold encrusted with diamonds?"

Chuckling, Ajay shakes his head. "No, no, just a miniature brass statuette, depicting a sacred Kamadhenu cow with her calf."

"That sounds like a perfectly acceptable gift, Ajay."

"Does it?" Ajay's brow furrows in concern. "Won't I be breaking a social rule or two? I've lived in France for many years now, but certain social codes still elude me."

"I'm not aware of any social faux pas involving the gift of bovine statuettes from the vice president of an HOA to its president." Zack turns to his companions. "Are you, guys?"

They assure Ajay there are no such rules.

"What about… religious rules?" Ajay looks from face to face. "Would my gift be appropriate?"

"Religious etiquette is not my forte, but I don't see why not," Zack replies.

"She won't find it offensive?" Ajay presses on. "Does a cow even belong in a Catholic Nativity scene?"

"Take it from a lifelong atheist," Edgar says. "A holy cow totally belongs in a holy barn."

Cat and Christelle offer more reassurance. Ajay's shoulders relax at their collective approval. He thanks everyone and retreats to his apartment, his step buoyant now.

After he's gone, Zack turns to the group with a wry smile, "Ajay's gunning for the 'Most Thoughtful Vice President of the Year' award."

"How stiff is the competition?" Cat asks.

Zack's grin widens. "Ajay's running unopposed."

CHAPTER 11

Zack and his companions have been in the Garnier Palace for twenty minutes now, since three in the afternoon. The rehearsal is still underway. To kill time, they wander the majestic halls designed by Charles Garnier in the late nineteenth century in an opulent style called *Second Empire.*

Zack has been here twice before, both times with a date to see a ballet. The beauty of the decor hadn't escaped him, of course, but it hadn't been the focus of his attention. It is now. He takes in the grand staircase that leisurely curves upward, framed by ornate balustrades that gleam under the chandeliers.

But the most dazzling thing in the foyer is the monumental Christmas tree. A blend of immaculate white and gleaming silver with gold ornaments, it dominates the vista. The decorations extend beyond the tree, with tasteful festoons and velvety red ribbons draped along the railings.

Unlike his previous visits when Zack had focused on the performance, this time he's appreciating the beauty of his surroundings, multiplied by the enchantment of the holiday season.

Christelle voices his feelings. "Just wow! I look around and I hear Tchaikovsky's *Nutcracker* playing in my head."

"Napoleon III wasn't one to hold back on the decor," Edgar says. "The folks who did this place for Christmas clearly took their cue from him."

Zack smiles. "I feel like I should be wearing a top hat and tails."

"Fun fact," Christelle offers as they climb the imposing staircase. "*The Phantom of the Opera* was inspired by the hidden passageways of this building and the rumor that it was haunted."

"Did all of you guys spend the night doing research?" Zack teases. "It makes me feel better about my all-nighter."

"I already knew everything there is to know about the Garnier opera house," Edgar boasts. "We teachers come from the womb with facts and trivia preinstalled."

As the group approaches the auditorium, the once-closed doors are now invitingly open. The realization that the rehearsal is finally over sends a thrill down Zack's spine. They file in. Inside the great concert hall, each team veers in a different direction.

Zack takes in the vast space around them. It's dominated by rows of lush red velvet seats that fan out from the orchestra pit. Above, a balcony and five tiers of loges are stacked vertically, each draped in gold leaf embellishments that catch the light. Zack's gaze travels upward to the expansive fresco that crowns the hall.

Marc Chagall's vivid strokes contrast with the grandeur of the venue—but in a good way. The ceiling fresco is a burst of modernity and freshness in this classical setting. It's divided into several thematic panels, each painted in a distinct color scheme. One dazzles with deep blues and greens, depicting a serene scene from *The Magic Flute*. Another explodes with the fiery reds and oranges of *Carmen*... And this being Chagall, each segment blends childlike whimsy with real emotional depth.

Right in the center of the fresco, the massive chandelier hangs like a behemoth of crystal and light.

Cat points at it. "Did you know it fell down once?"

"Over a century ago," Zack chimes in, showing off his homework. "Killed one, injured a bunch…"

His voice trails off as he scans the ceiling again, hoping for a trace of Lenepveu's fresco.

Several moments later, he turns to Cat, gesturing upward vaguely. "Remember my working theory?"

"That the clue might be embedded in the original fresco under Chagall's?"

"Yes." He releases a heavy breath. "Well, looks like that's an untestable hypothesis."

Cat's lips curve into a half smile. "Unless you brought your X-ray goggles?"

"I wish I had! Unfortunately, real X-ray specs are still a fictional piece of technology."

"The clue must be here somewhere," Cat insists.

They weave through the aisles, eyes darting around, searching for a sign, an anomaly, anything. Zack stops for a moment to take in the multilayered complexity of the auditorium.

Cat pauses beside him and grimaces. "We could be looking for a needle in a haystack…"

"Then let's hope it's a particularly shiny one!" He cocks his head. "Should we split up to cover more ground? I could take the left flank, and you, the right."

Cat nods but doesn't move. Her gaze rests on the ceiling again, intent.

"That's the panel in lithograph number four hundred thirty-four over there, right?" she asks.

Zack follows her gaze. "It could be."

Cat's focus on the ceiling doesn't waver as she reaches into her tote bag, a bear-with-me smile on her face.

"Ta-da!" She pulls out a pair of miniature black and gold opera binoculars.

"Kudos! You came prepared."

Cat grins. "I remembered I had them as I was leaving this morning. My grandma gave my twin sister and me each a pair ten years ago."

"You have a twin sister?"

Cat nods. "We aren't as close as people expect twins to be. Julie moved back to Provence three years ago."

"Funny, I don't hear the South in your accent."

"Seventeen years is long enough to lose the singsong." She trains the binoculars on the ceiling. "This is actually the first time I'm giving them a spin since I'm not much of an operagoer."

"Are they any good?"

"See for yourself." She hands him the binoculars.

He takes them and peers through the lenses, first with his glasses on, then without. The details of the ceiling fresco come into sharp focus. Cat was right. The panel they are observing is the one depicted in volume 3 of the Mourlot catalog—a fragment of it, to be exact. Dedicated to the art of ballet, it features dancers and musicians against a yellow background.

Wasn't the lithograph's background green?

Zack reaches into his pocket. "Hey, I came prepared, too!"

He pulls out a folded sheet of paper and opens it to reveal a low-res print of the lithograph. Despite its quality, the effort earns a grunt of approval from Cat.

She leans closer to get a better look. "How did you get this?"

"Snapped a pic last night at the chapel and printed it out this morning just in case."

They huddle closer, comparing the details of the ceiling segment to Zack's printout. The background color isn't the only difference. The lithograph probably shows an early study for that segment, rather than a copy of the finished work.

While Cat has the binoculars, Zack surveys the crowd in

the auditorium. He can't see Edgar or Christelle, but across the hall, he spots Dalila and Cedric. They're engaged in an endeavor very similar to Cat and Zack's. Cedric holds his phone's camera up to the ceiling, then zooms in and shows the images to Dalila. Their eyes shift between the ceiling, Cedric's phone, and Dalila's screen.

Did she also take a picture of the lithograph last night?

They don't have binoculars, but the naked eye and digital zoom should do the trick.

"Spying on our competition?" Cat teases, passing him the binoculars.

"Guilty as charged." He gives her a wink. "May the best team win!"

"So, we have to win."

"Agreed."

She passes him the binoculars, opens her notebook, and scribbles furiously. "I'm listing all the discrepancies. The inscriptions 'Swan Lake' and 'Giselle' that you see in the fresco are missing from the print."

He squints through the lenses. "You're right! Also, the orange donkey with a bouquet in the lithograph has become a white moon up there."

"Let's recap," Cat says, when he hands the binoculars back to her. "We have the donkey, the text, the color, and the number of dancers."

"Is the number different, too?"

"There are thirteen in the lithograph and twelve in the fresco," she replies.

"Sniff, someone didn't make the cut from paper to plaster."

With their list complete, Cat caps her pen. "We'll take this to Wiet tomorrow. Hopefully, these discrepancies are the right answer to this imprecise puzzle."

"Yeah, I'll take a cryptogram over this any day, all day!"

Cat sticks her phone, notebook, and binoculars back into her tote bag, and they leave the auditorium.

As they walk down the grand staircase, Zack looks over at Cat. "So, team dinner to strategize?"

He hopes his words came across exactly as he'd meant them—a suggestion of a casual business meal.

Because I sure as hell wasn't asking her out.

Zack has found every woman he's been with either too silly, too crazy, or both. This, despite the fact he's only dated exceptionally normal ladies with remarkably conventional jobs, pigs will fly before he'll have a fling with a clairvoyant.

Also, I have work to catch up on.

Cat will probably say no anyway. She must have plans for tonight or clients booked—or a visit from spirits.

"Sure," Cat replies. "I know a place on the Boulevard des Italiens—"

"How about we go back to my apartment?"

What? Why did I say that?

So, it wouldn't look like a date, of course! If they had a proper dinner in a nice restaurant, she might misinterpret it as him making advances. Which is why he'll just cook some pasta at home. They already had an informal get-together at his place today with Edgar and Christelle. This one will be just like that! They'll eat, discuss the scavenger hunt, and then he'll call her a cab.

There won't be the slightest hint of anything romantic. Zack isn't looking for a serious relationship or planning to settle down—not until he and his potential partner are too old to start a family, at any rate.

Cat is, what, thirty?

That's a no-go.

Her age aside, she's simply wrong for him to consider even for a hookup. It doesn't matter if she sincerely believes she has supernatural abilities or if she's a fraud. Neither is something Zack wants to be around. On the famous Hot Crazy Matrix, a psychic would be squarely in the right upper quadrant—the Danger Zone. *Chaos and destruction.*

Zack has a strict policy of avoiding that category. It's a

policy that has served him well, and he's not about to abandon it now.

Not even if Cat makes the first move.

That being said, he'd be thrilled if she did.

CHAPTER 12

Cat steps into Zack's delightful courtyard. It's her second visit of the day, yet the charm of this quintessentially Parisian setting captivates her anew. The limestone dates from the same proud and audacious time as the Palais Garnier—an era of technological revolution. Cat saw a documentary about it last month. The Western world had just invented the tools to start mass-producing things. Railroads, factories, and steam engines were springing up everywhere. Yet, their designers still put in the effort and resources to make them aesthetically pleasing.

Granted, labor was cheaper, but that wasn't the main reason. The Belle Époque was a time when the insipid and the vulgar were equally frowned upon and beauty was highly prized.

Just like today, only the opposite.

Zack and Cat climb the stairs covered with carpeting that muffles their steps. The scent of old woodwork fills the stairwell and mingles with a hint of Zack's annoyingly yummy eau de cologne.

As they enter his apartment, the ambient smell changes

subtly. The wood is still present, but there are notes of freshness and modernity to it. It isn't that the interior is resolutely modern—because it isn't, not resolutely, anyway. It's rather that the charm of the building's exterior continues inside. The honey-colored parquet floor is intricately patterned and stretches down the hallway that leads them to the spacious living room. Cat glances up at the high ceiling decorated with ornate moldings all around.

Those features aren't Zack's work, of course. They came with the walls. To his credit, Zack has furnished the place well without excess but with a respectful nod to the builders' vision. There's a graceful feel to the room, and enough uncluttered space to allow the craftsmanship of the original artisans to shine through.

Cat squints to get a better idea of her surroundings in the twilight.

My place would be pitch dark at this hour!

Zack flips a switch, and the chandelier in the center of the room comes to life. The light from its many tiny high-tech bulbs bounces off the crystal pendants and fills the room with a golden warmth.

Cat tries to imagine the chandelier in her own studio apartment. The bookcase would be a goner, the ficus would have to find a new home, and she'd need a helmet to navigate around its imposing presence.

Get a grip, Catherine!

It's unfair and also disingenuous to compare her shoebox on the ground floor in a big, soulless block, where hardly anyone says hello, to Zack's glorious abode. Cryptography pays a lot better than clairvoyance—that's a fact. She chose her profession because it seemed a shame to let her gift go to waste. She wanted to help people. And if she could go back in time, she'd make the same choice all over again.

"It's only five-thirty," Zack says, heading for the wall bar. "A little early for dinner… unless you're starving?"

"Not at all!"

"How about an *apéritif*? I'll have a Bordeaux." He steps aside to let her examine the contents of the bar.

"A *Martini Bianco* would be perfect."

He motions her to the sofa and fixes her drink.

"What do you think our odds are?" he asks as he hands her the martini.

"I'm starting to hope they're not too bad."

He settles into the sofa, a glass of red in his hand, and a decorous distance between them.

She raises her martini. "To our victory!"

"To victory!" He touches his glass to hers.

"By the way, if the next clue is anything like today's, we can use the 'phone a friend' option."

"Which friend do you have in mind?"

"Technically, it isn't a friend but my sister, Florence," she replies. "Flo has a degree in art history."

"I take it, you have two sisters, your twin Julie and Flo?"

"Three, actually," she grins. "Vero, the oldest, followed her husband abroad. Julie and Flo went back to Provence. They live in a small town we come from, near our grandmother."

"Which town?"

"Beldoc."

"Never heard of it."

"It's a quaint little place near Arles," she says. "Grandma Rose is royalty there."

He quirks a single eyebrow. "You mean, she's very influential?"

"That too, but also literally."

He blinks, confused.

She lifts her eyes to the ceiling. "Haven't you ever heard of the Provençal tradition of electing a pretty damsel as queen of this or that town?"

"Right. I have. But—"

"There you go! My gran was elected Queen of Beldoc."

Fighting back a smile, he asks, "How old is she?"

"Careful, young man! That question could get you banned from ever setting foot in Beldoc."

He slaps his forehead. "What an idiot! Everyone knows you should never ask a woman her grandmother's age."

"I'm glad you saw the error of your ways, Monsieur Rigaud," Cat says pertly.

They laugh.

Hang on, am I flirting with him?

A sticky wave of panic rises in Cat's chest.

I can't! I mustn't!

It's too soon and she's not ready. It's imperative that she maintain her relationship moratorium until she's purged herself of all neediness and is demonstrably self-sufficient. The cost of dating again before she's "clean" will be too high. If her fourth boyfriend dumps her like the previous three have done, Cat fears she will never heal from the heartbreak.

"What about your parents?" Zack asks. "Are they in Paris or down South?"

"Dad is here in Paris," Cat replies. "Mom passed away when I was fifteen in an accident."

The room falls silent for a moment, the air thick with unspoken words.

Then, he clears his throat. "I'm sorry to hear that."

"Thank you." She smiles to show she's made peace with it. "What about you? Any siblings?"

His eyes dart to the clock on the wall. "No, just me."

"And your parents? Do they live in Paris?"

He sets his glass down and stands up abruptly. "I'm starving! How about we start with the spaghetti? I promised you dinner, and Zachary Rigaud always keeps his promises."

Cat follows him into the open kitchen. He fills a large pot with water, twists the knob on the stove and ignites the burner with a soft whoosh.

The water is just starting to boil when a vintage landline

phone on his counter rings. With Cat's permission, he answers it.

"Good evening, Zack, are you coming?" a man asks on the other end, his voice loud enough for Cat to hear. "Everyone's here already."

Zack's face loses color. "Oh no, I completely blanked on the meeting tonight!"

"What meeting?" Cat whispers.

"Hold on a sec," Zack mumbles into the phone, then covers the receiver. "It's the Christmas Planning Committee." He holds up the phone. "This is Ajay."

"Your neighbor we bumped into this morning?"

Zack nods. "I can't believe I spaced out on the meeting tonight!"

"Go." Cat leans against the counter. "It sounds like a matter of national security."

"It's not."

Ajay's voice cuts in from the phone, "Yes, it is!"

Cat gives Zack a small, understanding smile. "Please, go. Save Christmas! I'll head out. We can strategize world domination later on the phone."

Ajay pipes up again, "Hey, Zack, you can bring your friend."

Zack hesitates and then pleads with Cat, "Come to the meeting with me! It won't take long, I promise."

"Our president runs a tight ship," Ajay chimes in. "We'll release you back into the wild in thirty minutes, tops."

Zack clasps his hands together in mock desperation. "Please, don't make me a promise breaker! I dangled a pasta dinner in front of you, and I intend to deliver. You can't go home hungry!"

Feeling a sudden surge of playfulness, Cat straightens up. "Oh well, why not?"

Zack turns off the heat under the pot. They step out onto the landing and descend two flights of stairs to Ajay's place.

"They'll do their dance asking me to host the Christmas party," Zack briefs Cat in the stairwell. "I'll dodge as usual, and then we'll check out."

She points to her feet. "We're lucky these boots are good for running. You know, just in case your dodging skills are off today…"

CHAPTER 13

When Zack rings the bell, Ajay opens the door immediately and ushers them into his meticulously tidy apartment. The furniture is sparse, minimalist, and drab with the notable exception of a well-stocked wall-to-wall bookshelf and the splash of color provided by two pieces of fabric. Hanging on the wall is a green silk banner with red tassels and a multiarmed goddess painted on it. A bright Indian throw drapes over the couch.

Two women sitting on that couch greet them. Cat introduces herself. The older woman is the president of the HOA board, Lucile. A graceful blonde in her early sixties, she wears her hair in a cheek-length French bob, and her reading glasses low on the bridge of her nose. Cat realizes that Lucile must be the intended recipient of the cow figurine Ajay had been agonizing about this morning.

The younger woman is Monica, the concierge. In her mid-forties, her sharp eyes seem to miss nothing of Cat's appearance. Fortunately, the sparkle of mirth in them tempers the overly inquisitive gaze.

Without further ado, the meeting, chaired by Lucile, gets underway around Ajay's dining table.

"Did you buy all the garlands and twinkling lights?" Lucile asks Monica.

"I did," the concierge reports. "But let me tell you, it's hard to stay on budget when you want the lobby to feel like you're walking into Santa's living room!"

Ajay leans back in his chair. "Speaking of Santa, I met him this morning."

"At a mall?" Monica asks.

"No, he was with Zack and Cat," Ajay replies.

A girly laugh escapes Cat as she looks at Zack.

Zack grins at her before turning to the others. "His name is Edgar, and yes, he looks exactly like Santa."

Lucile leans over to Cat, her tone conspiratorial and warm.

"I'm so glad Zachary brought you to this meeting, dear! Do you think you can persuade him to host the condo's Christmas party?"

"We'll take care of the refreshments, decorations, and the music," Ajay says to Cat.

"And we'll clean up after," Monica volunteers, also addressing Cat.

"All he needs to do is provide the space," Lucile adds.

That's hilarious! They think I'm his girlfriend.

Cat opens her mouth to tell them she has no control over Zack's decisions when Monica interrupts her, a hand over her heart. "My boys will be on their best behavior, I promise!"

"And I," Zack finally speaks, "promise to pay for the venue of your choice, drinks and snacks included!"

Instead of thanking him, as Cat expected after such a generous offer, the committee members exchange looks of disappointment. Monica sighs in exasperation. Ajay avoids making eye contact with him. Finally, Lucile suggests they decide on the venue at the next meeting.

"The final item on our agenda is apartment window treatments," she announces.

Ajay and Zack shift uncomfortably in their seats.

Lucile's eyes sweep over the group before settling on the two men. "I've noticed that neither of you have begun to decorate your windows. Do you need any advice or assistance?"

"I'm all set, thanks!" Zack flashes a confident smile. "I'll tackle mine this weekend."

Ajay rubs the back of his neck. "Actually, I could use some advice, but not for the windows. I'm thinking of getting a Christmas tree. It'll be a first for me."

"Oh, Ajay, that's a great idea!" Lucile exclaims, gesturing vaguely around her. "A nicely decorated tree will certainly brighten up your home."

Visibly boosted by her support, Ajay leans forward. "I might put up a Christmas crèche, too."

Lucile claps her hands together. "That's wonderful! A Nativity scene is a surefire way to bring the spirit of Christmas into a home."

"Do you think it's a good idea to include some animals in the manger?" Ajay inquires cautiously.

Lucile nods. "Animals make a Christmas Nativity scene complete. A lamb, a donkey, and a bull are the traditional Christmas crèche figures."

Ajay's eyes light up at the mention of a bull.

He ventures further, eyes on Lucile, "I noticed that your superb Christmas crèche is missing a cow. Would you consider adding one this year?"

There's a pause.

Lucile's smile fades to a glummer expression. "I appreciate the concern, Ajay, but I think my late husband's crèche is perfect as it is."

Ajay's face falls.

Unaware or indifferent to the effect her remark has had on him, Lucile adds, "I wouldn't change a thing about it!"

Ajay's entire body seems to deflate like a punctured

balloon. Sensing his disappointment, Cat is overcome with sympathy for him. She may not be alone. The atmosphere in the room thickens with the awkwardness of crushed hopes.

Fortunately, Cat's phone comes to life. She picks up at once.

On the other end, Dalila's voice booms with unbridled excitement. "Turn on the TV right now! You won't believe it!"

"I'm afraid I can't, I'm not at home."

Even as Cat utters those words, Ajay is already on his feet, fumbling with the remote.

"We're on the evening news!" Dalila shrieks into the phone.

Cat's eyes widen in surprise as the TV flickers to life with a report on their scavenger hunt. The segment covers yesterday's sorting and the first round of tests. Cat gapes, realizing for the first time that cameras were present in the chapel and filming them.

All eyes in Ajay's living room are glued to the screen as the footage shows Damien Wiet talking about his brainchild. The camera pans over the participants gathered in the beautiful venue, then cuts to the end of the evening and zooms in. Suddenly, Cat's happy face fills the frame, followed by Zack's. In the background, Wiet's voice announces them as one of the night's winning teams.

On this side of the screen, the Christmas Planning Committee erupts in squeals and cheers. Hearty congratulations ring out as Zack's neighbors react with animated glee.

"Look at you two, celebrities now!" Monica exclaims.

"Well done!" Lucile beams. "This is going to be the talk of the town for days."

"Not to mention the building," Ajay chimes in, recovering after his disappointment.

Zack rubs the back of his neck, his eyes flicking to Cat. "I guess we missed the memo about the reporters in the chapel."

"Yeah, but we should have seen it coming when we waived the rights to our image," Cat says, recalling all the paperwork she had to sign before the game.

She shifts her gaze back to the screen as the segment wraps up.

Ajay turns off the TV. The conversation centers on the scavenger hunt for a few minutes, after which the gathering naturally breaks up. The neighbors drift to the door and say goodbye.

Cat and Zack dart upstairs.

"Well, that was unexpected," he chuckles, glancing over at her.

"Totally," she agrees.

He unlocks the door to his apartment and ushers Cat inside. "Ready to tackle that spaghetti?"

His voice is light, but something in his darkened gaze, in his towering stance, and in how close he stands to her makes Cat's heart skip a beat. She knows where this is going. Panic swells in her chest.

I can't do this. I'm not ready!

"Um, you know what?" she stammers. "It's late and I live far away."

"Don't worry about it! I'll make sure you get home safe."

She swallows hard.

"Unless it's pouring down," Zack carries on, "in which case I'll put you in a cab. I'll deliver you personally on my metal horse!"

She grabs her coat. "Thanks, but I really should be going."

He steps aside.

Her bag feels unusually heavy as she slings it over her shoulder and steps over the threshold. In her haste she stumbles.

He reaches out and steadies her by the elbow. "Are you sure?"

No, I'm not.

But she's already on the first step.

"Thank you for the lovely evening!" she mumbles awkwardly in a rush. Without waiting for his response, she races down the stairs, her emotions all over the place.

CHAPTER 14

The morning sun shines on the checkered marble floor of the privatized lobby of the Rodin Museum, where eight teams of scavenger hunters have gathered for a lavish brunch.

The air is filled with the rich aromas of freshly brewed coffee and hot chocolate. Waiters in crisp uniforms glide between the tables, balancing platters of smoked salmon on blini, petits fours stuffed with fine ham and cheese, and delicate little pastries. Cat almost drools as she gazes at their pastel- and candy-colored icings. Her twin sister Julie makes that sort of stuff day in and day out, what with being a pastry chef. But for Cat, who never learned to bake, they're something truly special.

She shares a table with Zack, Dalila, and Cedric. They're positioned next to the glass doors, which affords a perfect view of the garden dotted with Rodin's magnificent statues. At one end of the lobby, a large Christmas tree sparkles with silver and gold ornaments. Though it lacks the pizzazz of the tree in Garnier Palace, it's glamorous enough that it should've been the center of attention. But Cat and—judging by the tense chatter in the room—everyone else can think of one thing only.

Dalila looks from Cat to Zack. "Do you think you got the opera ceiling puzzle right?"

"We certainly hope so," Zack replies.

Cedric pops a petit four into his mouth. "So do we."

"I have a good feeling about this." Dalila turns to Cat. "Remember our deal, eh? If one of us wins the prize, she's paying the rent on the shop for a year!"

"Of course, I remember," Cat replies. "But let's not get ahead of ourselves."

As the brunch winds down, the servers clear the tables, and Wiet's assistants invite everyone to gather around the lectern. The murmur of conversation fades as Wiet steps forward. He's greeted by a round of applause. Cat, now attuned to how this works, notices the cameraman setting up discreetly off to the side, his lens trained on Wiet.

"Ladies and Gentlemen," the philanthropist begins, "what we wanted you to do at the opera house was to spot the differences between the lithograph number four hundred thirty-four and the actual ceiling."

"So far so good," Cat whispers to Zack.

He squeezes her hand in silent celebration and then immediately releases it as if scalded.

Wiet continues, "Five teams identified their mission correctly, but only three found all the differences."

The room holds its breath.

"And the teams that will go on are..." Wiet pauses for effect, "Marguerite and Lorenzo, Christelle and Edgar, and Catherine and Zachary. Congratulations!"

Amid cheers and disappointed expletives, Dalila jumps up and throws her arms around Cat, nearly knocking her over in her enthusiasm. "I knew it! That's my girl!"

The camera zooms in on Cat, making her self-conscious.

She waits for it to point elsewhere before turning to Zack. "Can you believe it?"

"We did it, partner!" He grins.

Should I hug him now? She gives him a thumbs-up instead.

Spotting Christelle who's squealing with joy next to Edgar, Cat goes over hugs her. "Congratulations to you all!"

"You too, dear!" Christelle says, patting her on the back.

As the applause dies down and the camera rolls away, Cat finally gives in to the rush of adrenaline mixed with a hearty dose of pride and punches the air. "Woohoo!"

Wiet's assistants call everyone's attention back to the front.

The atmosphere in the lobby pulsates with renewed anticipation as Wiet says, "May the three winning teams step forward?"

The teams do as requested.

"Are you ready to embark on your next challenge?" he asks, his voice tinged with mystery.

Zack, Cat, and the others exchange bewildered looks. This brunch was to announce the winners of yesterday's test. The invites said nothing about the next one.

"I have a working lunch and a staff meeting later," Zack mutters.

Cat leans toward him, her voice a low hiss. "And I have two clients this afternoon. How are we supposed to juggle this?"

"You mean, now?" Edgar's voice rises, expressing everyone's concern. "Personally, I'm between jobs and free as a bird. But not the others."

Wiet offers a reassuring smile. "You'll get the puzzle now, but you don't have to start working on it straight away. The answer is due by tomorrow at four."

The contestants process the information while Wiet shuffles through the papers in front of him.

"This leg of the hunt is special," Wiet says. "The psychic and the mathematician on each team will be working together to solve the puzzle. Ladies and Gentlemen, get ready for some poetry!"

The mention of poetry raises some eyebrows.

Wiet clears his throat. "First, I'll read a poem written by yours truly in a traditional Korean three-line format called sijo."

An impressed murmur runs through the room.

He flashes a hand. "My poem is not very good. But, please, don't judge me too harshly! I'm merely an amateur at this."

Another cough, and he begins to recite his creation.

Beneath the chandelier, you all searched, and some of you found.
But above, where the Phantom retires to watch the Iron Lady twinkle,
A hidden, humming cove crowns the house of music.

When Wiet is finished, the audience claps. He bows, clearly enjoying the moment. His assistants hand out envelopes to Cat, Zack, and the other four finalists. Each envelope is sealed with an elaborate wax stamp. Cat runs her fingers over the textured craft paper and the thick reddish-brown stamp that's too beautiful to break.

"Go ahead and open it," a female assistant says, noticing her hesitation.

"What's inside?" Cat asks the aide.

The woman chuckles, "Nothing sharp! Just the text of the poems that make up the puzzle."

Cat unseals the envelope, pulls out a folded sheet of paper with two short poems, and lifts her eyes to the aide, "Your boss's sijo was good."

"Surprisingly decent for a mathematician," Zack chimes in. "I could never write a poem like that!"

The assistant glances around and then blurts out in a low voice, "He didn't write it."

Cat stares at her, taken aback.

"What do you mean?" Zack asks.

"I mean, like he said, it's no Baudelaire…" the aide trails off.

"But?" Cat presses.

A brief hesitation, and then, "But if you do want to compliment someone, then it should be me and that guy." She points out the aide handing an envelope to Christelle. "We composed the sijo for Monsieur Wiet."

With that, she retreats to her spot behind Wiet.

Cat and Zack trade a look. There's a funny expression on his face, but he makes no comment.

A hushed silence falls over the lobby as Wiet raises his hand to gain everyone's attention.

"The next piece," he announces, "is by a professional poet. I chose these three lines." He reads in a measured cadence:

All at once, he paints
He grabs a church and paints with a church
He grabs a cow and paints with a cow

As the last word hangs in the air, Wiet scans the room, his gaze sharp. "The poems will lead you to a place where you'll find a date. Email that place and date to me before four in the afternoon tomorrow!"

What?

Cat glances at Zack. He answers with an equally confused look. The others appear just as bewildered.

Zack breaks the silence. "Monsieur Wiet, does that mean there's another puzzle waiting for us wherever these poems lead?"

"Yes," Wiet replies. "You should also know that this test is trickier than the previous one. Good luck to all!"

With that, he strides off with his assistants scurrying behind him.

As the crowd begins to disperse, Cat and Zack head for the exit. Cat checks the time on her phone—it's eleven.

She turns to Zack, apologetic. "I have to dash to my shop before my noon client shows up."

"I have to run, too," Zack says. "And tonight, I have to be at a speed dating event between startups and business angels. Can't miss that."

Cat nods, all too aware that putting off the work on the puzzle until tomorrow morning with an additional one to solve right on the heels of it is risky.

"Why don't I swing by your shop this afternoon at three?" Zack asks, as if reading her mind. "Will you be done by then?"

"Yes."

"Good. We can squeeze in a few hours of brainstorming before my speed dating event. Text me the address."

Cat's thumbs dance across her screen. "Done. Bring your geekiest glasses!"

"I'll bring a helmet for you," he says. "In case we figure out the place and decide to check it out straight away."

"I salute your optimism!"

They share a brief, nervous laugh, before parting ways outside the museum. As Cat hurries to the métro, her mind swirls with the cryptic poems and… the image of Zack in the snow globe.

Where did that come from?

She shakes her head.

There—gone.

CHAPTER 15

At three sharp, a knock echoes through Cat and Dalila's shop on Quai Valmy. Cat opens the door to find Zack with two motorcycle helmets under his arms. She invites him in. As he enters her colorful world, his eyes widen with each step.

"Is this your first time in a psychic's lair?" she teases, amused.

Zack nods, a look of awe on his face. "Your decor… It's a total mind trip compared to my office in La Défense! I feel like I accidentally took a psychedelic and slipped into another dimension."

"Welcome to my galaxy!" Cat gestures him farther in. "Coffee?"

Zack sits down at the round table covered with an indigo tablecloth. "Please. Black, no sugar."

Cat prepares two cups of coffee. As its aroma mingles with the sandalwood from the incense burner, she covertly glances at Zack as he scans the room. From the corner of her eye, she notices his gaze lingering on the various mystical objects on the shelves, including… the snow globe!

Cat tenses, waiting to see how he'll react. But his gaze glides right over the glass sphere, unimpressed.

She hands him his espresso and opens her copy of the sheet with the poems. Zack unfolds his.

"Shall we focus on Wiet's poem first?" Cat asks.

"You mean, the one written by his aides that he passed off as his?"

Again, that funny look. And again, no comment.

"Yes, that one," she confirms and reads the first line aloud, "Beneath the chandelier, you all searched, and some of you found."

"But above," Zack picks up, "where the Phantom retires to watch the Iron Lady twinkle, a hidden, humming cove crowns the house of music."

"But above..." Cat repeats, her voice trailing off, as she looks up at Zack.

He lays his copy on the table and taps his finger on the line about the Phantom. "It has to be the roof of the opera house, right?"

"Sounds like it," Cat agrees. "But what's with the 'humming'?"

Zack rubs his chin. "No idea... Electricity? Machinery? Insects?"

"I don't know, and I don't see how the second poem fits in."

"Hmm, me neither."

Cat reads the second poem. "All at once, he paints. He grabs a church and paints with a church. He grabs a cow and paints with a cow."

"This poem could be referring to a church," Zack submits. "The question is which one."

"By the same logic, it could be referring to a cow."

"A cow on the roof of the opera house." Zack flashes all his teeth. "Eureka! That's the connection between the poems!"

Cat laughs. "A cow on the roof sounds a lot like something Chagall would paint, doesn't it?"

"It does," Zack agrees.

They fall silent.

Zack scratches the back of his head. "I'd say this poem is about Chagall. What do you think?"

"I'd bet money on it."

Suddenly, an idea strikes Cat. "Should we do an Internet search to see if those lines come up?"

"Go for it!"

She pulls her laptop off the shelf. "If the poet is a professional, as Wiet said, then he might've posted that stanza online."

"Unless he died before the Internet was invented," Zack points out. "But someone could've shared his poems online since then."

Cat opens her computer and types in the verse. Zack moves his chair closer, eyes glued to the screen. To Cat's surprise, the search engine brings up the lines and a name associated with them—Blaise Cendrars.

Ten minutes later, Cat and Zack have learned that Cendrars was a contemporary and friend of Chagall's in the 1910s. And he was, indeed, a published poet. The verse Wiet included in his clue was from a poem called "Portrait" that Cendrars wrote about Chagall.

"Can you find out when he wrote it?" Zack squints at Cat.

She clicks a few more links. "Looks like it was published in 1919, as part of a collection titled *Nineteen Elastic Poems*."

"Could 1919 be the answer to the date part of Wiet's riddle?"

They stare at each other before turning back to the screen.

Cat tsk-tsks. "Wiet warned us that this test would be tricky, remember?"

"I do."

"Well, I feel like *1919* came too easy," Cat says. "It could be a trap."

"I don't disagree, but as a mathematician, I must ask. Are you familiar with Occam's razor?"

She shakes her head.

"It's a principle of logic and science," he begins. "If you have more than one idea to explain something, you should always go with the simpler one."

She gives it some thought. "It tracks. But then, what's the purpose of the first poem?"

"To confuse us?" He slaps a hand on his forehead. "Of course! That's what he meant by *tricky*."

She can't explain it, and she doesn't dare contradict a principle of science and logic, but something about this simple solution feels off.

She cocks her head. "Wiet said we must follow the poems to a place where we would find a date. But we found this date before we had a place."

They both scratch their heads. When they set their hands back on the table, Zack's accidentally brushes Cat's. She catches her breath at the contact and yanks her hand away.

To counter the awkwardness of the moment, she puts her fingers back on the keyboard. "Why don't I dig a little deeper into Chagall's poet friend, Blaise Cendrars?"

"Sure, why not?"

"Here we go!" She flexes her fingers and begins to poke around the web.

"Hang on, stay on this page, please!" He points to the bottom of the screen, just as she's about to close a page of Cendrars's poems. "Read this one."

"The one titled 'Studio'?" She shoots him a glance. "You think it's about Chagall's studio?"

"The date at the bottom is 1919. It must've been published in the same collection as 'Portrait.' "

Cat scrolls up and zooms out, so that the entirety of the text is visible on the screen. Silently, they read the poem.

It begins with:

The Beehive
Stairs, doors, stairs

And it ends with:

Chagall
Chagall
In the ladders of light.

"Yeah, it's definitely about Chagall's studio," Zack sums up.

Cat grabs Wiet's printout. "My gut tells me these texts are related."

"The Iron Lady twinkling… That's obviously a reference to the Eiffel Tower. The place we're looking for could be a point from where one can see it." Zack leans in, his face dangerously close.

"A hidden, humming cove," she quotes from the first poem. "Humming… Let me check something!"

Frantically, she types in a question.

He reads from the search box on her screen. "What is special about the roof of the Garnier opera house?"

Most of the results that come up talk about Chagall's ceiling. But one mentions bees. Turns out there's a small beekeeping operation on the roof of the famed opera house.

"That's what's humming!" Cat cries out, the pieces clicking into place.

"A beehive!" Zack exclaims. "The first line of Cendrars's 'Studio' poem is, 'The Beehive'!"

"Do you think Chagall had a studio on the roof of the Palais Garnier, among the beehives?"

"Sounds unlikely."

Cat returns to her keyboard and searches for combinations of keywords including *beehive, Chagall* and *Blaise Cendrars.* A location comes up. It's an old but functioning artists' colony in southwest Paris. The place is called The Beehive. And, yes, Chagall rented a studio there during his first stay in the City of Light.

Cat shifts her gaze from the screen to Zack. Their eyes meet. His expression is triumphant, a feeling Cat shares fully.

"We have the place," he declares. "Let's go work out the date."

"Now?"

He looks at his watch. "It's only four. My event starts at eight and it's on the Left Bank, an easy ride from The Beehive."

She hesitates.

He asks gently, "What about you? Any immutable commitments this afternoon?"

"No, I'm free."

He stands up. "Then, what are we waiting for?"

CHAPTER 16

Zack picks up the helmet he brought for Cat—*good thinking, man!*—and holds it out to her when her phone trills.

She gives him an apologetic smile as she answers the call. "Hi, Dad!"

"Should I wait outside?" Zack mouths, moving to the door.

She'll want some privacy to talk to her father.

But Cat whispers back, "No, no, it's fine," before shifting her attention back to the phone.

Her father's voice booms through the device. Zack can't make out his exact words, but the loud undulations of pride and excitement are impossible to miss. He pulls out his own phone and thumbs through unread emails, but his focus is split.

"No, they haven't called yet," Cat replies to her dad. "You do know that none of my sisters own a TV, right? And Grandma only turns hers on to watch her favorite show. You're the only news junkie in the family!"

A hearty laugh comes from the phone in response. Zack finds himself smiling along even as a pang of envy creeps up on him. The effortlessness of their conversation, the warmth in Cat's father's tone, the way she rolls her eyes while looking mighty pleased...

Zack forces himself to focus on his phone screen again, but it's too late. His mind has drifted to his own parents. He never had such an easy relationship with his dad or with his mom while she was alive.

Well, that's not entirely true.

He does have some happy memories from when he was very young before his parents shipped him off to boarding school. Unless, of course, his eight-year-old brain fabricated those memories during his first and roughest year in Lille. They helped him feel less desperate, less angry, less... unwanted.

Here's the sad truth. The closest thing Zack has to family are his employees. And maybe also—*pathetic, but there you go*—his intrusive neighbors.

As Cat's conversation winds down, Zack's envy melts into a kind of detached admiration for the bond she shares with her father, for their camaraderie. And that right there is the main reason he refuses to start a family of his own. If he did but failed to connect with his children, they would be the ones to pay the price for his selfishness. And that would be unfair to them.

Cat wraps up the call with a promise to visit soon and turns to Zack. "Sorry about that!"

"No worries!" He hands her the helmet. "Shall we?"

Cat slips into her puffer jacket and a pair of sturdy boots, slings a backpack over her shoulders, and snaps the helmet on. He follows her out the door into the cold but sunny afternoon and leads her to his scooter parked just down the street.

"Ready for an unforgettable ride, Madame Cavallo?" Zack asks over his shoulder as he saddles his sleek machine.

She climbs on behind him, securing herself with a firm grip around his waist. "Full steam ahead, Captain Rigaud!"

He kicks his Yamaha into life, and they pull away. Zack stays on the bank, skirting the Canal Saint-Martin with its waters reflecting the changing sky. The festive garlands along their route add a cheerful sparkle to the cityscape.

After leaving the canal, Zack takes them through Le Marais. It's always a pleasure to revisit the oldest and quaintest neighborhood on the Right Bank, with its densely packed medieval buildings lining the cobblestone streets. This being mid-December, the narrow lanes are decorated with Christmas ornaments strung from lampposts. Pop-up vendors sell seasonal treats. Shops and restaurants are decked out in glitter.

"I love this area," Cat comments, her voice raised to carry over the hum of the scooter.

"It's hard not to," he shouts back.

They whiz past the Gothic Saint Jacques Tower, reaching skyward in all its lavish splendor, and then cross the Seine on the Pont Notre-Dame, which offers a breathtaking view of the wide river.

"Never gets old, does it?" Zack shouts, turning slightly toward Cat.

"Never!"

As he steers the scooter onto Cité Island, the traffic thickens. Cars and cyclists swarm around them, a chaotic ballet that demands his full attention. But it's the tightening of Cat's grip around his waist that takes center stage in his mind. Her hands clasp him tighter than before and her body presses against his back. Her closeness sends a ripple of something alarmingly pleasant through his veins. The sounds of the city buzz around them as he struggles to ignore the subtle shifting of Cat's body with every curve they lean into.

She's holding on to me for safety, nothing more!

Zack remembers how she fled last night, making him feel like a fool. She's not interested. He should mind the road instead of being distracted by the woman behind him, the feel of her hands, the warmth of her breath…

Pull yourself together, man!

Zack focuses intently on the Yamaha's path as they ride across the island. Once on the Left Bank, they glide into the Latin Quarter, which is a welcome distraction. Hordes of tourists blend together to form a colorful human patchwork.

Regaining his composure, Zack calls over his shoulder, "Can you spot any locals?"

"Those two over there?" Cat points to an older couple. "They're not gawking or taking selfies, and they're walking faster than a snail."

"Bingo!"

Her laughter floats forward, and her grip loosens a notch. Zack takes a deep breath, grateful for the respite as they continue south and west.

Soon the Montparnasse Tower comes into view, and he dutifully grumbles about its utter lack of charm. In keeping with Parisian custom, Cat agrees with that view. The last leg of their journey takes them along the narrow Passage Danzig. As they reach their destination at number 2, Zack is torn between relief and regret that the ride has come to an end.

CHAPTER 17

Zack cuts the engine. The street is as quiet as it is empty. They dismount and take off their helmets.

"Thanks for the ride!" Cat says. "It was fun."

"Glad you enjoyed it. There's nothing like crossing Paris on two wheels!"

They approach the gate and peer through the beautiful wrought iron gate at the quaint structure nestled in a picturesque garden. It's a four-story rotunda with large windows and a spectacular conical dome. The first and widest level of the dome is covered in classic terracotta tiles that match the color of the brick below. The tiles curve upward to the second level made of glass. It culminates in a pointed metal copper cap, judging by the oxidized green.

The rotunda's masonry is as weathered as that of the surrounding buildings. Vines hang from its façade. Its front entrance is a green door flanked by two Greco-Roman sculptures, each resting on a stone pedestal. The dignified gatekeepers give the cozy brick-and-iron place a touch of classical gravitas that's anachronistic and slightly preposterous. But only slightly.

Off the beaten track and far from the hustle and bustle of

central Paris, the shabby yet imposing Beehive offers a quirky serenity as if it were something…

"I've never seen anything so completely out of time!" Cat exclaims, echoing Zack's sentiment.

She leans closer to the ornate gate, her face brushing the metal as she peers inside.

Zack scans the wall for a buzzer when the green door of the rotunda swings open. A man in a crisp, dark blue suit and a tastefully understated tie steps out. He walks toward Cat and Zack, smiling pleasantly.

"Bonjour, I'm Sofian," he says as he unlocks the gate.

"Catherine, nice to meet you."

"I'm Zack. We're—"

"From the scavenger hunt, yes, I know," Sofian interrupts Zack. "I'm an assistant to Monsieur Wiet. I wasn't present at the ceremonies, but I've seen your files. It's my job to supervise your visit here at The Beehive."

"We were allowed into the opera house unsupervised," Zack jokes.

Sofian's face remains impassive. "This site is private property, Monsieur Rigaud. No visitors are allowed without a guide."

Cat turns to Zack. "The good news is that Sofian's presence here means we got the place right, don't you think?"

"I do." Zack winks at Sofian. "Do you?"

"What I think is irrelevant," the aide replies smoothly. "Please, follow me."

He leads Cat and Zack between the busty Roman statues and through the green door. Zack glances around the lobby. In browns and off-whites, it has an undeniable retro charm even if it's not as original as the exterior.

On either side of him, mailboxes and billboards cover the walls. Straight ahead is the base of a remarkable wooden staircase with its sturdy beams exposed. On a pedestal below the stairs, a sculpted Venus embraces a creature of indeterminate species. It could even be Groot from *Guardians of the Galaxy*.

Would Venus have a thing for tree aliens?

Why wouldn't she? Gods are weird.

On a small table next to Venus and Groot, Zack notices a scale model of The Beehive. Sofian informs them that the rotunda was put together in 1903 by a wealthy sculptor named Alfred Boucher, using the bits and pieces from the Paris Exposition of 1900.

The lobby's Christmas decorations are sparse, especially in comparison to Zack's building. Clearly, The Beehive's Christmas Planning Committee isn't living up to its full potential. Or—and he shudders to think—maybe The Beehive doesn't even have a Christmas planning committee.

Sofian leads them farther into the heart of the rotunda. The cozy circular space is the antithesis of Zack's sleek office building. Tall wooden beams stretch upward, dividing the curved wall into panel-like sections. A simple wooden door is embedded in each of these sections.

"You must keep your voices down," Sofian whispers, pointing at the doors. "The Beehive is still an active artists' colony. There's a painter or sculptor working behind every door you see."

"Speaking of artists, can we visit Chagall's studio?" Zack asks.

"I'm afraid you can't," the aide replies. "It's currently occupied by another artist."

Cat expels a frustrated sigh. "Shame."

"Chagall's studio was emptied when he returned to Russia from 1914 to 1922," Sofian says. "Later, it was extended and redone. You won't find a trace of him in there."

"Damn shame!" Zack laments.

Cat looks at Sofian from under her eyebrows. "Um… Would you happen to know what Monsieur Wiet meant when he asked to find him a date?"

"Whether I know it or not is irrelevant," Sofian replies.

Zack guffaws. "Nice try, Cat!"

"Thanks," she deadpans, then turns back to Sofian. "Can you at least tell us if any other team has been here today?"

Sofian nods. "Madame Djossou and Monsieur Jaume came in around noon and spent a few hours poking around."

Ah. Well, the good news is that Marguerite and Lorenzo haven't worked out the place. The bad news is that Christelle and Edgar have.

Zack moves closer to Cat in the center to get a better look at the wooden staircase. It's robust and refined at the same time. Some, but not all, of the elegant balusters are painted a muted teal.

Intentional? Left unfinished? Work in progress?

The smooth, well-worn handrail runs the length of the staircase up, up, up, turns at a landing, and goes up again. Zack tilts his head back.

Wow! From this vantage point, he can see the entire stairwell with its winding steps and sturdy handrails, leading all the way to the third floor. The glass layer of the dome above allows the last rays of the day to pour in and create patterns on the stairs.

"Chagall, Chagall, in the ladders of light," Cat recites, her face turned upward.

That sounds familiar… It's the last lines of the second poem!

Cat turns to him, eyes bright. "I totally get what Cendrars meant!"

Me too, Zack means to say, but then he tumbles into her hazel eyes and forgets to speak.

"Would you like to see the upper floors?" Sofian asks.

"Yes, please," Cat answers.

She turns away from Zack and follows Wiet's assistant into the ladders of light.

CHAPTER 18

Over the past hour, Cat and Zack checked every nook and cranny of every floor—except for the inaccessible studios—under Sofian's watchful eye. Nothing jumped out at either of them. Nothing screamed a specific date.

They're back on the ground floor now, rechecking what they've already seen. Zack tries to remain upbeat, but his spirits have been dampened. There's no denying it.

How long before Sofian asks them to leave?

The aide pulls out a tablet. "If you're done with the tour, would you like to watch a short documentary where Chagall talks about his years in The Beehive?"

"Sure," Cat replies.

Zack nods.

Anything to drag out the time, hoping for some inspiration!

Sofian taps Play on his tablet. For the next fifteen minutes, Cat and Zack listen to Chagall, filmed in his eighties, reminisce about The Beehive. In the years before World War I, when he lived here, the area wasn't yet urbanized, and The Beehive was surrounded by farms and cows.

He grabs a cow and paints with a cow!

In the documentary, Chagall tells the interviewer that none of The Beehive residents were eager to sell their paintings. In those days he felt, Chagall explains, that if he sold a canvas, he'd have to paint the same one again, because it belonged in the studio in The Beehive. His friends felt the same.

Picasso, Modigliani, Léger, Delaunay, Soutine, Apollinaire… They were ridiculously poor. Chagall, with a tiny stipend he'd secured from Russia, wasn't the worst off. Still, a half sardine was often all he could afford for dinner. He painted in his underwear so as not to stain the only set of clothes he owned.

"Ah, The Beehive," Chagall muses onscreen, his expression part nostalgia, part mischief. "One came out of there either dead or famous."

Cat's eminently kissable lips curl up into a smile. "Picasso and Chagall were lucky to come out famous."

"So did Modigliani," Zack offers, tearing his eyes from her mouth. "Except, he was dead before he was famous."

When the movie ends, Cat and Zack huddle together to brainstorm. They've just explored every corner of The Beehive, watched a documentary on its history, and listened to Chagall himself talk about it, yet the crucial piece of the puzzle—the date—still eludes them.

"Could it be 1903, when Boucher built this place?" Zack wonders aloud.

Cat rubs her chin. "It could also be 1912, 1913, or 1914, when Chagall lived and worked here."

The four possibilities spin in Zack's head. It's a bummer they haven't found any clues to point them to the one that's the solution to Wiet's puzzle.

He turns to Cat, half-joking, half-desperate. "Any psychic vibes on which year we should pick?"

"No vibes, sorry." She shrugs an apology.

He's about to suggest she pick one at random, when

Sofian approaches them. "Um… If you're done…" He gestures toward the lobby.

Hanging their heads, Cat and Zack follow him to the exit. At the door, the aide wishes them good luck. Zack thanks him for his help. Cat says nothing, making Zack realize she's fallen behind. He scans the lobby. She's standing in front of the billboard encased in glass on the wall, studying it.

Curious, Zack joins her. The billboard displays maps of the grounds, lists of residents, and three photographs. Two show a bearded man, posing proudly next to sculptures.

"That's Alfred Boucher, the founder," Sofian clarifies, following their gaze.

But it's the third photo that has Cat spellbound. Zack steps closer and adjusts the glasses on his nose to examine a woman in the picture standing under a clock on the wall.

"Is that Madame Boucher?" Zack asks Sofian.

"I don't know," the assistant says.

The details of the setting are clear—she's in The Beehive. Zack can see the distinctive vertical beams and the foot of the central staircase, meaning that the picture was taken on the ground floor. Behind the lady, several paintings are propped up against the wall. One of them, although only a quarter of it is in the frame, is undoubtedly by Chagall.

"That photo…" Cat begins, her gaze fixed on the picture. "The vibe you asked about earlier, I'm feeling it."

"Maybe what you're feeling is something else," Zack says.

She shoots him a quizzical look.

The gears in his head turn at full speed. "Maybe it's your logic that's intervened, subconsciously."

"What do you mean?" She furrows her brow in confusion.

"The date we need could be right in front of us."

The crease between her brows deepens. "I don't understand."

"There could be a date on the back of that picture."

She blinks, then lifts her eyes to the ceiling. "Duh!"

"Can we look at the back of that photo?" Zack asks Sofian.

"Of course." Wiet's aide pulls a small key from his pocket and unlocks the glass case.

He carefully unpins the photograph and hands it over.

Zack holds his breath as he flips it, but the back is disappointingly blank. A mixture of disappointment and frustration clouds his thoughts. Through the fog, his own sixth sense—or, rather, logic—tells him there must be another way to "see" the date. He stares at the front of the photo again. Clarity comes like a sneeze that's been building up for a while.

Hot damn!

He points at the partially visible Chagall painting in the photo. "Do you recognize this painting?"

"I don't," Sofian says.

"It looks familiar…" Cat leans closer. "I think I've seen it in a book or online."

Zack peers at the fragment of the canvas that shows a man with two faces looking through a large window at Paris. Against the sky, the smoky white Eiffel Tower stands tall—much taller than the buildings at its base. Three other human figures float through the cityscape, two horizontally and one, downward dangling from a kite.

"Found it!" Cat, who was searching online while he studied the photo cries out.

She holds up her phone with the same painting, but in full and in color.

"It's called *Paris through the Window,*" she says. "Painted in 1913."

Cat and Zack look at each other.

"We have the date!" she announces. "1913! High five, partner!"

She raises her arm, fingers spread. Zack does the same, and their palms meet in the air with a gratifying slap.

"Actually, we can do better than just the year," he says. "We can give Wiet the day and month, too."

"How?"

"Thanks to the clock above the woman's head. What time does it show?"

She peers. "Three twenty-two in the afternoon."

"Yes, this is, clearly, a daylight shot."

She eyes him expectantly.

"Look at the shadows on the floor," he says, pointing.

"Is there something wrong with them?"

"No, what I meant, is that their length and direction are clues. They can tell us about the position of the sun when the photo was taken."

"Okaaay."

He points at the warm coat the woman is wearing. "She's dressed for cold weather, right?"

"Uh-huh."

"That's a helpful detail, because the sun's path changes with the seasons." He searches her face. "Have I lost you?"

"Totally."

He pulls out his phone. "I'm going to plug a few possible dates, plus the known time of day and location, which is Paris, into an online solar calculator."

"And then?"

"You'll see."

With a few taps, Zack enters the data for January 1, 1913, and notes the sun's elevation and azimuth. He repeats the exercise for January 21 and February 21 of the same year.

"I'm running iterative tests," he explains, "to find the sun's elevation and azimuth that would best match the properties of the shadows in the photo."

She watches over his shoulder as the results populate his screen.

Minutes pass by as Zack makes his calculations.

Finally, he looks up. "It's February 11, 1913. The shadows line up best with the sun's position on that date."

"Are you sure?"

"I'm not saying my method is foolproof," he admits. "But it's sound."

Cat nods. "All right, let's do this! Let's email Wiet our answer."

She composes a short message in the email app on her phone:

> Place: The Beehive at 2 Passage Danzig
> Date: February 11, 1913

And then she hits send.

By the time they get back on Zack's scooter, it's already dark. Cat puts her arms around Zack. He takes a deep breath and starts the engine. Whether the answer they just turned in was right or wrong or whether they stay in the game or drop out, there's no denying that these past few days have been the most fun he's had in years.

CHAPTER 19

Zack enters the quiet sanctum of the conference room. Not that his office isn't quiet, but he needs a change of scenery. The paper cup in his hand warms his fingers, sending up clouds of fragrant steam. With fingers itching to pull out his phone, he sets the cup down on the mahogany table and rereads Wiet's email he received a few minutes ago.

After sending in their answer to the day's puzzle yesterday, Cat and Zack rode back to the Right Bank. Zack dropped Cat off at her place in the 20th arrondissement and then raced to his own building in the 9th. At home, he changed into a tux and took a cab to the speed dating event with the potential investors. Luckily, he got there on time.

The first thing he did this morning while still in bed was to check his inbox. But there was nothing from Wiet. Zack kept refreshing compulsively all day until his last refresh at five, an email appeared. It was short, but that didn't diminish the thrill Zack felt—and still does—at the news it announced.

He unlocks his phone and reads the message a third time:

Dear Catherine and Zachary,

Congratulations! You are one of the two teams that submitted the correct answers and will continue the hunt for Father Christmas.

You will soon receive another email with a cipher. The solution will be your next clue.

Good luck,
Damien Wiet

The words echo in his head with the sweet melody of victory. Grinning to himself, he dials Cat.

She picks up on the second ring, her voice bright. "Hey, Zack! Did you see the email?"

"Yeah, just now. No ceremony this time, huh? He just moves on to the next cipher."

"Could this be a sign we're in the home stretch?" she inquires.

"I hope so," Zack replies.

No, I don't.

She chuckles. "Unread emails piling up?"

"That and a bunch of other stuff."

"I hear you," she sympathizes.

"Have you found out who the other team is?"

"It's Christelle and Edgar," she replies. "No surprise there, right? They got to The Beehive before us."

"Any idea how they figured out the year?"

"No clue," she admits. "But I'll ask."

The conversation tapers off. There's a finality to Cat's tone and the unmistakable air of an impending goodbye. For no apparent reason, Zack panics.

"Hey, I have an idea," he hastens to say before he can second-guess himself. "Since Wiet isn't celebrating this win, why don't we? How about the four of us have dinner tomorrow night?"

There's a brief pause before Cat says, "That's a great idea, Zack! But it has a big flaw."

"I don't see any."

"What if the next cipher drops tonight or in the morning? By tomorrow night there might be only one team left," she says. "Or none."

His mind ticks through those options. "Then we should celebrate tonight! I'll call Edgar, and you see if Christelle's free. I'll cook."

The last words are out before he can think better of them. He'd meant to say, my treat, and suggest a restaurant, but his tongue misspoke. Perhaps, being the stubborn son of a gun that he is, he wants Cat to have the dinner she ran away from last time. Only this time, it won't be spaghetti. And they won't be alone, so she has no reason to head for the hills.

"I'll make something special," he adds quickly, hoping to entice her further into his plan. "How about eight o'clock?"

His mind is already working out the logistics. If he leaves at six-thirty, he'll be home by seven-fifteen, and he'll have at least three-quarters of an hour to cook. Fortunately, he restocked the fridge and pantry two days ago. Since he buys groceries to cook in bulk, there's enough to improvise a dinner for four.

That should work.

"That's not going to work, I'm afraid," Cat says. "I'm actually in your neighborhood right now."

He raises an eyebrow. "Oh? What brings you to the 9th?"

"I just finished a reading for a client on rue Bleue."

"Rue Bleue is practically next door to where I live!"

"Usually, clients come to my shop," she says, the sound muffled by the roar of a passing motorbike. "But this lady is a regular, and she's recovering from an operation, and she hates virtual sessions."

"I hate video conferencing."

"Not a fan, either," she chimes in. "Makes it hard to tap into the client's physical energy."

"Or properly read the room including looks, expressions, and body language."

Belatedly, Zack realizes she might interpret this as him saying that her "tapping into energy" is just paranormal mumbo-jumbo for interpreting nonverbal cues. Mind you, that's what he actually thinks. But he's polite enough not to share that fact with a woman who firmly believes in her esoteric shit.

Will my attempt to establish a rapport backfire?

"Anyway," she says, a hint of weariness in her voice. "The reading drained me. I'm going straight home. And, once I'm on my couch, there's no way I'll make it out again tonight."

"Matter of fact, I'm wasted, too. I was just about to call it a day. I can be home around five-thirty."

Zack glances at his half-empty cup of coffee before downing it. Letitia will have to reschedule his six o'clock update with Marketing.

A moment of silence stretches between them as Cat hesitates.

Zack plows ahead. "Just stick around, yeah? Stop by a café or do some shopping. It shouldn't take me more than thirty minutes, and I'll call you as soon as I get there."

"OK," she replies. "I'll call Christelle."

As soon as they hang up, Zack dials Edgar.

The math teacher answers with his usual peppy cynicism. "Let me check my social calendar. Oh, wow! It's as full as my bank account. I'll be there."

Satisfied, Zack ends the call and hurries back to his office. He gathers his things while instructing Letitia to reschedule his six o'clock.

"Something personal and urgent came up," he adds. "I have to go out."

"Is it about the scavenger hunt?" Letitia asks. "Everyone here is rooting for you!"

He gives a dramatic look over his shoulder like a spy

preparing to reveal top-secret information and presses a finger to his lips. "Shh. And, yes, it is."

It's true, actually.

Sort of.

CHAPTER 20

Clutching a paper cup of tea from the coffee shop around the corner, Cat arrives at the gate of Zack's building. It's five twenty-five. He hasn't called her yet. The traffic is even heavier than usual for this time of day, but he was extremely punctual every time they met. He must've factored the traffic in when he estimated how long it would take him to get here.

He'll call any minute now.

The gate swings open behind a departing resident, and Cat glides into the courtyard. She's been here twice in a week, but she finds this hidden haven just as unexpected and enchanting as the first time.

More, actually.

Twilight has transformed the space into a fairy-tale tableau. Strings of garden lights have come on, emanating a soft, multicolored glow. The sprawling tree in the middle—a magnolia?—sparkles with those lights. Ahead, the lobby's glass doors frame a handsome Christmas tree decorated with sparkling ornaments. From where Cat stands, the tree is a little hazy, like a vision, which only adds to the magical feel.

A festive spirit envelops not only the courtyard, but the entire U-shaped building around it. Every window twinkles with tiny LEDs or candles. That glowing warmth inside the apartments creates a striking contrast to the slate blue of the sky. Snowflake stickers embellish the windows. On the balconies, glittering reindeer and hanging Santas sway in the gentle breeze.

In the background, the soft strains of a Christmas carol waft through the air. Cat listens, trying to figure out where it's coming from. Likely, a speaker in the concierge's box.

The Christmas Planning Committee can give themselves a pat on the back!

Near a wall, Cat spots a quintessentially Parisian bench, styled with curved armrests and a rounded back. Its dark green paint is chipped in places, revealing hints of the wood beneath. It looks dry. Cat runs her hand over the seat to be sure, then settles down. The bench offers a perfect vantage point from which to enjoy her tea and the heartwarming surroundings while she waits for Zack.

Just then, the lobby door opens, and Cat's attention snaps to the figure stepping out into the courtyard. But it isn't Zack. It's Lucile, the HOA board president, with her distinctive blond bob. After throwing her trash in the dumpster, Lucile notices Cat and approaches with a curious smile. The women greet each other.

"I'm waiting for Zack," Cat says. "He should be here any minute. We're having a little get-together for the last two teams in the scavenger hunt."

"Did you find the Chagall painting yet? I haven't seen anything new on TV."

"Not yet," Cat admits. "But I think we're getting close."

"How exciting!" Lucile clasps her hands. "On the subject of gatherings..."

Cat tucks a loose strand of hair into her hat. "Yes?"

"You know, it's funny. Zack's place is ideal for them, and he seems to enjoy hosting soirees for his employees and now fellow treasure hunters. Yet he balks at the idea of the condo Christmas party."

Cat adjusts her scarf, unsure of what to say.

Lucile gestures broadly around the courtyard. "The condo is small and look at how well we keep things. It's not like we're going to mess up his apartment!"

"I'm sure you wouldn't."

"Could it be that he doesn't like kids much? We do have a few in the building. Monica's boys and some younger ones from other units. Any insight on that?"

Does she still think I'm his girlfriend? "Honestly, I have no idea why he's hesitating."

"Oh, well," Lucile says. "We still have ten days to make him change his mind."

Cat expects Lucile to retreat into the building at this point, but the older woman sits down on the bench instead, pulling her thick cardigan closer against the chill.

"I've always loved Chagall," Lucile says. "The way he painted Paris is exactly how I see it, too. No other artist really captures that feeling."

Cat nods enthusiastically. "I did quite a bit of research on him in preparation for the treasure hunt. Did you know that he once said, 'My art needs Paris like a tree needs water'?"

"No, I didn't." Lucile's eyes sparkle in the light of the courtyard's decorations. "But I remember reading somewhere that he called himself a dreamer who never woke up."

"That explains the flying couples, doesn't it?"

"Oh yes, and the donkeys, too."

They smile.

Lucile studies Cat's face. "They said on TV that each team is made up of a psychic and a mathematician, and since you're Zack's teammate and he's a mathematician…"

"Then I'm a psychic," Cat fesses up. "Excellent deduction!"

"I was a psychotherapist before I retired," Lucile reveals. "You know, our professions aren't that different."

"No?"

"Both psychics and psychotherapists try to help people deal with their emotional problems."

"True," Cat agrees. "By the way, I like psychology a lot. Self-help books are my favorite bedtime reading."

"It's called bibliotherapy. But be careful! Not all self-help books are worth your time. Some are excellent, some are just nonsense."

"Really?"

"Books on cosmic ordering, for example, are often little more than pseudo-intellectual word salads," Lucile warns.

"I mostly read books on relationships."

"Do you, now?"

"I'm trying to correct a flaw I have that ruins all my romantic relationships."

"What flaw?" Lucile asks.

"I'm too needy, you see."

Am I opening up to a virtual stranger because she's a therapist, or because I'm desperate?

Lucile frowns. "What makes you think you're too needy?"

"Where do I begin?" Cat sighs. "Let's just say, every man I was in love with ended up dumping me."

Before Lucile can react, Cat's phone buzzes. She glances at the screen and puts it to her ear. "Hey, Zack!"

"I'm here," he says. "Just parked my scooter. Where exactly are you?"

"In your courtyard."

"Oh, cool! I'll be there in three minutes."

Lucile gets to her feet. "I'll leave you two to your plans. It was great talking to you, Catherine."

"Likewise."

As Lucile disappears into the building, the concierge's door swings open, and a boy of about eight scurries out, clutching a bag of trash. He leaves the door ajar. Seizing the opportunity, a red tabby makes a stealthy escape.

Just then, Zack strides into the courtyard, an apologetic expression on his face. "I'm so sorry I'm late!"

"Only fifteen minutes. It's fine, really," Cat reassures him with a genuine smile. "I had a good chat with Lucile. And your courtyard is quite a festive sight!"

A loud rustling draws their attention. The boy from earlier is now high in the branches of the magnolia tree.

How did he get there? Zack and Cat go to him.

"I was trying to get Nemo," the boy stammers.

Is Nemo the red tabby cat I saw? He doesn't seem to be in the tree.

"Did you get him?" Zack asks.

"He jumped down and went back in," the boy replies. "But now I can't come down. I'm too scared."

"Underage humans should be supervised at all times," Zack whispers to Cat, frustration coloring his tone. "They're a danger to themselves and to the social life of their neighbors. Ugh."

Lucile may have been onto something…

To the boy, Zack says, "Hang on, Paulo! We'll get you down."

He hands Cat his helmet and steps closer to the trunk. With measured movements, he begins to climb. The branches look sturdy, but his ascent is complicated by the fairy lights spiraling around the trunk.

Cat is impressed by Zack's agility as he gets closer to Paulo.

"I got you!" Zack assures the boy as he reaches his perch.

Wrapping an arm around Paulo, he starts their cautious descent. The boy clings to the man. It's obvious from the way Paulo avoids looking down that he has a fear of heights. He must've climbed the tree in the heat of the moment before his phobia kicked in. Zack takes his time maneuvering Paulo back to safety.

I hadn't pegged Zack as a firefighter at heart.

That's because he's not! If anything, this episode has

shown how much he dislikes children. It doesn't take a psychic to see the writing on the wall if Cat ever lets their obvious mutual attraction turn into a fling.

Verboten! Stop! Go back! Falling for this man is out of the question.

Back on solid ground, Paulo looks like he's about to cry, overcome by a strong emotion. Cat wonders if it's relief or shame that he was too chicken to climb down on his own.

"Please, don't tell my mom I let Nemo out!" he begs Zack in lieu of thanks. "We have to keep him in at dusk, so he doesn't hunt."

At that, he turns on his heel and bolts into the loge.

Zack turns to Cat. "Well, this is not how I wanted to start the evening."

"Paulo's safe," she reminds him. "So are you and so is Nemo. It could have been much worse."

He takes his helmet from her. "Shall we go in? I have a three-course dinner to whip up before Christelle and Edgar get here."

"I'll give you a hand." She follows him into the lobby. "Let's hope the rest of the evening is more... um, grounded."

CHAPTER 21

Cat places the last poached pear on the table, and steps back to admire her handiwork. After the *oeufs cocotte* with mushrooms and the *magret* with mashed potatoes, the four scavenger hunters are about to dig into their well-deserved desserts. Zack pours muscat wine into glasses and sits down across from Cat.

This went well, she tells herself. Neither she nor Zack are particularly skilled at cooking. To make up for it, they chose recipes that were simple without being trivial. Besides, their limited culinary skills proved to be complementary.

Cat takes a spoonful, and her palate confirms that she can be proud of her pears. Zack grins at her from across the table, his expression telegraphing, *We make a good team, you and I.*

Christelle tastes her dessert. "Mmm, I love it!"

"Did you really make it yourselves?" spoon in mouth, Edgar looks from Zack to Cat.

"It's the only dessert I know how to make." Cat shows her palms. "These little hands did all the peeling, melting, and poaching, while Zack took care of the main course."

Edgar pretends to tip a hat. "Bravo!"

"To the cooks!" Christelle raises her glass. "And may the best team win the scavenger hunt!"

Everybody drinks to that.

They finish their desserts. Zack refills the glasses. The conversation flows as smoothly as the wine. Zack's spacious dining room is brimming with a jolly, holiday atmosphere despite the conspicuous absence of seasonal decorations—save for the window stickers mandated by his building's Christmas commissars.

"About yesterday's leg of the hunt," Zack says, his gaze on his teacher. "Cat and I were wondering how you guys figured out the place and the date?"

Cat lifts her eyes to Christelle. "Come on, spill the beans! I told you ours, now tell me yours."

"As for the place," Christelle begins, "it was the poems that led us there, just like they did for you. Regarding the year..." She looks at Edgar.

"We narrowed it down to 1903, 1912, 1913 or 1914. After that we got stuck," he says.

"How did you get unstuck?" Zack eggs him on.

Edgar points to his teammate. "Christelle here picked 1913, and that's what we sent in."

"Just the year?" Zack asks.

Edgar nods. "And the place, of course. Fortunately, that was enough to pass."

Cat turns to Christelle. "Fa divination?"

"I didn't have my figurines with me, so I performed a ritual dance," Christelle replies.

"Or maybe it was just a lucky guess," Edgar says.

Zack nods, skepticism written all over his face.

Cat and Christelle roll their eyes.

"What about you?" Edgar asks. "What made you pick 1913? Christelle hasn't had a chance to relay it yet."

Zack tells him how Cat spotted the photo on the billboard, how they found the fragment of the painting on it, and how he figured out the exact date using solar calculations.

With a surprisingly pleased look on his face, Edgar sits back. "The student has outdone his teacher!"

"Only because Cat noticed the pic." Zack gives her a tender look.

Her cheeks suddenly warm, Cat averts her gaze. She catches Christelle shifting her eyes from said cheeks to Zack with an amused expression on her face.

Grr, how embarrassing!

Cat racks her brain for a new topic. Thankfully, a detail that has been in the back of her mind for several days now comes to the fore. It's been bothering her but not enough to override the other, more pressing concerns. Now seems like the perfect time to air it out.

"Remember," she says to Zack, "when Wiet's assistant told us Wiet hadn't written that poem about the Opéra Garnier beehives?"

"He didn't?" Christelle and Edgar exclaim in unison.

"No," Zack confirms before turning back to Cat. "The assistant told us it was her and another aide who wrote it for their boss."

"Do you believe her?" Edgar asks.

Cat nods. "Ever since then I've been thinking about why Wiet didn't disclose it? Why lie about such a minor detail at the risk of upsetting and alienating his assistants?"

"Maybe he didn't think their feelings were any more important than his reasons for passing off their efforts as his own," Christelle suggests.

"That's the thing," Cat retorts. "What reasons? I see none, other than dumb vanity."

"It could also be the pressure of the expectations he's raised by presenting himself as a puzzle whiz," Edgar joins in. "Not that it justifies such inelegant behavior, of course."

Christelle scoffs, "What expectations? Wiet is a mathematician and a businessman. Nobody expected him to be able to write halfway-decent poetry."

"So, vanity," Cat sums up.

Zack scratches the back of his head. "Hmm… Doubtful."

"Why?" Cat asks.

"Wiet is a successful entrepreneur," he begins. "I would understand if he lied to save his company and his employees' jobs. But out of vanity? I don't know… It feels gratuitous."

"Which begs the question." Edgar leans forward. "If he was so cavalier with the truth about such a minor matter, what else has he lied to us about?"

Everyone looks at Edgar, pondering his question.

In a flash, Cat catches his drift. "The whole scavenger hunt!"

"Bingo!" Edgar cheers. "What if Wiet designed it to be too hard?"

Christelle peers at him. "You mean unwinnable?"

"If no one wins, he gets to keep his money," Edgar says, "all while reaping the benefits of good publicity."

Zack shakes his head at Edgar. "Your negativity is getting the better of you."

"You think?" his teacher asks.

"If no one wins, people will come to the same conclusion, that Wiet had planned the game that way. The contestants, the public, the press, the museums he promised money to—everyone will be terribly disappointed. Wiet's reputation would take a big hit."

"I see what you mean," Christelle concurs. "Reputation is everything in business. I don't think Wiet would risk his for a bit of publicity he doesn't really need."

The argument sounds convincing enough for Cat to nod.

Edgar begins to say something, when four smartphones come to life at once with three pinging and one buzzing. Everyone reaches for their device. Unless there's been a nuclear attack, or an alien invasion—in which case sirens would be wailing—there's only one person who'd send a message to all four of them at once.

Damien Wiet.

CHAPTER 22

Cat, Zack, Christelle, and Edgar each open their phones. The screens light up with a new challenge from Damien Wiet.

Cat reads silently, her chest tight with apprehension:

Good evening!

Here's a binary code cipher for you. It spells out the place where you will find your next clue. Go to that place, and from there, follow your logic and intuition to the next stop of the hunt.

You're getting very close.

Good luck,
Damien Wiet

Below the signoff, rows of binary codes sprawl across her display.

01000010

01100101
01100001
01110101
01100010
01101111
01110101
01110010
01100111

Beside her, Zack and Edgar exchange puzzled looks.

"What do you think?" Christelle asks them, concern in her voice.

Cat chimes in, just as worried as Christelle, "Too hard?"

"Too easy, actually," Zack says.

Edgar nods, "Suspiciously so."

Zack's fingers fly over his phone's screen. "Each of these sequences is just an 8-bit binary number that corresponds to a letter."

"This cipher is a basic ASCII conversion," Edgar mutters, opening up some website. "All we have to do is translate it back."

Christelle and Cat hold their breath, but not for long. It only takes a heartbeat before Zack and Edgar look up from their screens.

"Beaubourg," they declare in unison.

Christelle and Cat clap their hands.

"That could refer to either the neighborhood or its main attraction, the Pompidou Center," Christelle says.

"True," Edgar agrees. "Most people use *Beaubourg* as a shorthand for the cultural center."

Cat jumps in, "The Pompidou Center houses the Museum of Modern Art, which has a permanent collection of about a dozen Chagall paintings."

"Sounds like a good place to start," Zack says.

"I suggest we hit the museum first thing in the morning," Christelle says to Edgar, her tone firm.

Edgar smiles. "Best to beat the crowd. The line outside can stretch into eternity."

"I have a full schedule tomorrow morning." Zack casts Cat a regretful look. "A meeting, a videoconference in the morning, and then a working lunch. I won't make it until three."

Cat meets his gaze. "Three it is, then. I'll sync my schedule and make sure to book those skip-the-line tickets."

She smiles to hide her disappointment. It's clear that prize money means less to Zack than it does to the others at the table, including her. He can afford to prioritize his work at the risk of ceding the victory to Edgar and Christelle. It's unfair!

Am I mad enough at him yet?

The question gives Cat pause. And the answer, too obvious to pretend she can't see it, irks her even more.

I'm trying to work up a grudge big enough to help me leave in a few minutes.

Christelle picks up her empty dessert bowl and wine glass from the table. "Thanks for tonight, Zack!" She looks at Cat. "And Cat, for the delicious poached pears. I had a wonderful time."

"This was needed," Edgar adds, rising from his seat and reaching for some empty bowls.

"Oh, no, please, don't worry about it!" Zack interjects with a friendly wave of his hand. "You're my guests. Let me take care of the cleanup. I insist!"

Quickly, before she can change her mind, Cat stands up. "Well, if you put it that way, who are we to argue with the host's wishes?"

The air between her and Zack crackles with unspoken words, so she tosses him a thank-you and heads for the door, Christelle and Edgar in tow. She avoids looking at Zack and is grateful when the door closes behind her, shielding her from temptation.

Next to Zack, Cat stands in the skip-the-line queue to get into the Pompidou Center, taking comfort in the fact that it's the shorter line.

The building, a bold statement of modernism, towers with its exposed skeleton of colorful tubes, pulsating with the energy of hundreds of visitors. There is always something fun going on. It might be a mind-bending exhibit, a rare film projection, an event, or all the above. But Cat hasn't even looked at the program today. Her mind is preoccupied with the task at hand.

Did Christelle and Edgar crack the puzzle this morning?

Cat almost called Christelle an hour ago to ask, but then decided it would be inappropriate. And awkward. Anyway, she'll find out soon enough.

At last, Cat and Zack enter the building. In the atrium, they turn left and step onto the escalator enclosed in a clear tube. Aptly nicknamed *caterpillar*, it climbs up the glass wall to the Museum of Modern Art on the fifth floor.

Once in the museum area, they wind through the maze of galleries until they reach the room dedicated to Marc Chagall. Excitement bubbles in Cat's chest as they enter the room behind a group of Japanese tourists.

"This isn't what I expected," Zack says, looking around.

Cat scans the walls of the rectangular room. Instead of the paintings in the museum's permanent collection, her gaze meets an entirely different assortment. She heads for the introductory panel on the right. Zack follows. Silently, they read the text on the plaque.

Aha!

This is a surprise ephemeral exhibit titled, *Chagall: Lost and Found.* It's a one-day event featuring a curated selection of the works recovered by the police in 1994, five years after Luc Stratte stole them from Chagall's widow Valentina.

Cat smirks. "I bet it's Wiet who arranged for and sponsored this show."

"I agree," Zack says. "This can't be a coincidence. The

1952 *Father Christmas* painting we're looking for was one of the works that Stratte had snatched."

She turns her attention back to the canvases on the walls. "I don't see that *Father Christmas* here."

"If that painting was here, that would be the end of the hunt, wouldn't it?" He flashes a playful smile.

Lightheaded from the effect, she agrees, "True."

They begin to study the lithographs and paintings in the ephemeral exhibit, trying to find the clue Wiet referred to in his text message. None of the works are Christmas themed or portray a Santa. Two lithographs depict identifiable cities, Paris and Vitebsk, Chagall's hometown. But neither shows a specific location within those cities.

"What are we missing?" Cat mutters, frustrated.

At Zack's suggestion, they focus on the text labels next to the artwork. Once again, they walk around the room, reading and photographing the captions. Along with the name of the painter, the title of the work, and the date of its creation, each text contains the story of its recovery. Not an actual story, but a summary of where and how the police found the work after Stratte was caught.

When they're done, Zack and Cat huddle over their collected data.

"Our con man didn't mind traveling for work," Zack notes, scrolling through the images on his screen.

"Saint-Paul-de-Vence in the South… Néchin in Belgium… Chartres, southwest of Paris," Cat adds. "These places keep coming up."

He lifts his gaze from the screen. "Wiet could've rehidden *Father Christmas* in one of them."

"Which means we might have to plan some road trips to follow Stratte's trail of breadcrumbs."

He surveys her. "You really think we should visit those three locations?"

"Not all three, if we get lucky on the first or second one."

Or if Christelle and Edgar beat us to it.

Zack shakes his head in mock dismay. "This is getting out of hand. What next? A sleigh ride to the North Pole, just to keep things interesting?"

"Seriously, though," Cat says, "where would you start?"

"In Chartres."

"Why?"

"It's the only day trip," he replies. "But I do recognize that my choice is influenced by Chartres' proximity to Paris—"

"In other words, by convenience."

"Yes," he admits. "And that may not be the best guiding principle in a treasure hunt."

They consider the options for a few minutes.

"Let's go to Chartres," Cat says with a determined nod.

"Convenience for the win!"

"That's not why I picked it."

He squints at her. "Then why?"

"Because…" She shrugs. "Call it a hunch."

He replies with a teasing smile. "Sixth sense for the win!"

"Come on, we're done here," she declares. "I have a virtual reading at seven. No time to waste."

Her tone deliberately crisp, Cat turns on her heel and heads for the exit.

CHAPTER 23

Cat listens to the rhythmic clacking of wheels and the murmur of her fellow passengers as the TER train rumbles toward Chartres. The city where Stratte spent the last years of his life from 2014 to 2016 is an easy, ninety-minute ride from Paris on the regional train. It's where she and Zack are headed on this Wednesday morning.

Is it best to start in Chartres?

Cat is far from sure. She didn't have a vision or even a strong vibe like with the photo at The Beehive about this destination. It was more of a vague feeling. If she's being completely honest, she can't rule out that it wasn't a subconscious preference for practicality. Zack made the same choice for the same reason, but at least he was aware of it.

In contrast, Christelle picked the less convenient possibility of Néchin. It's a small Belgian town where Stratte lay relatively low for a while, after his trial and public disgrace. He'd been slapped with a 10 million tax adjustment, but he managed to avoid jail time by convincing the experts and judges that he was mentally disabled.

I kid you not.

Next to Cat, Zack pores over a map of Chartres spread out on his lap. "Any hunches where in Chartres we should start?"

"If it worked that way, I would have found the painting on day one."

"Would've been nice!" He points out a spot on the map. "Well, then I suggest we start with the cathedral. It's what Chartres is most famous for."

"Sounds like a plan."

"I hope it's the final leg of this hunt!" he exclaims. "I hope what we'll find won't be yet another clue, but the painting itself."

Ouch.

"Me too," she mutters.

Just days ago, Zack was openly flirting with her, but look at him now! He can't end their acquaintance fast enough.

Thank God I didn't give in to temptation!

If she had, she'd be head over heels in love with him by now, which is to say emotionally dependent, vulnerable, and miserable. And Zack would be exactly where he is now—eager to move on. By standing her ground, she saved herself some heartache. And buckets of awkwardness for both.

Cat's gaze drifts out the window to the passing scenery. The train speeds past the town of Rambouillet. The landscape outside is a sad tableau of wintry, melancholy fields. The frost clings to the sparse vegetation and bare branches that seem to tremble in the faint sun.

I wish it were snowing! The heavenly fluff would cover the depressed vista with a glistening white blanket and make everything better.

"Did you know," Zack says, staring at a beautiful picture on his phone, "that Chagall created amazing stained-glass windows for various places of worship in France, Europe, and Israel."

Cat points to the church window on his screen. "Where is this one?"

"In Reims Cathedral."

"Did he paint any windows in Chartres Cathedral?"

He shifts his gaze to her. "The windows in Chartres Cathedral are ancient, from the thirteenth century. They're known for that deep, intense blue—"

"The famous Chartres blue?"

"Exactly," he confirms. "No one's been able to replicate it since the Middle Ages."

"Really?"

He nods. "I read about it when I was researching Chartres for our visit. Apparently, it's a big mystery in the art world. The technique has been lost."

"That's a shame."

"Yeah, makes you wonder about all the knowledge, art, literature, and other amazing things created by geniuses and lost to time and morons."

Cat grunts in agreement, but her thoughts are already far away from the blue of Chartres.

God, I'm such a loser!

While she gazed at the scenery, getting all emotional and depressed, Zack spent his forced downtime *productively*. He was researching Chartres in preparation for their visit.

For crying out loud! Her untreatable sentimentality annoys Cat so much she would burst into tears right now if she were alone. Since she isn't, she turns her gaze back to the window where the countryside rolls by.

"Wiet's been awfully quiet since his last message, don't you think?" Zack says.

"Has he?" Cat watches her breath fog a small circle on the glass. "It's only been two days..."

"Still, his communication style is different now."

"In what way?"

"It's more hands-off," he replies. "Starting with the binary code cipher, he hasn't asked the competing teams to report their solutions to him and wait for the next puzzle."

She considers that observation. "Right. His last

instructions were to follow our logic and intuition and see where they might lead."

"See? That's new."

She shrugs. "So, he's switched up his MO to keep things fresh for us."

"I guess... It's all part of the mystery, right? Maybe he's setting the stage for a dramatic finale."

"Or maybe his assistants went on strike, and he ran out of poems to pretend he wrote," she jokes, finally regaining some of her confidence.

He laughs. "Either way, I feel we're closing in."

"Should we call it a hunch, or did I just witness the awakening of your psychic powers?"

He responds with a hearty laugh. "So, this psychic thing, does it work for predicting lottery numbers, too?"

"I wish! But unfortunately, it doesn't."

"Please don't take this the wrong way," he begins gently, "but have you considered that so-called psychic powers are nothing more than magical thinking plus chance?"

She leans back and folds her arms over her chest. "As in, even a broken clock is right twice a day?"

"Something like that."

"I can't speak for others, but in my case it's not magical thinking."

"Are you sure?"

"Beyond a shadow of a doubt." She unfolds her arms. "There is one aspect, though, that I'm not sure about."

"Will you tell me what that is?"

"You see, when I do a reading for a client, I usually get a vision, a glimpse into their future... But for my loved ones and myself, all I get are vague intuitions."

Well, there was one exception last year, when hitmen were after me, but that was a fluke.

"Maybe money has to change hands for you to get a vision?" Zack asks with a mock-serious expression on his face.

"If that were the case, I'd never get visions for nonpaying clients, or for strangers, would I?"

"No, you wouldn't." He searches her face. "Is that the *aspect* that's bothering you?"

"What bugs me is that without the clarity of a vision, it's hard to judge how seriously to take this or that warning."

He frowns. "I don't follow… If you truly believe those intuitions are real, why wouldn't you take them all seriously? They give you an edge over everyone else—such a boon!"

"More like such a pain."

His frown deepens. "Please explain."

"I'll do my best." She takes a moment to put her problem into words. "Say, I have a gut feeling that tells me to do A rather than B. Are you with me so far?"

"Yes."

"Problem is, I have no idea if doing B will cause something terrible to happen, or if the consequences will be insignificant."

"If I understood correctly," Zack recaps, "your intuitions leave you in the dark about the consequences of noncompliance."

"That's right! So, when it's easy to comply, I just do it. But when it's hard, I have to make split-second decisions about whether to heed the warning or ignore it."

"Can you give me an example?" Zack asks.

"Say, I need to cross the street. There's a crosswalk some twenty meters ahead, but my gut tells me to cross right where I am."

"Before the marked crosswalk?"

"Correct," she says. "So, I have to decide what to do about my premonition without knowing what caused it and what the penalty for ignoring it would be."

"Hmm… Not sure I understand."

She sighs.

"Like, I don't know what will happen if I don't comply. Will I get a planter on my head, or just step in a puddle?"

"I see. That's a tough one." He gives her a sympathetic look. "Do you usually comply?"

"I've tried blanket compliance for a while, followed by systematic noncompliance. I've also tested alternating compliance and noncompliance, as well as complying randomly."

"That's very thorough of you!" he exclaims. "What was the result of your tests?"

"There doesn't seem to be a clear advantage to any one of those approaches."

"Very impressive."

She raises her eyebrows. "Which part?"

"The part where you ran a series of empirical tests and analyzed their results to verify a hypothesis," he replies. "I find that hilariously scientific for a psychic."

Was that a compliment or an affront?

She narrows her eyes. "You don't believe in psychic powers, do you?"

"I believe that you do," he declares. "There's no doubt in my mind that you're not a scam artist preying on vulnerable people."

"Um, thank you, I guess." She turns back to the window.

Outside, the landscape has changed. The fields have given way to the outskirts of a city. It's Chartres! A few minutes later, the train pulls into the station.

As they get off, Cat realizes her mood has improved after the frank conversation she's just had with Zack. She walks beside him into the heart of Chartres, her steps quick, her body energized, and her mind ready for the challenge.

CHAPTER 24

The majestic silhouette of Chartres Cathedral looms in front of Cat and Zack, and they enter its vast nave. The air inside is cool but not unpleasant, perfumed with the scent of wax from the candles flickering in various corners. Cat pauses, overwhelmed by the grandeur of the place. The towering columns reach up to the vaults high above, drawing her gaze to the famous stained-glass windows.

"Chartres blue," she whispers, her voice hushed in reverence.

"Beautiful," Zack concurs.

They move slowly down the aisle, necks craned to take in the details of the windows depicting biblical characters and their deeds. Cat read somewhere that because most people in the Middle Ages were illiterate, the religious scenes on the windows served a very practical purpose. They were in fact educational tools used to teach the Bible to the poor.

After a thorough walk around, double-checking even the most inconspicuous corners for any potential clues, they find nothing.

Zack checks his watch. "It's lunchtime. Are you hungry?"

"Not really," Cat says. "I'd rather maximize our time here."

He nods. "In that case, we can check out the Fine Arts Museum. It should be a stone's throw from the cathedral."

Cat looks it up on her smartphone. "Let's see… The museum has works by Soutine, one of Chagall's friends from The Beehive days, but it doesn't look like they have anything by Chagall himself."

"OK, I'm open to other suggestions."

I wish I had one!

She could have thought of something on the train ride from Paris if her mind had been on Chagall instead of Zack…

She slides her phone into her purse. "Let's check out the museum, anyway. You never know."

Once inside the museum, they hurry through the less relevant exhibits and then linger in front of Soutine's works, scanning them for anything that might be a clue. But their scrutiny yields nothing, and Cat's psychic sense remains stubbornly off.

When they return to the museum lobby, Zack vents his frustration, "I feel like we're looking for a needle in a haystack."

"We could shift our focus from Chagall to Stratte…"

"Sure, why not?" He points to the lockers. "Should we get our coats now that we're done here?"

"In a minute."

She pulls out her phone, accesses the online White Pages, and types "Luc Stratte" into the search box. The results flicker on her screen, and she scrolls through them.

"No Luc Stratte in Chartres," she says. "But there is an entry for a Luc Stratte in Néchin."

It looks like Christelle is on the right track… Did I screw up?

"That's where our competitors went, isn't it?" Zack asks.

"You aren't helping."

Cat shifts her gaze away from Zack to a group nearby. A spark of recognition makes her zero in on the tour guide, a lively woman with a flair for dramatic gestures. Cat had noticed her upstairs. The guide says goodbye to the people in her group, who thank her profusely. The notion forming in Cat's brain is still so imprecise it can't even be called an idea, but she decides to seize the moment. She strides over to the guide, her boots clicking on the polished floor. Zack follows behind.

"Bonjour," Cat begins, offering her brightest smile. "I'm Catherine Cavallo and this is Zachary Rigaud. We're participants in a scavenger hunt involving a rather notorious art theft."

The guide's eyes light up. "Oh, I saw something about it on the evening news! You must be having so much fun!"

"We're trying to track down places connected to Luc Stratte, the con man who'd stolen Chagall's *Father Christmas*," Zack chimes in. "He lived in Chartres for a while a few years back."

The guide ponders his question. "I don't know much about him, but I know someone who might. Just a second."

She whips out her phone. "A friend of mine, also a tour guide here in Chartres, is a local history buff and a fan of Chagall."

She scrolls through her contacts and taps Call.

A moment later, a deep voice answers. "Melanie! How are you doing?"

"Great, thanks! Carlos, I'm calling you on behalf of a team from that scavenger hunt you mentioned the other day."

Carlos says something inaudible, and Melanie nods, "Yes, the one where they're hunting for a Chagall. Can I put you on speakerphone?"

A second later, she taps the speaker icon. "So, our adventurers are investigating Luc Stratte, the swindler who stole from Chagall's widow."

"I'm familiar with the story," Carlos says.

Zack leans closer to the phone. "Stratte lived in Chartres from 2014 to 2016. Any idea where?"

"I heard that Sylvester Berg—you know, the art dealer—allowed him to live on his property as a guest."

"A guest?" Cat's eyebrows shoot up. "For three years?"

Zack's eyes meet hers. "That would explain why we couldn't find an address for him in Chartres. It was an informal arrangement."

"One wonders why a respectable art dealer would be so nice to a convicted thief," Carlos says.

Melanie offers a guess, "Old friends?"

"I doubt it," Carlos replies.

Zack leans in closer. "Do you have a theory, Carlos?"

"I do, but I have no proof, so I'm not going to cast aspersions."

Zack turns to Cat. "Sounds like Berg's house is our next stop."

She looks down at the phone. "Carlos, do you happen to know where Berg's place is?"

"My parents live in that village, so yes, I do."

Cat scrunches her face in confusion. "I thought he lived in Chartres."

"It's the most village-like part of the city," he replies. "I'll text Melanie the address."

Her phone pings almost immediately.

"Got it," she announces, turning the screen toward Cat and Zack.

Cat quickly types the address into her own phone. "Thank you so much, Melanie! And Carlos, we really appreciate your help!"

Zack adds his thanks.

Melanie crosses her fingers. "Good luck to you!"

"Go win that contest!" Carlos cheers before hanging up.

A few minutes later, Zack and Cat retrieve their coats from the lockers and exit the museum. Outside, the chill of the evening air bites Cat's cheeks. Zack hails a passing cab, and soon they're weaving through the streets of Chartres, blurred by the foggy weather.

It's still midafternoon, but it feels like evening as the taxi pulls up to a gated compound. Zack insists on paying the fare, and they get out. The sprawling grounds behind the wrought iron fence are shrouded in the gray of winter. Leafless trees cast gnarled shadows on the lawn and the brick mansion beyond. A decorative pond at the edge of the lawn lies still, its surface littered with fallen leaves. Despite the bleakness of the season, Cat can easily imagine how beautiful this place would look in full bloom.

Zack presses the buzzer on the gate, but there is no answer. In fact, there isn't a living soul around, except for Cat and Zack. The estate seems deserted.

"What do we do now?" Cat asks.

Zack points to the cluster of houses in the distance. "We're here, so let's try the 'village.' "

They walk toward the beating heart of the village, the boulangerie. Just like Julie's pastry shop in Beldoc, this bakery also serves hot drinks. The air smells of fresh bread and coffee.

What a comforting reprieve from the cold outside!

They order coffee at the bar. Cat begins to sip hers, feeling Zack's gaze on her face, on her lips…

She abruptly turns to the bartender, a slender woman in her forties. "My sister runs a gluten-free patisserie in Provence."

"Our bread isn't gluten-free, but it's made from heirloom grains my husband buys from organic farms in the area."

A well-upholstered man with a friendly, open face appears in the service window behind his wife. "Like my Cathy said, ancient grains still contain gluten, but they're much easier to digest and don't cause inflammation like modern high-yield wheats."

Cat grins at Cathy. "My name is Catherine, by the way."

"Isn't it just the best?" her namesake smiles.

Meanwhile, Zack's attention wanders to the round rolls in a basket on the bar.

"They look yummy..." he says.

The longing in his eyes is so intense that Cat purses her lips to keep from laughing. *Aww, you poor thing!* He must've been hungry already when he asked her if she cared for lunch. And now he's starving.

"They look delicious," she agrees.

He almost begs, "Would you like some?"

"I'd love some."

He buys three for each.

"We were just at Sylvester Berg's estate," Cat says to the bakers after wolfing down her first roll. "It seemed pretty quiet. Do you know if anyone's there now?"

"Oh, the Bergs?" Cathy says. "They hardly ever stay there this time of year. They prefer their apartment in town."

"Villa Berg is more of a summer retreat," her husband chimes in, dusting flour from his hands.

Cat and Zack finish their rolls and coffees and thank the bakers. Back outside, they agree to hike to the train station instead of trying to find a cab. During the half-hour trek, guided by an app on Zack's phone, their arms and hands touch every now and then.

OK, *often.*

So much, in fact, that even a mathematically challenged person like Cat knows that such a rate of accidental brushing is a statistical impossibility.

CHAPTER 25

It's only seven o'clock, but it's already completely dark when Cat and Zack get off the train from Chartres at the Gare du Nord. After the Villa Berg and the bakery in the village, they visited another museum and Sylvester Berg's gallery. He wasn't there. They found nothing that stood out in either of those places.

Cat's shoulders hunch slightly against the chill as she and Zack step from the station. Zack stops and turns to face her. Their eyes meet. It's time to say their goodnights and head off in opposite directions to their respective homes. There's nothing more they can do today. They followed Cat's gut feeling to Chartres, explored the town, and came up empty.

Except, every bone in my body resents saying goodbye…

Zack's voice cuts through the rush hour noise. "Hey, I have an idea I want to run by you."

"Oh?" She tries not to sound too eager. "Now?"

"Yes, before I forget. And maybe some food will help the thought process." He smiles. "There's this fantastic Indian place just a few blocks from here. What do you say?"

Dinner sounds good. And dinner with Zack sounds irresistible.

"Sure, I could eat," she blurts out, before her mind has a

chance to remind her that she's still nowhere near self-sufficient and that Zack is the wrong kind of guy for her.

They take the short walk to the restaurant. It's a quaint little place, bathed in warm light and tantalizing aromas that hit Cat as soon as she crosses the threshold. Inside, the atmosphere is full of bright colors and silky textures. Bollywood music plays softly in the background. It's as if this place were aiming to be the absolute contrast to the dark, cold evening outside.

They choose a small table in the back away from the low hum of other diners. Cat orders a korma, and Zack, a curry.

As they wait, Zack leans forward. "OK, here's what I'm thinking. Stratte and Berg—something's off about that setup, right?"

"Right."

Their fragrant food arrives. For a moment, nourishment sidetracks them. The korma is warm, rich, and comforting, and Cat welcomes the sensations.

"I mean," Zack picks up where he left off, "why would Berg harbor a known thief for years unless there's more to their relationship?"

"It's weird, for sure," Cat concurs. "Do you think Berg participated in the thefts?"

"Not directly, but I think Stratte had something on him."

"Like what?"

Zack dabs his mouth with a napkin. "What if Sylvester Berg was one of those unscrupulous art dealers who bought stolen Chagall works from Stratte?"

"And then Stratte blackmailed Berg into offering rent-free accommodations?"

He searches her face. "Does that make sense to you?"

"Totally!" She wipes her mouth. "The question is, how does that help us find *Father Christmas*?"

"I haven't gotten that far in my thinking yet."

The waiter clears the table and returns with chai and dessert.

Cat wraps her hands around her cup. "We need to look into Berg's business dealings."

"Especially the deals he made in 1990, but also during the years Stratte holed up in Villa Berg," Zack agrees. "Maybe there's a trail of breadcrumbs there for us."

She nods. "Are the transactions of art dealers and galleries a matter of public record?"

"I'm sure such records exist, but I doubt they're public... Hang on."

He taps on his phone, reads, then looks up. "As I thought, they're private. But apparently, there are services that give subscribers access to these proprietary databases so they can track art sales and provenance."

"Can anyone subscribe to such a service?"

"Sure, if they're willing to pay." Before she can ask if he knows how much, he adds, "I'm totally willing to pay."

"Cool."

He does some more tapping and scrolling. "There are different tiers of subscriptions with different levels of information available."

"OK." She nibbles her carrot pudding.

He digs into his cashew fudge. "It just occurred to me—some info will only be available to tax authorities or regulatory bodies that oversee compliance with laws."

"What kind of info would that be?"

He counts off on his fingers. "Exact prices of private sales, financial information of buyers and sellers, other sensitive data protected by privacy laws."

"That's annoying."

"I beg to differ! Privacy laws protecting personal data are essential in a democracy." He winks at her. "Not to mention that companies like mine get contracts to manage the technical aspects of such protection."

She perks up. "Then you'd know how to hack through them, wouldn't you?"

"Hacking isn't my strong suit."

"But you could try?"

He shakes his head and puts the phone down. "I'm not going to, and I'm not going to ask my developers, either. We're a cybersecurity company, Cat!"

"Would this be the first time a cybersecurity outfit dabbles in a bit of hacking?"

"No." He smiles wryly. "Still, I won't do it."

She sighs and swallows the last of her pudding. "That's a shame. I don't see how else we can check Berg and Stratte's private transactions."

He doesn't answer, concentrating instead on his dessert. When their plates and cups are empty, he signals for the check.

Outside the restaurant, they stall again.

Cat's heart is fluttering with indecision, reluctant to say goodbye. Zack doesn't seem to relish the prospect, either. The way he looks at her—the way he's looked at her all day—leaves no doubt as to what's on his mind. You don't need psychic powers to tell how he would like to conclude this pleasant evening. Cat wants that, too. But she knows she'll regret it.

I haven't fixed myself yet.

If she sleeps with him now, she'll ruin this fragile thing between them, just as she's ruined her other relationships. It might take a day or a month, but eventually he'll want out. And she'll be left with another heartbreak to nurse.

You're not ready, Catherine Cavallo.

She exhales forcefully. "I guess this is good night, then."

Before she can turn away, Zack closes the distance between them, pulls her into a tight embrace, and kisses her senseless.

~

Cat's memory is hazy as to how they got to the gate of Zack's building. They walked. The only thing she can remember is that they stopped every few minutes to kiss, like a couple of giddy teenagers. Now they're standing in front of the massive green gate. She's dizzy from all the smooching and feverish with anticipation, caution be damned.

I'm suspending my vow of celibacy. I want to give this a chance.

As Zack punches in the code, someone stops right behind them. Cat turns to see that it's Zack's neighbor, Ajay.

They exchange greetings.

Ajay sniffs the air around Cat and Zack. "You smell like curry."

While Zack explains why, Cat sniffs at Ajay's coat. "So do you."

Oops. If she hadn't been kiss-drunk, she would never have allowed herself such familiarity with someone she barely knows.

To her relief, Ajay cracks up. "That's because I also had dinner at an Indian restaurant with my son, daughter-in-law, and grandchildren."

"You have grandchildren?" Cat gives him a once-over. "You look young."

"I'm sixty-two," Ajay replies, still chuckling. "I married young back in Mumbai and was widowed young. My son is thirty-six."

"My age," Zack comments.

"It's a good age to start a beautiful new chapter in your life," Ajay says with a quick glance at Cat. "Unfortunately, I was foolish to think it was still possible past sixty."

Cat frowns. "Did Lucile say no?"

Ajay's head jerks back as he looks from Cat to Zack. "Is my affection for her that obvious?"

Cat and Zack respond with sympathetic smiles.

"Ah, I guess it is." Ajay shrugs. "She didn't need to spell it out. You saw what happened when I suggested a cow figurine for her Christmas crèche. The message was quite clear."

Zack wrinkles his nose in apology. "I'm afraid I don't remember her exact reaction."

"She said she preferred her crèche just the way it was," Cat sums up, before turning to Ajay. "Aren't you reading too much into this? She didn't say she preferred her *life* just the way it was."

"She's a trained psychologist," Ajay reminds her. "I'm sure she can read me, and I don't think her answer was *only* about her Christmas crèche."

He pushes open the gate and steps into the festively lit courtyard. Cat and Zack follow, Cat's mind processing Ajay's argument. As regrettable as it is, he's probably right. If his feelings were so obvious to Cat—and even to Zack—there's no way Lucile could have missed them. It's also likely that she was so categorical about her crèche simply to nip Ajay's courtship in the bud.

They enter the lobby.

"How is your scavenger hunt going?" Ajay asks. "I hope you guys are still in the game."

"We are," Zack replies.

Cat squints at Ajay. "Wait a minute, didn't you say you worked as a software engineer?"

"Yes, ma'am."

"Can you hack into proprietary databases?" she asks, as they start to climb the stairs.

"Well, it depends…"

"Cat, come on—" Zack begins.

She covers his mouth with her hand and speaks over him, "We're stuck right now. And to get unstuck, we need to hack into a database that holds information on the transactions of a certain art dealer."

Ajay takes a moment to digest her words before pointing at Zack. "I'm sure Zack here can do it even faster than I could."

"I have no intention of hacking into proprietary

databases," Zack says firmly. "And neither should you. Please ignore Cat's request."

Ajay stops in front of his door. "Consider it ignored. Good evening, Cat, Zack." His eyes crinkle. "And good luck with the hunt!"

Cat follows Zack up two more flights of stairs. He unlocks the door and lets her in, all while glaring at her in feigned anger.

"Oh, please!" She rolls her eyes. "Can't blame a girl for trying."

He backs her up against the wall and braces his arms against it on either side of her face. "All right then, I won't. Can I kiss you now?"

His mouth covers hers before she has a chance to say, "Finally!"

CHAPTER 26

Zack lies still, watching the gentle rise and fall of Cat's breathing. The faint rays of the early-morning sun peeking through the slats of the blinds create a warm haze over her serene expression.

God, she's beautiful!

The instant that thought takes shape, a ripple of panic stirs in his chest. Why is he so into her? What does this mean for him? He's not looking for anything serious until he's in his late forties. That life choice has been the guiding star of his adulthood. Every hookup he's ever had, every decision he's ever made has been informed by it.

What's changed?

Could it be the fact that last night was perfect? Not just in general, but in all the ways that matter. Everything clicked on every meaningful level, be it physical, intellectual, or emotional. That unexpected intense compatibility between them makes him to want more. It also makes him resent the impending denouement.

And therein lies the rub.

With a heavy sigh, he pushes these thoughts to the back of his mind and glances at his watch on the bedside table. It's half past eight. High time to start the day, regardless of the mess inside. Quietly, he slips out of bed and makes his way to the bathroom. When he's showered and dressed, he heads straight to the kitchen, where he turns on his fancy coffee maker and citrus juicer.

While the coffee brews, he meticulously arranges everything on the kitchen table: freshly squeezed orange juice, morning cereal, yogurt, milk, almond milk, toast, butter, and jam. Then he returns to the bedroom, steaming cup in hand.

Cat is still asleep. Apparently, the light coming in through the blinds isn't enough to wake her. He sits on the edge of the bed and holds the mug up to her nose. The aroma of the brew is strong—it should do the trick. Smiling, he watches it work its magic on her.

When her eyelids flutter open, he greets her with a kiss. "Good morning!"

"Good morning!" She sits up.

He hands her the coffee.

She cradles it between her hands and takes a tentative sip. "Mmm, what a way to wake up!"

"There's a full breakfast waiting in the kitchen. I thought we'd start the day right."

Her laughter fills the room with warmth. "Is this your subtle way of telling me I need to leave soon?"

"Not at all," he replies quickly. "Well, I do have a busy day at work, but no meetings until noon, so there's no rush."

She nods a thank-you. "Can I take a shower?"

"Of course! There are clean towels on the rack."

Half an hour later, she's buttering her toast in the kitchen. They chat about his plans for his company and her psychic readings.

"Have you always had these visions and intuitions?" he asks.

"Nope. It started when I was fifteen after the accident."

"What accident?"

She hesitates for a split second before replying. "A rented summer house exploded and collapsed on us. The contractor had left a hole in the gas pipe."

"Damn fool!"

She looks at him from under her brows. "Remember I told you my mom died in an accident? That was the accident. It was a miracle my sisters and I got out nearly unscathed. Anyway, I'm telling you this because Vero, Julie, and I started getting visions after that."

"Not Flo?"

"No, not Flo."

"Are Vero and Julie clairvoyants like you?"

She shakes her head. "Their gifts are different."

They eat in silence for a few minutes, before Cat speaks again, "Tell me about your parents."

"There isn't much to tell."

She probes gently, "Then tell me what little there is."

He shrugs. "OK, if you insist. My father and I are estranged. My mother died in an accident, like yours."

"Oh, I'm so sorry!" She gives his hand a little squeeze. "What kind of accident?"

"She was crossing a busy street at a red light and was hit by a truck."

"Oh, God." Her eyes brimming with sympathy, she asks, "How old were you when it happened?"

"I was fifteen and in a boarding school in Lille."

"Same age as me! You must've been devastated."

He doesn't say anything, so she adds, "I was inconsolable when I lost my mom."

"I wasn't."

Her eyes widen in surprise.

"You see," he explains, "in order to lose someone, you have to have them. At that point, I no longer had her."

"What do you mean?"

"Years before she died, she had removed herself from my life," he says. "Or rather, she had removed me from hers."

He watches the orange juice in his hand blur into a blinding yellow-white stain like the sun behind his father's head. Zack is eight again, standing in the train station and looking up at the towering figures of his parents. He cries and begs as his entire world tilts.

His mom, beautiful as always but unusually pale, avoids his gaze. Instead, she concentrates on adjusting the collar of his stiff new jacket.

The only thing his dad has to say in response to Zack's pleas is, "It's for the best, my boy."

Desperate, Zack turns to his stern grandfather who's going to deliver Zack to Lille. "Papy, please!"

"It's for the best, kid," Grandpa Charles repeats like a parrot.

"But I don't want to go!" Zack's voice cracks. "Please don't send me away!"

He tugs at his mom's hand, searching her face for any sign of wavering. "Please, don't make me go!"

Her lips press into a thin line. She still won't meet his eyes. She busies herself with his luggage, then smooths out imaginary creases on his jacket... Even when she wipes his cheeks with the back of her hand, her gaze is not on him but on the stone tiles of the station floor.

"It's a wonderful school, sweetheart," she says. "You'll make friends, and you'll learn so much!"

"Yeah, it'll be a great adventure," his dad piles on. "You'll thank us later."

Both his parents glance at the station clock, again, and at the departure board, again.

"It's time," his dad says brightly like it's a good thing. "Let's get you on the train, buddy!"

Zack feels a wild, uncontrollable thing growing in his chest. It makes him want to scream and run as fast as he can. His dad grabs his hand as if he can sense Zack's urge.

Sobbing with misery, Zack pleads again, "Please, I'll be good. I won't be any trouble!"

"Son, it's decided." His dad's other hand lands heavily on Zack's shoulder. "You're going, and that's final."

His parents nudge him toward Grandpa Charles who leads him to the train. As they walk down the platform, Zack looks over his shoulder at his waving parents, the people around them, the pigeons scavenging in the station café—all witnesses to his being cast aside.

Moments later, Grandpa Charles and Zack board the train. The hiss of the doors that seal his fate is deafening. Zack sits down at the window as instructed by Grandpa Charles and presses his face against the cool glass. He can't see his parents from here.

The train lurches forward.

The station fades into the distance.

Zack tells himself that his childhood is over, and with it everything good in his life. He's afraid of the unknown that awaits him. He feels betrayed by the two people he never expected to abandon him.

Cat's voice brings him back to the present. "It's all right if you don't want to talk about it. I understand."

"Thank you."

"Of course."

When her face comes back into focus, he forces a smile. "Let's talk about our strategy for the rest of the hunt, what do you say?"

CHAPTER 27

Zack stirs his second coffee—this one with a shot of milk—and watches the steam rise in delicate swirls. Across the kitchen table, Cat picks at her croissant.

"So, we agree then?" she says. "We're focusing on Luc Stratte instead of Marc Chagall?"

"Yes," he confirms. "Focusing on Stratte makes more sense now that Wiet has switched to a hands-off style for the final stretch of the competition."

She nods, a satisfied smile on her face.

He sets his cup down. "I'm blocking off my late evening, as soon as I get back from the office, to dig deep into Stratte's background. I'll gather as much info as I can online."

"I'll do the same on my end," she says. "We can sync up first thing in the morning, compare what we've found."

Does her reply mean she understands we won't be spending the night together?

Zack tends to think so, but he'll have to send another probe later to be completely sure.

Cat's phone on the table starts to vibrate.

Her face lights up with recognition before she answers. "Hey, Dalila!"

The other psychic says something.

Cat nods, "Drinking coffee and plotting for the hunt, darling. But I have a client at ten-thirty, so I'll be at the shop by ten."

The corners of her eyes crinkle as she listens to her friend's animated chatter. After a moment, her face lengthens with surprise, and she glances at Zack.

"I'm going to put you on speaker, Dalila," she says. "Zack needs to hear this, too."

"Zack, huh?" Dalila repeats, loud enough for him to catch the amusement in her voice.

He braces himself as the phone clicks into speaker mode.

"Good morning, Zachary!" Dalila begins, her tone heavy with implication. "Strategizing fresh out of bed, are we?"

Best to sidestep the innuendo. "Morning, Dalila."

Her tone becomes more serious. "I take it you didn't hear the news last night?"

"What news?"

"On TV, dummy! As I was just telling your teammate, they had another segment about the scavenger hunt," Dalila informs him.

"Oh." He realizes his expression is mirroring Cat's from moments before. "Did they interview Wiet? We haven't heard from him in over twenty-four hours."

"He came on and said there were two teams left in the race, each following a different lead," Dalila says. "He was very succinct and enigmatic."

"Was that it?" Zack asks.

"No, the journalist then interviewed Christelle and Edgar, live from Néchin. Our friends sounded pretty confident about their lead."

Cat leans into the phone. "We're feeling pretty solid about our direction too!"

She looks at Zack, clearly expecting him to jump in.

He hesitates. Loyalty compels him to support Cat's optimistic assessment, but he forces himself not to.

Crossing his arms, he says instead, "Néchin makes a lot of sense, considering it's where Stratte hid out in the late nineties after his trial."

The conversation wraps up with promises to keep each other posted. Cat ends the call and puts the phone down.

Her eyes linger on the darkened screen before turning to Zack. "You don't sound convinced."

Zack picks up a piece of bread to do something with his hands. "It's not that I'm not convinced, it's just…"

"What?"

"Being too sure can blind us to other possibilities."

"Right." She looks away and then back at him. "You still refuse to hack into Berg's transactions?"

"I do."

"Fine." She sits back, exhaling. "But we should still go back to Chartres and try to learn as much as we can about Berg's and Stratte's dealings."

"How do you suggest we do that?"

"We'll visit Berg's gallery again, try to talk to him and his employees. We should also go back to Villa Berg and talk to the neighbors."

"You do that," Zack says. "I'll head south and spend the weekend in Saint-Paul-de-Vence."

She blinks and looks him in the eye. "You think we should investigate separately?"

"Yes." He meets her gaze and holds it. "If we're lucky, and Néchin turns out to be a false lead, I'm sure Christelle and Edgar will go to Saint-Paul-de-Vence next. We should beat them to it."

Zack can see that Cat isn't too keen on his idea. Objectively, she might be right. It might be wiser to divide their time and brainpower within each of these places rather than across them. They could both go to Chartres tomorrow, spend the day there, and cover as much ground as possible, one in the gallery and the other in the village. And the day after that, they could travel together to the Mediterranean coast and search Saint-Paul in the same way.

Unfortunately, this plan has one big flaw. It means that Cat and Zack will spend more nights together. He can't let that happen. The risk of him getting emotionally involved is too high.

"Why do you think Saint-Paul is a better lead than Chartres?" Cat asks.

The answer comes to Zack easily. "Put yourself in Damien Wiet's shoes when he planned the scavenger hunt."

"OK. And?"

"*Father Christmas* was stolen in Saint-Paul," he points out. "If I were Wiet, I'd hide the painting there."

"Why?"

"To bring things full circle," he replies. "It's neat. Wiet studied mathematics, and mathematicians like neat solutions."

"Isn't it neater to hide *Father Christmas* where Stratte originally hid it, and where Wiet found it with a seer's help?" she counters.

"That place could very well be Saint-Paul."

She says nothing.

He cocks his head. "We can't rule out that your gut feeling about Chartres could be wrong, Cat, whether you like it or not."

More silence.

He carries on, "Frankly, I don't see why Villa Berg or any other place in Chartres would be where Stratte would have stashed the goods."

"Why not?"

"For one, because some fifteen years separate his stay in Chartres from the theft in Saint-Paul."

She purses her lips. "Hmm."

"If I were Stratte, I'd hide the stolen paintings somewhere that didn't involve smuggling them across the country, or abroad."

"But when Stratte got caught, the police must have been all over Saint-Paul and the surrounding area," she says. "If *I* were him, I'd find a way to move the haul to a safer location."

He releases a sigh. "Shall we agree to disagree?"

"I'm not disagreeing that Saint-Paul is worth our time. All I'm saying is we finish with Chartres first, pooling our complementary skills." She looks up at him. "That's how we've done it so far—and with success!"

"But we're at a dead end now, so why not change tactics?"

"We haven't given Chartres our best effort yet," she argues. "If we do that and find nothing, we'll head straight to Saint-Paul."

He racks his brain for a good reason to decline her suggestion.

Finding none, he resorts to empty rhetoric. "Do you still want to win this competition?"

"Yes, of course."

"Then there is no time to waste." He sets his hands flat on the table. "We should work in parallel. Double down on research tonight and fieldwork tomorrow. We bring each other up to date morning and evening or as soon as one of us uncovers something noteworthy."

She hangs her head, visibly defeated. "Sounds like a plan."

"Good." He springs to his feet and busies himself clearing the dishes.

She gives him a hand.

A few minutes later, he brings her the spare helmet. "Shall I drop you off at the shop?"

She hands it back to him. "Thanks, but I'd rather walk. I need to clear my head."

Zack holds the door open for her. They step out into the brisk Paris morning and say goodbye.

He doesn't lean in to kiss her.

She doesn't hold up her face to be kissed.

CHAPTER 28

Zack pulls his scooter into the parking garage down the street and then enters his building. He crosses the courtyard, bypasses the main lobby, and heads straight for the concierge's box.

He received a text message this afternoon while he was at work. He immediately assumed it was Cat, and the warm fuzzies that came with that assumption took Zack completely by surprise. He hadn't thought about her all day. Well, except during lunch, when he congratulated himself for not thinking about her all morning. She'd popped into his head again during a conference call in the afternoon, but only for a brief moment, and only because the meeting was boring as hell. So, overall, he'd done great.

The cold wave of disappointment when he saw that the text wasn't from Cat caused him much consternation. He told himself he was upset because he'd hoped Cat had dug up something on Berg or Stratte. He also reminded himself that disengagement takes time. It hadn't been a day since he'd held Cat in his arms. Better to be realistic and adjust his expectations.

Moving on after her will take a little longer than usual.

The text message was from Lucile, the president of the HOA board. It sounded innocent enough—a quick board meeting about an urgent matter—but experience had taught him to be wary. The Unholy Trinity had been relentless in its attempts to corner him into hosting the condo Christmas party.

Is this yet another ploy to browbeat me into submission?

Zack pushes open the door to the box and steps into the warm, cramped living quarters that double as Monica's command center.

The first thing his senses register is the aroma of fresh tea mingled with the scent of pine from the Christmas tree near the window. The room is modest but cozy with a small kitchenette cluttered with the day's utensils and a bunk bed peeking out from behind a folding screen in the back. That's probably where Monica's boys sleep. The two other doors could be a bathroom and Monica's bedroom.

Lucile, Ajay, and Monica sit around a compact table covered with various papers and mugs of tea. Ajay, who usually sits next to Lucile, is as far away from her as the table will allow. Paulo and Tiago are so eerily quiet that they must be either fast asleep or out. Nemo the cat is dozing on top of the closet, one paw twitching in sleep.

Zack greets everyone.

Monica pulls a chair out. "Tea?"

"That'd be great, thanks!"

Lucile flashes him a smile. "Thank you, Zack, for coming on such short notice!"

"Just doing my duty as an HOA board member." He eases into the offered chair.

Monica pours tea into a mug for him.

"Where are the boys?" he asks.

"Over at the Gantzes', playing video games." She sits down. "Madame Gantz saw you save Paulo from the magnolia tree the other day. I'm so grateful, Zack!"

He waves off the praise. "It was nothing, really. Just glad I could help. Paulo is all right, I hope?"

"He's in a lot of pain."

Zack's eyebrows knit in concern. "Scratches? Muscle strain?"

"Third and final day without dessert," Monica explains. "But he won't let Nemo out again at dusk."

Zack chuckles. "Sounds like a fitting punishment."

As they sip their tea, Lucile turns the conversation to the agenda at hand. "We need to decide whether to upgrade our intercom system as the building manager has suggested."

That was the emergency? I was right to be suspicious!

The intercom discussion flits around for the next fifteen minutes with technical specs and budget considerations tossed back and forth. Zack listens in, interjecting occasionally and bracing himself for the subject to turn to the Christmas party.

Sure enough, as soon as the intercom matter is settled, Lucile looks at Zack. "We were wondering if you would reconsider hosting the Christmas party?"

Zack adopts a grave expression. "I'm afraid I won't."

"But you have the perfect space for it!" Monica's eyes cloud over. "The previous owner of your apartment, Madame Delarue, always hosted our Christmas party. She also made delicious canapés and pastries—"

"I don't bake," Zack says dryly.

Lucile gives Monica a look that says *You're not helping,* and then turns back to Zack. "No one expects you to cook. I won't, either. In fact, I hate cooking. We'll pitch in and get some drinks and snacks."

"Come on, say yes!" Monica urges him with a tone that is both a challenge and plea. "It's only once a year."

"No can do, sorry." Zack flashes a bright smile. "But my offer of sponsorship still stands!"

Ajay waves a dismissive hand at Monica. "Leave him be.

Sometimes the other person really doesn't care about the same things we do, and that's just the way it is."

Was that about Zack's reluctance to host the party, or about Ajay's failed attempt to woo Lucile?

"True," Lucile interjects. "We'll look at other options, Zack."

Finally!

Zack finishes his cup and stands up, smiling. "Have a good evening, everyone, and thanks for the tea, Monica!"

Stepping out into the crisp night, Zack is pleased with himself for having finally dodged the Christmas party. He rushes upstairs to his lair, eager to pop a frozen pizza in the oven and get to work researching the thirty-year-old art theft in Saint-Paul in preparation for his trip tomorrow.

Three hours later, Zack leans back in the swivel chair in his home office and rubs his hands. He's made excellent progress, despite some initial frustration. The transcripts of the 1994 trial when con artist Luc Stratte was found guilty of art theft turned out to be inaccessible online. All Zack could find were press articles covering the case at the time. But they were quite detailed, so in the end it was all right.

Zack learned that after Chagall's death in 1985, his widow, Valentina "Vava" Brodsky, chose to live out her days surrounded by mementos of her husband at La Colline, the couple's villa in Saint-Paul.

Stratte traveled from his native northern France to the South in 1989. According to press accounts of the case, the move was motivated by a news report about Vava's life in La Colline amid the Chagall paintings she hadn't put up for sale. Stratte had a plan. He hoped to befriend the widow and gain access to her home.

Unfortunately, Vava wasn't interested in his friendship.

Undeterred, the devil managed to charm her housekeeper,

Yvette. In exchange for a share of the profits from future sales, he persuaded Yvette to steal Chagall's artwork stored in the house. Paintings, lithographs, watercolors, drawings—you name it, Yvette snatched them one at a time every week for about a year. Stratte sold them by forging the paperwork and posing as a legitimate art dealer. The looting continued until February 1990 when Yvette decided she was better off without her husband. She told him she was leaving him, and he stabbed her to death.

Vava passed away in 1993. It was an anonymous phone call in 1994, reporting suspicious dealings between an art gallery and Stratte, that sparked the police investigation. According to press accounts, police recovered about twenty-five works in the aftermath of the murder investigation. He hid most of them in the homes of his accomplices, the housekeeper, and her adult children.

And that's just some of the promising information Zack has been able to dig up in the last three hours.

Reason over fortune-telling!

Reason is the only force that moves humanity forward. Everything else is just comfort food for minds that aren't demanding enough to feed on reason alone.

Zack looks at his watch. It's ten o'clock. Cat hasn't called him yet, but he feels he has enough juicy information to share and that this is a good time for a mutual update. As he picks up his phone and finds her name in his contacts, he's giddy at the prospect of hearing her voice.

That is, her update.

CHAPTER 29

Zack hesitates, his finger hovering over the Call icon, the weight of the morning's awkward goodbyes weighing heavily on his mind. He rubs the back of his neck, tells himself to stop being such a wuss, and taps Call.

When she answers, Cat's voice carries a chill that does nothing to ease his stress.

"Hey, Cat," he begins.

"Hi."

"Um, still no new instructions from Wiet," he says, stating the obvious by way of introduction. "It's been over forty-eight hours now. Don't you find that odd?"

"I do." The edge in her tone is palpable.

He tries to work around it. "So, I've now spent three hours digging into Stratte's escapades in Saint-Paul, and I have things to report. How about you?"

A breath is held and then released on the other end. "I've uncovered a few things myself. But let's hear yours first."

"No, ladies first. I insist!"

"Well, if you *insist*... So, there's this art historian, André

Dafoe. He wrote a long blog article about Stratte a few years back."

"OK." He nods eagerly even if she can't see it.

"According to Dafoe, Stratte must've extorted not only money but also works of art while living at Villa Berg."

"From the owner of the villa?"

"Obviously but not exclusively," she replies, her voice growing animated. "He also squeezed other art dealers who'd bought stolen Chagall paintings from him back in 1989."

Zack whistles softly. "Wow."

"And here's the kicker. He apparently got one of them to hand over several Brancusi and Giacometti sculptures worth millions."

"Seriously? Is there a paper trail?"

"No, of course not," she says.

"Then what makes André Dafoe think it happened?"

"Persistent rumors, his excellent knowledge of the case, and putting two and two together."

Zack feels a shift as the excitement of the hunt seeps into their conversation. *Good.* He'd hoped Cat would prove mature and sensible enough to remember that they're teammates with a common goal and last night shouldn't change that. It was a moment of human weakness, a stumble in their highly constructive collaboration—something to be put behind them and forgotten as quickly as possible.

"What happened to those valuable sculptures?" he asks. "Did Stratte manage to sell them on the black market?"

"It's unclear."

"Does Dafoe discuss Sylvester Berg's past dealings with Stratte in his article?"

"Not directly, but it's heavily implied."

"That's quite a find, Cat! We should track down André Dafoe and talk to him. I'm sure he has more insight."

Cat's tone drops as she replies, "That would've been great, but he passed away last year."

"Damn!" Zack winces at the missed opportunity. "Anything else?"

"Well, I still don't know where Stratte tucked away *Father Christmas*, but I'm hoping to find out tomorrow, after I snoop around Villa Berg."

"You still think Chartres is our best lead?"

"Yes." There's a brief silence and then she says, "Now, your turn."

"Where to begin?" Zack scans his notes. "OK, when Marc Chagall died, he left behind thousands of works from large paintings to doodles on scraps of paper."

"Did you just say, 'thousands'?"

"Yes," he confirms. "Chagall was very prolific in his twilight years. He painted until his last breath in 1985 at the age of ninety-seven."

"How many thousands are we talking about?"

"Shockingly, no one really knows. Probably ten."

"How is that possible?" she asks, incredulity lacing her voice. "He was world-famous in his lifetime."

"You see, the only complete inventory we have for Marc Chagall is Mourlot's catalogue raisonné."

"The catalog of his lithographs we saw in the Petits-Augustins chapel? The one Wiet used for his second set of puzzles?"

Zack smiles. "The very same. Like he explained, lithographs are limited-edition prints. Even when signed, they aren't nearly as valuable as original paintings."

"Are you saying that the only complete inventory humanity has of one of its finest painters contains only his least valuable works?"

"For the moment, yes," he replies. "Chagall's heirs have launched an ambitious attempt to inventory everything. But that will take time."

"I see. So, what happened to the ten thousand or so works Chagall left behind when he died?"

Zack finds the marked passage in his notes. "Everything

was divided into three lots of roughly equal value among Chagall's heirs—"

"Who were they, exactly?"

He checks his notes. "His daughter from his marriage to his muse Bella, his son from a relationship that followed Bella's death during the war, and his second wife, Vava."

"Thank you. Go on."

"The heirs each drew a lot at random," he continues. "Vava's share remained at La Colline, his villa in Saint-Paul where she chose to live after her husband's death."

"Enter the talented Monsieur Stratte!" she says with theatrical flair.

"Not immediately," he points out. "First, the heirs commissioned the then director of the Fondation Maeght, an art foundation in Saint-Paul, to take an inventory of everything over the course of a year."

"I thought there was no inventory except for the lithographs?"

He laughs, pleased at her keen interest in what he has uncovered. "Patience, madame, I'm getting there! The Fondation Maeght began to inventory Vava's share but never finished."

"Why not?"

"Please bear in mind that Vava was eighty-eight years old, alone, and grieving. When appraisers started visiting to make a detailed catalog of the works, she was overwhelmed. Strangers wandering around the house, looking everywhere, moving things around, taking pictures—it was all too much."

"But it was important work!"

"I'm sure she was aware of that," he says. "Initially, she just asked for a time-out."

"And then?"

"And then, the break stretched into years, and years turned into never."

She exhales audibly. "Stratte was one lucky SOB!"

"Indeed, he was."

He goes on to recount the events of 1989 when Stratte showed up in the village and persuaded Yvette to steal dozens of paintings from under Vava's nose.

When Zack is done, Cat makes small noises, like she's mulling over something.

"A penny for your thoughts?" he asks.

"I have this feeling—"

"Ah."

She clucks her tongue. "Must you show your disapproval quite so often? You don't believe in psychic powers—I get it, and I'm not trying to convert you." The edge in her voice is back.

Zack feels like hitting himself with the heaviest pan in his kitchen for ruining the fragile rapport between them.

"I'm truly sorry, Cat! Please, can we rewind to before my inane interjection?"

She releases a sigh. "The irony is, I didn't even mean anything paranormal. I used *feeling* in the sense of *suspicion*."

"Suspicion? Tell me more, I'm begging you!"

There's a tight little laugh on the other end. "This whole hunt, I don't know..."

"Something's bothering you?" he prompts.

"Nothing big, but little things like Wiet letting us improvise off-piste, Stratte who might've amassed a small fortune in various works..."

"Are you saying that this game is turning into something more than just chasing *Father Christmas?*"

"I wouldn't go that far, but doesn't it make you wonder if Wiet's reasons for putting this scavenger hunt together go beyond philanthropy and good publicity?"

He looks out the window, pondering her words. Night has now completely enveloped Paris. It's quiet, except for the distant, barely audible hum of traffic.

He shifts his gaze to the phone. "Are you suggesting that Damien Wiet has a hidden agenda?"

"I know it sounds wild, and it's probably just my overactive imagination."

"Assuming for a second it isn't, what would he be after?" Zack thinks aloud. "Is he trying to get his hands on a hidden fortune or hidden ledgers that contain damning information about his dealings with Stratte?"

"Wiet told us in his intro that he only found out about the theft recently, after Stratte's death, remember? He claims he never met the guy."

"I'd say the same thing if I'd bought ill-gotten art from a thief, wittingly or unwittingly!"

Cat chuckles.

"Joking aside," Zack says, "tomorrow, we should keep our eyes open not just for clues about Stratte or *Father Christmas*, but also about Wiet himself."

"Agreed."

They end the call with plans to touch base tomorrow evening. That night, Zack has a particularly hard time falling asleep. The excitement of the scavenger hunt, which may have just become more than a game, keeps his eyes open. And when he manages to stop thinking about it, memories of last night rush in and take over.

What a mess!

CHAPTER 30

Cat steps off the bus into a cold mid-December morning in Chartres. Wrapping her scarf tighter around her neck, she makes her way to the local bakery where she and Zack had coffee and rolls the day before yesterday.

The doorbell chimes, and a welcome warmth envelops her the moment she walks in. Cathy greets her with a smile from behind the counter.

Cat orders an espresso.

When there's a lull between customers, Cat tells Cathy about the scavenger hunt and why she's back in Chartres.

"Have you or your husband ever heard of a man named Luc Stratte?" Cat asks.

Cathy shakes her head as she wipes down the counter. "The name doesn't ring a bell. But I can ask my husband tonight. He's out of town right now."

"You can tell him Stratte stayed at Villa Berg from 2014 to 2016."

"Oh, then I doubt he'd have heard of him," Cathy says. "We've only been in Chartres five years."

Maybe I'll have better luck with the neighbors.

Cat finishes her coffee, thanks Cathy, and walks out the door. Immediately, the damp chill in the air seeps into her bones. She heads toward the imposing silhouette of Villa Berg, the frosty ground crunching underfoot. As she walks, her mind circles back to Zack, and her irritation bubbles up again. Not at him specifically, but at herself for being such a loser.

Has my journey to emancipation been cut short? Will I ever get back on track after this relapse?

She'd vowed to bury her old clingy self and become a new, independent woman who didn't need a man to feel complete. The kind of woman she'd always wanted to be. It had been a year since she'd sworn off men. She was doing great, making slow but steady progress toward her goal.

Unfortunately, she hadn't reached it yet when Zack came along. She knew she wasn't ready. She also knew he wasn't looking for a serious relationship. He'd made that clear. And yet, she broke her vow and slept with him. Worse, she woke up the next morning with a subconscious expectation of commitment, of coupledom in the making. Zack recognized it at once and promptly crushed it.

How could I let myself down like that? Because of that damn snow globe!

The glimpse of Zack she'd seen inside the globe had nothing to do with destiny. It wasn't about him being her future or any of that sentimental crap. The brief vision simply foreshadowed their partnership during the scavenger hunt. She'd just seen the banner in the métro, which had tuned her mind to what was about to happen without her realizing it. Thus primed, her senses were open to receive another sign regarding Wiet's game while she was gift shopping in the Tuileries. An image of her future teammate was that sign.

What a fool I was to read more into it!

Shaking her head to dispel those thoughts, Cat focuses on today's mission and the specific task she must tackle. The villa sits secluded and surrounded by a large plot of land. The iron fence, aged but stately, separates her from the mansion and its dormant gardens. She takes in the strangely beautiful desolation of the place through the gaps in the fence.

Apart from the birds, there's not a living soul in sight.

She circles the corner of the property. Her spirits rise when she catches sight of a neighboring house where an elderly couple tends to their garden.

Cat approaches them with a tentative smile. "Good morning!"

The husband and wife look up. They return Cat's greeting, their expressions guarded but curious. She introduces herself and briefly explains her involvement in the scavenger hunt.

"You might've seen it on TV?" she adds.

The woman shakes her head. "We don't own a TV, dear."

"We get our news online and in the paper," the man explains. "And for entertainment, we prefer to read a book."

"Good for you!" Cat says.

The woman wipes her hands on her apron. "What brings you to our quiet corner?"

Cat shifts from one foot to the other, wishing Julie were with her to ask the questions. *It comes so much more naturally to her than to me!*

"Villa Berg," she finally replies.

The woman looks in that direction. "What about it?"

"Um, were you here ten years ago?"

"We've lived here for twenty-five years," her husband says.

"Do you by any chance remember a man named Luc Stratte who stayed at Villa Berg?"

The couple trade glances.

"We don't know a Luc Stratte," the man replies, drawing out the name. "But we do remember a Luc Verst. He was a friend of Monsieur Berg's, stayed over at the villa for a few years."

Luc Verst? Was that Stratte's alias?

"A memorable fellow," the woman adds.

Cat arches an eyebrow. "How so?"

"Big, green-eyed, charming but also troubled." Smiling at something she doesn't share, the woman clips a dead twig. "Oh, dear, the parties he threw! And the odd hours he kept!"

"Yes, always something going on over there," the man adds.

Cat listens intently.

"Except when Luc disappeared to sunnier shores, which he did often," the woman says. "And sometimes he'd bring back these handsome young men he'd met on his travels."

Her husband chuckles. "And the drinking, dear lord! It got worse every year. By 2016, he was quite a spectacle around here."

Cat leans forward. "In what way?"

The woman's nose wrinkles at the memory. "He'd come out in the evening and pee on the flower beds. That summer, he also hired our local contractor to dig wells all over the Berg property."

"There's no water around here, mind you." The man gestures broadly from Villa Berg to the distant hills. "I asked him once why he was digging. He said he was looking for the Templar gold."

"Did he think it was buried here?" Cat asks.

The man nods. "Yep, right under our noses!"

Cat raises her eyebrows. "Did he find it?"

"Not that we know of," the man replies.

The woman nods. "And once, when he was drunk, he bragged to my husband here that he was stinking rich."

"Rich, right!" her husband scoffs. "And yet, there he was, mooching off Sylvester Berg. If he was so rich, why was he freeloading in a friend's house?"

"That's curious indeed." Cat's mind churns to grasp the implications of what she just learned.

Was Stratte really after the Templar gold? Or were those holes intended for some other purpose, like burying the stolen art until this settled down and he could fence it?

When the couple runs out of tender memories of Stratte's antics, Cat hands them a business card. "Anything else you can remember might help. Please call me even if it seems unimportant."

"Catherine Cavallo, clairvoyant and psychic consultant," the man reads aloud before lifting his eyes to Cat.

"We will, dear," the woman assures her. "You take care now and good luck with your hunt!"

Cat thanks them and resumes her exploration. She turns the next corner, and the couple and their house disappear from view. Ahead, a chimney peeks through the bare trees on the downhill slope.

She pauses, weighing her options. Should she go to that house, knock on the door, and risk being treated as a nuisance? Her twin Julie would totally do it, but Cat is too fond of her comfort zone, especially when it comes to pestering strangers. She was lucky that the couple she just talked to was out in their backyard, but what are the odds of that happening again?

I'm sure Zack could calculate them on the fly.

She pictures his face, the way he's been looking at her since they met... and the way he distanced himself yesterday morning.

Argh! She mustn't—*she won't*—think about him right now. She'll ponder the task at hand.

What could be less unpleasant than knocking on random people's doors? Hmm, she could sneak onto Sylvester Berg's property, study the grounds, and try to find those mysterious holes the neighbors told her about.

Is she more comfortable trespassing than bothering people in their homes?

Hell, yeah!

CHAPTER 31

Cat makes her way to the fence around Villa Berg, scanning the area to make sure no one is watching. Within seconds she finds a spot where the barrier looks pregnable. With a determined grunt she begins to climb it.

Halfway up, a piercing alarm goes off.

Her heart leaps into her throat. She drops to the ground and bolts, silently praying there are no security cameras nearby. Lungs burning, she sprints down the street until she reaches the bus stop and collapses on the bench to catch her breath. She almost squeals with delight moments later when a bus appears and rolls up to the stop.

On board, she slumps into a seat, still panting, half expecting to see police lights in hot pursuit. Her adrenaline levels drop a bit as the bus staggers forward. She wipes some of the condensation from the steamed-up window and peers out. No one is chasing her.

She's safe now. No one saw her.

What was I thinking?!

"Of all the harebrained stunts," she mutters to herself, massaging her temples.

As the bus trundles back into the heart of Chartres, Cat tells herself she could get off at the railway station and catch the next train to Paris. But that would be a shame. She cleared her schedule for today so that she could stay in Chartres until dark if she must.

And that's exactly what I'm going to do!

First off, she's going to revisit Sylvester Berg's art gallery and see if she can talk to him. Cat pulls out her phone and finds the address she wrote down the first time. The bus slows to a stop in the historic center of Chartres, a stone's throw from the gallery.

Cat gets off, straightens her coat, and walks down the street until she reaches the gallery. The building looms large and authoritative, fit for Banque de France or something equally important. Its wide windows offer glimpses of the contemporary artwork inside—vivid paintings and sculptures bathed in deliberate light. Each piece is a statement, as bold and intimidating as the next, against the whitewashed walls.

Gathering her resolve, Cat pushes open the door and steps inside.

For the next ten minutes, she wanders the empty gallery, her eyes darting over the abstract works. The air is cool, rich with the scent of oil paint and wealth. The same two young employees as last time are watching her from the reception desk.

Cat doesn't need to look at them to be aware of their amused scrutiny. It's not that they're being mean—at least, she doesn't think so. It's just that without Zack's assertive presence at her side, she can't help but feel that she shouldn't be here. Her cheap puffer jacket, worn-out jeans, and dirty hiking boots are hysterically out of place in this sanctum of the refined.

She takes a deep breath and approaches the desk.

The young woman, her hair pulled back in a sleek bun,

looks up with a practiced smile. Beside her, the tall, thin young man pauses in the middle of arranging pamphlets.

Cat clears her throat. "Bonjour. I'm here to see Monsieur Berg."

"Which one?" the young man asks.

Cat blinks, taken aback. "I… uh, the owner?"

"Monsieur Sylvester Berg senior retired two months ago and moved to Monaco," the young woman clarifies. "His son is running the gallery now. He's currently in Japan on business."

Cat tries again, "Perhaps you can help me with something else. I'm looking for information about a Luc Stratte. Does the name ring a bell?"

The employees exchange a quick, puzzled glance.

The young man shakes his head. "Never heard of him, sorry."

"Could you maybe check your database?" Cat asks.

"No," the clerks reply in chorus.

Cat's heart sinks a little more, but she forces herself to hand her business card to the female clerk. "Please give this to your boss when he gets back from Japan and ask him to call me. It's important."

The employees take the card and stare at it in fascination. With a background in deep purple, it features a mandala design and shimmering gold lettering that spells out Cat's title.

The young man chokes back a laugh.

"Will do," the young woman assures Cat, keeping her face more or less straight. "I'm sure he'll call you back."

Cat forces a smile. "Thank you."

Burdened by the weight of her fruitless visit, she steps out into a city indifferent to her frustration.

What is the probability I'll get a call from either Sylvester Berg?

There's no need for Zack's sophisticated calculations to answer this one. *Zero.*

Back on the street, she wanders aimlessly, her thoughts a swirling mess of frustration and self-doubt. Should she return to the Fine Arts Museum? Seek out the tour guide, Melanie, in the hopes that her friend Carlos can provide another insight?

Today, Cat's intuition is a blank slate. The subtle nudges from the universe that usually guide her life, scrambled and confusing as they may be, are simply not there.

"Come on, anything!" she begs.

Nothing. Not even a whisper.

Julie would've had this wrapped up by now.

If only I had my twin's skills and moxie!

But Cat is no detective. She's just a psychic who's out of her depth and in over her head. She feels a twinge of envy for her twin, who's solved several crimes in the past few years. Just because Julie and Cat investigated a case together last year doesn't mean Cat can do this by herself.

If Julie were here now, she'd know exactly what to do.

Should I call her and ask her advice?

But then Cat would have to tell her everything from the beginning. Right now, Dad is the only person in the family who knows about the scavenger hunt. Julie would be furious that Cat hadn't clued her in until she needed help. She'd help, of course, but… Cat would love to solve this mystery like the adult she is without her family's help!

Her phone buzzes, and she looks at the screen. A message from Dalila:

Any luck?

Cat doesn't reply. What can she tell her friend? That she tried to trespass on private property, set off an alarm, and had to run for her life?

Cat shivers and rubs her frigid hands together. She's lost. She's demotivated.

I could just quit and go back to my comfy life.

The idea, which would've seemed absurd only an hour

ago, sparkles enticingly in Cat's mind. Granted, Dalila would kill her for walking away from one hundred grand, but honestly, does Cat really believe she can win this thing?

No, I don't. I never did.

The more Cat thinks about it, the greater the appeal of quitting becomes. No more scavenger hunts. No more fruitless searches, rescheduled appointments, pushing herself outside her comfort zone.

And—the biggest, shiniest upside of all—no more Zack.

CHAPTER 32

As Cat's feet tap an uneven rhythm on the sidewalks of Chartres, her mind rumbles as much as her empty stomach. She tells herself she should stop somewhere and grab a bite. But she's too restless. She's also lightheaded from indecision and an eerie feeling of being watched that sends shivers down her spine. But every quick glance over her shoulder or in the reflecting glass of the shop fronts reveals nothing.

Paranoia, surely.

She must be experiencing a delayed side effect from triggering the alarm at Villa Berg during her aborted attempt to break in this morning.

Her phone vibrates against her thigh, cutting through the fog of her thoughts. She stops and pulls it out. It's Zack:

> I may have found something here in Saint-Paul. Will dig deeper. Can't wait to tell you!

Those three short sentences have an unexpected effect on Cat. They reignite her competitive spark, and her motivation is back. She doesn't want to give up anymore. She'd rather keep going so she can impress Zack with her own findings when they talk later.

She quickly taps out a reply:

> Can't wait to hear it. Got spooked this morning, but not beaten. Hope to have more to report tonight.

The Send button swooshes, and Cat tucks her phone into her pocket with a renewed sense of purpose. She lifts her gaze to the spires of Notre-Dame de Chartres high above the buildings around her. Bathed in sunlight, they stretch toward the heavens like hands reaching for the divine.

Her gaze drifts from the spires to the majestic building across the street. Arches and carvings dance around its windows and doors. A set of wide steps leads to the double doors of the grand entrance, flanked by ironwork. But its most striking feature is the steep slate roof, topped with a narrow spire that gives it a half-Gothic, half-Renaissance fairy-tale vibe.

She crosses the street and comes closer to read the sign near the entrance. It's a public library called L'Apostrophe.

And then it comes—the urge, the impulse, that familiar "gut feeling" she hadn't experienced all day.

I must go in.

Cat runs up the stairs and pushes through the double doors. Without stopping to admire the interior, she makes a beeline for the nearest librarian's desk.

A middle-aged man with glasses looks up from his computer with a questioning smile.

Cat greets him, thinking on her feet. It's unlikely that she can get information about a user just by asking nicely. She's not here in any official role. The library owes her nothing. And chances are the librarian doesn't own a TV and has never heard of Wiet's scavenger hunt.

"I was wondering," Cat begins timidly, then stops.

The librarian tilts his head. "Yes?"

"Um, I was wondering if you could help me with something?"

"I hope so. Are you looking for a book?"

Oh well, let's just get it over with. "No, a person."

The librarian's eyebrows arch.

Cat plows on, "Do you think you could check if a man named Luc Stratte ever used this library? Maybe around 2014 to 2016?"

"That's an unusual request."

He's going to ask if I have a warrant or something.

She smiles her sweetest smile. "I know."

"Luc Stratte, you say?" He narrows his eyes. "Why does that name ring a bell?"

"Because he frequented your library?"

"No… I heard it very recently…"

But of course!

"You heard it on TV," Cat claims, perking up. "There were two news reports this month about a scavenger hunt called Looking for *Father Christmas.*"

"That's it! Was he the con artist who stole a painting from Marc Chagall's widow? And the point of the game is to find that painting, right?"

"Exactly right!" She grins. "All but two teams have been eliminated. I'm one of the finalists."

He gives her a thumbs-up. "Exciting! Let me check our records."

Nothing ventured, nothing gained! Turns out, the old adage isn't just empty pep talk. Sometimes, if you push through the negative thinking and step out of your comfort zone, you actually get somewhere. Or at the very least, you give yourself a fighting chance.

The librarian types on his keyboard then stares at his screen, then types again, and stares again.

Cat waits, her heart drumming a nervous beat in the silence of the grand, book-lined hall of L'Apostrophe. Seconds stretch into minutes. The librarian's pursed lips suggest his queries are coming up empty.

"If you can't find a Luc Stratte," Cat says before he can put his body language into words, "could you check for a Luc Verst?"

"Sure. Give me a moment."

Finally, he looks up. "It seems there was a Luc Verst who visited a few times during those years."

Holy guacamole! A rush of excitement steals Cat's voice.

She clears her throat. "Do you have any records of what materials he read or borrowed here?"

"Let me see what I can find."

As he delves deeper into the digital records, Cat listens to the hum of quiet conversations and the rustle of pages turning around her.

The librarian peers at his computer screen, then nods. "The book Monsieur Verst consulted is, *Cryptic Mastery: An Expert's Guide to Advanced Cryptographic Techniques.*"

"Is it currently available?"

He zeroes in on an area of his computer screen. "Yes. Would you like to look at it?"

"Yes, please!"

Smiling, he pushes his glasses higher up his nose. "You'll find it in section 5B, on the second floor."

"Thank you so much!" She hurries to the stairs.

On the second floor, Cat navigates the orderly rows. The air here is muskier, subtly scented with ink and binding glue.

"Yesss!" she whispers when she finds the book nestled among other hefty volumes.

She pulls it off the shelf and settles into a secluded corner of the reading room to peruse it. The book turns out to be exactly what it says on the cover—advanced. The chapter headings are complex and the paragraphs dense. The technical jargon is overwhelming, not to mention the codes and formulas that twist her brain into knots.

What were you up to, Luc Stratte?

She recalls that early in the game, Damien Wiet had mentioned that Stratte, much like himself, was an avid lover of puzzles and ciphers. Could it be that Stratte read this book as part of a hobby, something to keep his mind sharp and for pleasure rather than purpose?

Or is it possible that during his stay at Villa Berg, Stratte used this book as a tool, a means to an end other than simple intellectual curiosity? What if he were creating coded instructions for his accomplices—perhaps those "handsome young men" that the elderly couple told her about this morning?

She imagines Stratte hunkered down by a desk lamp late into the night as he concocted encrypted messages about where to discreetly hide the stolen artwork or how to smuggle them to eager buyers who lurk in the shadows of the black market.

The scenario does seem plausible, yet a part of her hesitates.

Is she letting her imagination run a little too wild, inventing a convoluted theory more suitable for a novel than the reality of a disgraced grifter's life?

Minutes tick by.

Half an hour…

An hour…

An hour and a half…

She keeps turning the pages, looking for any sign of Stratte's interaction with the volume—bookmarks, dog ears, notes in the margins, loose leaves, underlined sections—anything that might indicate what part of the book he'd been interested in. But she finds nothing at all. It's as if the book had been in the hands of a ghost who, for the obvious incorporeal reasons, left no trace of his presence.

With each passing minute, Cat's initial spark of hope fades. Discouraged, she closes the book. Her gaze drifts to the nearby window. Outside, the late afternoon sun paints everything in a golden hue. Her stomach rumbles harder than before. She's exhausted, thirsty, and hungry—and no closer to understanding Stratte's connection to the text than when she started.

Maybe there isn't one. Maybe her gut feeling about this library was wrong. Maybe this was just a dead end.

Reluctantly, she stands, stretches her stiff limbs, and walks back to the librarian.

"Can I borrow this book?" she asks, more out of desperation than hope.

Perhaps Zack might find something in it that I couldn't.

The librarian assists her with the membership forms and checking out the volume. Book in hand, Cat exits the library into the invigorating open air that resuscitates her optimism and boosts her morale for a full minute, until a gust of wind brings the doubts back.

CHAPTER 33

On this gray Sunday morning, Zack strides toward Santa's Grotto, a children's attraction in Saint-Paul-de-Vence.

He arrived in town around noon yesterday, having traveled by high-speed train and then by scooter, which he rented in Nice. Once inside the ramparts of this charming medieval bourg where Chagall spent the last quarter of his life, Zack checked into his hotel, showered, grabbed a bite to eat, and headed out.

First off, he went to La Colline, Chagall's villa. Unfortunately, there wasn't much to see or do there. Just like Chagall's studio in The Beehive, the house was occupied and not open to visitors.

Damn shame! But to be fair, what good would a second art museum do Saint-Paul when there's already a remarkable one for such a small place, the Fondation Maeght? Zack checked it out but didn't find anything relevant to his quest. He also stopped by the village cemetery, where Chagall was buried in 1985.

Homage paid, Zack tried to access the 1994 case file at the

local gendarmerie, which turned out to be permanently closed since over a decade. A visit to the nearest brigade in Vence yielded zilch.

On the plus side, he was able to identify one of the officers who worked on the case at the time as part of the cruelly understaffed OCBC—Central Office for Combating the Trafficking of Cultural Property. Commissaire Pierrick Essley had discovered Saint-Paul while investigating the case. He'd fallen in love with the village, and so had his wife—just like Marc and Vava before them. When the Essleys retired from the force, they settled here.

Thankfully, Pierrick agreed to talk to him. Zack took the Essleys to dinner at a cozy local restaurant. They'd heard about Wiet's scavenger hunt and were happy to help. Alas, there wasn't a whole lot Pierrick had to say about the case that Zack hadn't already gleaned from his extensive research.

Among Pierrick's meager scoops was that OCBC had arrested and obtained convictions for three art dealers who'd done business with Stratte. Unlike the impostor, who had feigned mental disability and served no jail time, the art dealers had been sentenced to prison.

It occurred to Zack that this lent credence to the theory that Stratte had extorted Sylvester Berg and other gallery owners. And why wouldn't he? His former business partners who slipped through the net in 1994 had the example of their imprisoned colleagues to put the fear of law into them.

The other thing Zack learned was that in addition to Stratte's known accomplices—the housekeeper Yvette Lujic and her two grown children—there was a possible fourth. René Guetta, a low-key young man with barely a digital footprint, had been Stratte's boyfriend at the time of the events. But because he'd disappeared before OCBC could get to him, his involvement in the theft was never established.

Pierrick kindly made some phone calls and got some friends to run the name through some databases. René Guetta was never officially found. However, a Frenchman with a different name, but matching Guetta's physical description, died in Thailand four years ago. He was buried there by his local boyfriend. The police suspect that the Frenchman was René Guetta. Unfortunately, a theory isn't enough to obtain an exhumation and DNA test in a foreign country.

After dinner with the Essleys, Zack went back to his hotel and spent the rest of the evening doing more Internet research. This time he focused on Stratte's two remaining accomplices, the children of the housekeeper, Yvette Lujic.

He found plenty of photos of her son Baptiste. Now in his fifties, the man is a voracious user of several social media sites. Zack tracked him to a local address.

At ten, he took a break and called Cat to give her an update. She told him about her misadventures in Chartres and about the book on cryptograms she'd borrowed from the public library. She sounded exhausted. Defeated, even.

He found himself longing to pull her to his chest and whisper words of comfort until she thawed enough to be kissed. Zack ended the call with a good night so dry he could have been talking to his stonehearted father rather than the most adorable woman he'd ever met.

This morning, he went to the address he'd found for Baptiste Lujic. He was expecting to see a large villa a bit like La Colline. What he found was a small, shabby house by the road in the least attractive part of the village. If there were more stolen Chagalls where *Father Christmas* came from, it didn't seem likely that Baptiste Lujic had access to them.

Zack rang the gate bell. A woman in her late fifties emerged from the house. She told Zack that her husband wasn't home. He'd taken their grandchildren to Santa's Grotto.

Hence Zack's current destination.

After passing a picturesque old fountain, Zack checks his map and takes rue Grande, the village's main street. Despite the grayness of this morning, Saint-Paul glows with a cozy warmth. Part is due to the Christmas decorations that drape every balcony and window. But most of it is inherent to the place with its narrow, cobbled streets and creamy houses with thick, rugged walls and pastel-stained wooden shutters.

Moments later, Zack finds himself in front of the attraction. Santa's Grotto is a dazzling display of twinkling lights and over-the-top festive decorations. Santa looms large, drawing children and their accompanying adults like a giant tractor beam. Zack heads for the ticket booth.

The cashier gives him a skeptical look. She must be wondering why a grown man would go into a children's mecca alone.

Zack grins and shrugs. "I never got to see Santa's home as a kid. Figured, it's now or never."

The cashier hands Zack the ticket, her smile as tight as his work schedule.

Once inside, he goes from room to room, scanning the visitors for a middle-aged man who resembles Baptiste. The ice cave shimmers with fake icicles and blue lights, leading into a Christmas village bustling with elves hard at work crafting toys. Zack makes his way to Santa's office, decorated in rich reds and golds, where he expects to find the jolly man himself answering fan mail. But Santa isn't there. He's hanging out in the gift store and posing for pictures with the delighted kids.

A man who looks a lot like Baptiste is here, too. He's supervising a boy and a girl, about four and six years old, respectively.

Zack stays back, never taking his eyes off the trio as they make their way through the maze of holiday cheer. Finally, the children sit down for a treasured photo with Santa, after which Baptiste ushers them toward the exit.

Outside, Zack quickens his pace and catches up with Baptiste, who's leading his grandchildren to the carousel.

"Bonjour, monsieur," Zack greets him. "My name is Zachary Rigaud. Can I ask you a few questions about Luc Stratte?"

Baptiste's face tenses. He sizes Zack up without a word of response.

To help him loosen up, Zack slips two fifty-euro bills into Baptiste's hand.

Baptiste stares into Zack's eyes.

"There's more where that came from," Zack says, "if you can tell me something I don't already know about the Chagall case."

That argument seems to do the trick.

Baptiste nods, gesturing toward the merry-go-round. "Let's talk there. My grandkids will be busy for a bit."

They move to the old-fashioned ride where Baptiste hoists the little boy into a rocket and the girl into a princess carriage, both children giggling with delight. As the carousel begins its gentle whirl, the two men stand side by side and watch the children orbit in their fantastical vehicles.

"How did you find me?" Batiste asks. "Are you a cop? A private investigator?"

Zack holds out his business card. "Neither. I'm just good at research."

"So, Monsieur Rigaud." Batiste lifts his eyes from the card. "What do you want to know about Luc?"

"Anything you can remember might help. His habits, people he associated with besides your family and his boyfriend, things he said."

"He mostly talked to my mother." Baptiste's mouth curls with a bitter twist. "She'd tell you more if my father, that pathetic excuse for a man, hadn't killed her."

My father, that pathetic excuse for a man… Zack could sign off on those words. The only difference in the way Baptiste and Zack feel about their parents is that Zack harbors just as much distaste for his late mother.

He shakes off those distracting thoughts and racks his brain for something to jog Baptiste's memory.

"What can you tell me about Luc's boyfriend, René Guetta?" he asks. "Do you think he was involved in the scheme?"

"Yes, he helped hide the paintings after my mother gave them to Luc."

"Are you sure?"

"Positive."

"Any idea where he hid them?"

Baptiste smirks. "I wish I knew."

"The police estimate that your mother carried off some twenty-five Chagalls, most of which have been recovered," Zack says. "Does that number sound right?"

"It's what Luc told them and what we all told them."

Zack squints at Baptiste. "Were there more?"

"I'd say at least five hundred."

Zack's mouth falls open.

Baptiste chuckles. "You should see your face! Trust me, I'm not making this up just to get the money you dangled in front of me. I heard it from my mother."

"That's huge if true." Zack knits his eyebrows. "Where did all that spoils go?"

"Luc sold some of them right off the bat. The rest... My mother handed the pieces over to Luc, who passed them on to René. I have no idea where René took them or what happened to them after that."

The merry-go-round stops, and Baptiste goes to extract his grandkids from their chosen vehicles. When he returns, Zack hands over all the cash he has on him—300 euros, to be exact —and bids him farewell.

As he walks away from the festive crowd, his mind is buzzing with questions.

Did Baptiste Lujic tell him the truth? Had Stratte really been in possession of five hundred or more works by Marc

Chagall? What did he do with them? How many did he sell? What did he do with the proceeds?

Is it possible that Damien Wiet got wind of this either from Baptiste or someone else?

And if so, what does that mean for the scavenger hunt? What's Wiet's endgame? Are Cat and Zack playing a role they've misinterpreted in a plot they don't understand?

CHAPTER 34

The spirit is willing, but the flesh is weak.

The aphorism plays on a loop in Zack's head as he steers his iron horse through the congested traffic on his way to Cat and Dalila's psychic shop. Urban legend has it that in the early days of machine translation, CIA agents asked a computer to translate this St. Matthew quote into Russian and then back into English. The result the machine spat out was, "The vodka is good, but the meat is rotten."

Zack smiles to himself. Vodka can be good, and he enjoys it once in a while, though not nearly as much as wine. As for his spirit, it's perfectly willing to resist the über-temptation that is Catherine Cavallo. Nevertheless, St. Matthew had a point.

The flesh is weak.

Which is why, when Zack texted Cat on the train taking him back to Paris, he suggested he stop by her shop after work. What his weak flesh craved was for him to take Cat out to dinner, hoping she'd end up spending the night at his place on rue du Faubourg Montmartre.

But here he is, turning onto Quai de Valmy, proving that man can overcome carnal weakness when vodka, aka the spirit, really means it.

Zack parks right in front of Cat's shop, cuts the engine of his Yamaha, and gets off the scooter. He knocks on the glass door decorated with swirling gold stickers of stars and moons. When Cat opens it, he steps into the dimly lit interior to the welcoming tinkle of the chimes above the door and the scent of burning incense.

Dalila brushes past him on her way out. "You two better win this thing, or else!" she tosses over her shoulder.

After she shuts the door behind her, he turns to Cat, who beckons him to the round table before heading for the kitchenette.

He settles into an upholstered chair. "Dalila seems really invested in the scavenger hunt."

"Tea?" Cat asks, filling a teapot with water.

"Yes, please."

"She has a good reason," Cat says over the sound of running water. "If we win, I'll pay a year's rent on the shop in advance."

"That's quite an incentive!"

While Cat prepares the tea, Zack tears his gaze off her shapely form and lets it wander around the room before it lands on the shelves along the wall. They're lined with everything from ancient tarot decks to books on astrology to modern tech.

His eyes linger on a tacky snow globe that seems out of place among the mystical paraphernalia. Besides, who buys tourist souvenirs in their own town? The globe depicts a cozy little house, a Christmas tree and the Eiffel Tower, all surrounded by fake snow.

"What's the story with the snow globe?" he asks.

Cat spins around, glances at the globe and then at him. For a brief moment, there's an odd expectancy in her eyes as if she was waiting for him to say something more.

Then she smiles wryly. "It was an impulse buy at the Tuileries Christmas market. Doesn't really fit the aesthetic, does it?"

"Unless it's predicting a snowy apocalypse at the Eiffel Tower," he jokes.

She sets the tea mugs down on the table between them. "Who knows, maybe it'll start a new trend in psychic decor."

They sit facing each other in silence. Zack inhales the hints of jasmine and mint carried by the steam from his mug. Cat shifts in her seat, visibly ill at ease.

"Have you heard from Christelle?" he asks. "Edgar and I haven't spoken since the dinner at my place when we received the binary code cipher."

She nods. "They're back in Paris."

"Still searching?"

"Yes."

They fall silent again.

All right, let's get this done and over with!

He recaps what he uncovered in Saint-Paul. She sums up what she learned in Chartres. They conclude that it's quite possible that Luc Stratte amassed a small fortune, both in kind and in cash, from the resale of the paintings, some of which may have fetched over 1 million each. Add to that the additional pieces of art he'd likely extorted from the unscrupulous art dealers who'd done business with him in the past, and the con man's secret treasure trove could be quite large.

"There's something I haven't told you about yet," Zack says. "I couldn't sleep last night, so I dug a little deeper."

"And?"

"A few years after his trial, Stratte set up a shell company and an offshore account."

Her eyes widen. "Really?"

"Yes. He did this while he was supposedly bankrupt and unable to pay the ten million he owed the French tax authorities."

"How did you find out about the account?"

"Stratte's name and company are in the Panama Papers."

"What's that?" she asks.

"A massive leak of documents from a Panamanian law firm that revealed the use of offshore entities by thousands of people to evade taxes and hide their wealth."

"So, our master fraudster both dodged jail time and squirreled away his ill-gotten gains, huh?" She flashes a toothy smile. "Does that mean that when he bragged to his neighbors in Chartres that he was rich, it wasn't a drunkard's tale?"

"Looks like there was at least some truth to it."

She narrows her eyes. "But if Stratte's name came up in that leak, why haven't the French authorities gone after his assets?"

"Mainly because Stratte had closed his shell company and the account in 2014, shortly before the publication of the Panama Papers."

She frowns. "Where did the money go?"

"No one knows."

"Stratte could've buried it, along with the unsold art, in the holes at Sylvester Berg's estate in Chartres," she muses.

He turns his mug, the tea in it swirling like the thoughts in his head. "Or René Guetta could've hidden it in the South to avoid traveling long distances with the goods."

"The other possible location is Néchin, where Stratte hid after the trial."

"And there are those sunny destinations he frequented, according to what Berg's neighbors told you." He meets her eyes. "Stratte's offshore account was in the Virgin Islands, by the way."

She makes a sad face. "Yes, but then he closed it. The money and the artifacts could be anywhere, really."

"Or spread over several places."

She trails her finger around the rim of her mug. "What if

Damien Wiet discovered the existence of the treasure, but not its location? Maybe he concocted this whole scavenger hunt to help him find it?"

"That thought has crossed my mind."

"And what do you think?"

He leans back in his chair. "Wiet could've heard about it from Baptiste Lujic like I did. Or maybe from someone else in Stratte's entourage."

"Or from Jacqueline!"

"Who's Jacqueline?"

Cat smiles. "Oh, only the most gifted clairvoyant in the world. Dalila and I believe she's the one who led Wiet to the *Father Christmas* painting."

"Then why didn't she take him to the rest of the treasure?" Zack asks.

"Maybe because the main cache wasn't in the same place as *Father Christmas*?" Cat shrugs. "Perhaps Jacqueline was unable to see where it was hidden."

"Hmm."

"Come on, that explains why Wiet opened the game not only to mathematicians like himself, but also to psychics!"

Zack doesn't comment, not wishing to appear rude. The truth is of all the hypotheses they just brainstormed, the Jacqueline lead sounds the least convincing to him.

Cat winks. "Can you believe it? The generous art patron and philanthropist Damien Wiet could be using us to find Stratte's haul!"

"I have no problem believing that."

"But he's already rich, so why bother?"

"It's a common misconception that rich people aren't as eager to increase their wealth as the man on the street," Zack points out.

"Right. I suppose they are."

"Totally! Besides, Wiet is a puzzle enthusiast. He could be doing this for love as much as for money."

"Then why doesn't he solve this mystery himself?" she asks.

"I'm sure he has tried and failed."

"It's easy to see why, because we face the same issues," she says. "Too many possibilities, not enough—"

"Vodka," he cuts in.

"Say what?"

"I meant *spirit*," he corrects himself. "And time."

They finish their tea.

Zack sets his mug down. "What about the cryptogram book you borrowed from the library in Chartres?"

"Want to see it?" Cat fetches the thick volume.

He leafs through it for a while.

"There's nothing there," she says. "It's clean."

Too clean, perhaps?

He pauses, the half-closed book in his hands. "Do you have a hair dryer in here?"

"A hair dryer?" she repeats, puzzled.

"Stratte was a cunning man, wasn't he?"

"Yes, why?"

Zack isn't at all confident this will work, which is why he's in no hurry to explain his hypothesis. "I'd like to check something."

Cat gets up. "Let me take a look in Dalila's things."

She disappears through the side door, leaving Zack to ponder all the ways his idea might not work.

Moments later, she returns, brandishing a hair dryer like a trophy. "Dalila's emergency kit for frizzy days!"

She passes it to him, and he accepts it with the solemnity of a knight being handed his sword. He plugs it in, turns it to a low heat setting, and directs the warm air over the open pages of the book.

For the next few minutes, the shop is quiet, save for the hum of the hair dryer and the occasional shuffling of pages under Zack's careful manipulation. Cat leans in closer, mouth slightly open. He tries not to think how close she is.

The pages flutter under the warm air stream. Suddenly, on a blank margin of page 69, the faintest writing begins to appear, not yet legible, but definitely there.

Cat gasps. "Zack, look!"

He nods, his focus sharpening. The writing become clearer by the second. Stratte's heat-reactive invisible ink is blooming like a flower in time-lapse. Careful not to overheat and burn the paper, Zack holds the hair dryer relatively far away. The downside is that the exercise becomes a test of patience.

"Invisible ink is a form of steganography," he comments while they wait.

"Stegano—what?"

He explains, "So, cryptography scrambles messages to make them unintelligible to the uninitiated, right?"

"Right."

"Well, steganography makes them invisible to the naked eye," he says. "In other words, it hides them in plain sight. Cyber attackers often use it to sneak malware past security systems."

He keeps his tone casual, hoping it doesn't show how thrilled he is about the opportunity to apply his narrow professional expertise to their joint undertaking. And to impress her.

When the writing is almost decipherable, both their phones buzz on the table, startling them.

"It's a text message from Wiet," Cat says, picking up her phone. "Should I open it?"

"Go ahead."

She reads it aloud:

> To both teams,
>
> You are almost there.
>
> Keep up the good work!

Your fans across the country and I can't wait to see which team finds Father Christmas first.

Sincerely,

Damien Wiet

CHAPTER 35

Cat whistles softly in surprise and shifts her gaze from her phone to Zack. "We have fans?"

"According to Letitia, my PA, there's a fringe group following our quest."

"Oh, wow! Which team are they rooting for?"

"Roughly half are Team Christelle, and half Team Catherine."

She beams with pride. Just as she's about to suggest to Zack that they thank their fans on social media, her eyes fall on the open page in front of him. The handwritten text in the margin is now fully legible.

"There!" she cries out.

He adjusts the hair dryer, holding it up to keep the page warm, as they both stare at the text.

It's a URL, and a rather unusual one at that. The web address consists of a string of random letters and numbers, followed by a period, and then by the word *onion*.

Cat points at the cryptic link. "What's that?"

"Probably a dark web address," Zack replies.

"Can we check it out? I'll get my laptop!"

"We can't just type this into a regular browser. We need something special to access it."

She furrows her brow. "I only have the standard browser."

"That can be fixed." He smiles. "Can you get your laptop?"

With a nod, she dashes to the back of her shop and returns moments later with her laptop in her arms. She sets it down on the table in front of Zack and opens it.

He scoots closer. "May I?"

"Be my guest!"

His fingers begin to dance across the keyboard with the ease of a lifelong geek.

"I'm downloading a secure browser that can handle dot-onion sites," he comments. "It'll let us see what Stratte was hiding."

"OK."

"And, don't worry, I won't put your computer at risk," he assures her.

"I'm not worried."

She hovers behind him as he sets up a peculiar browser on her laptop and installs additional security protocols.

"All right, I'm going in," he declares with mock drama, typing in the mysterious URL.

The screen flickers briefly before presenting them with a stark, empty page, save for a lonely password box.

Cat leans closer. "Try *MarcChagall*, one word."

Zack obliges.

The site's response is instant and unyielding.

The password must be ten characters.

"How about *ReneGuetta*?" Zack asks her. "He was Stratte's boyfriend and accomplice."

She nods. "Go for it!"

He types again, carefully. But the result is just as fruitless, and now with a more ominous warning:

One attempt left.

He stiffens, as if the finality of that message weighed on him. "I'm tempted to just enter the numbers zero through nine."

Eyes at Cat, he flexes his fingers.

She chews on her lip. "Try *LucStratte.*"

Was it inspiration or desperation?

He gives her a skeptical look. "Is that the clairvoyant talking?"

The truth is, it's not. Cat isn't getting any vibes or picking up any extrasensory information right now.

If anything, her suggestion is a product of logic. Based on what they've learned about Stratte's personality so far, the man was extremely full of himself. It takes a huge ego and tons of aplomb for a mole catcher, born and raised in the industrial north, to reinvent himself as an art dealer on the glittering Riviera. And not just any art dealer, but one who sold dozens of stolen works through some of the world's most prestigious galleries and auction houses!

Who would someone like Stratte love the most? *Himself.*

Part of Cat wants to admit to Zack that her suggestion was an informed guess. That would certainly appeal to his rational mind. But another, more twisted part of her burns to test how much he trusts her. He doesn't believe in the supernatural, and that's not going to change. But will he trust her, regardless?

"Let's call it a gut feeling," she says defiantly.

He seems to hesitate for a moment and then types in *LucStratte* and hits Enter.

They both hold their breath, watching the page refresh.

And then it happens. The password is accepted, and the security page peels away, allowing them access. A multirow and multicolumn table appears. It's a… ledger! Detailed and extensive, it lists artwork, transactions, names, dates, and prices—a full inventory of Stratte's illicit dealings laid bare.

Zack scrolls all the way down. "And look at this!"

At the very bottom of the page, there's a freestanding line of text. It's a woman's name, Fleur, and an address in Paris.

They trade excited looks.

Zack opens a new tab and enters the address into the search window. It takes a minute, tops, to get a name—Hanriot—and a phone number.

He checks his watch. "Is a quarter past nine too late to make a cold call?"

"It is, but screw that."

He barks an amused, "Yes, madame!" and dials the number.

After a few rings, someone answers. The voice is warm and mature but younger than Cat's grandmother's. It sounds like a middle-aged woman.

The "Fleur" from Stratte's secret website?

Zack puts her on speakerphone. "Good evening, Madame Hanriot?"

"Yeees…"

"My name is Zachary Rigaud, and I'm here with my colleague Catherine Cavallo. You might have seen us on TV."

"Really?"

Cat jumps in, "We're one of the two remaining teams in the scavenger hunt Looking for *Father Christmas.*"

"Yes, I've seen it," Fleur Hanriot says. "Um, how can I help you?"

Zack looks at Cat. "We're trying to find information on Luc Stratte."

"Oh. Right." There's a pause before Fleur says, "Yes, well, Luc Stratte was… um, quite a character."

"What can you tell us about him?" Zack asks.

She swallows audibly. "That's it, really."

You're hiding something, Fleur.

Zack shoots Cat a help-me-here look. She begins to spread her hands in apology, but then she remembers a bold tactic Julie used when they investigated together last year.

"Madame Hanriot," she begins as assertively as she can, "we *know* about the connection between you and Stratte. What we'd like to ascertain is whether he ever stayed with you or hid his haul in your house."

"I never met Luc personally," Fleur babbles in a panicked tone. "And he never stayed in our house, I assure you."

Oh my God, the trick worked! Cat punches the air in a soundless cheer.

"That's hard to believe," Zack jumps in, catching on.

"I'm not denying that René stayed in the house during the years I was abroad with my husband," she says.

René. As in, René Guetta, Luc Stratte's vanishing boyfriend? Who is he to Fleur Hanriot?

Zack gives Cat a thumbs-up and presses on. "How can you be sure that René didn't bring Luc in without telling you?"

"My half-brother may have kept questionable company at times," Fleur says, "but he never lied to me."

"If that's true," Zack counters, "then he told you about his involvement in the theft of the Chagall paintings, didn't he?"

Silence.

It's Cat's turn to give Zack the thumbs-up. The man is quick on the uptake, that geeky brain of his as nimble as his fingers.

Don't go there, Catherine!

"Madame Hanriot?" he probes.

What can Fleur say, the poor thing? She's cornered. If she continues to claim that René never lied to her, she'll have to admit that she knows about his involvement in Stratte's criminal enterprise. Her only way out is—

"René wasn't involved in that sordid affair," she finally says.

—that. Denial.

The thing is, Fleur Hanriot is an upstanding member of society, unlike her crooked half-brother. She's a trusting person, or she'd have hung up on them long ago. Lying doesn't come easily to such people. The delay in her answer and the dull, half-hearted tone in which it was delivered are additional clues. "René wasn't involved" sounded like a phrase Fleur had said many times, no doubt, to reassure herself and perhaps her husband without really believing it.

Cat sits down. "So, you didn't find any stolen art or money hidden in the house after you returned to France and moved back in?"

"No!" There's no hesitation in Fleur's reply this time. "We turned the house inside out and cleaned it thoroughly because René had transformed it into a pigsty. We found nothing of the sort."

"Uh-huh," Cat says, doubtful it's true.

"My husband is a civil servant from a family of military officers," Fleur goes on, "Trust me, if we'd found anything fishy, we would've reported it to the police the same day!"

Unless Fleur is a virtuoso liar, which she isn't, her words are as sincere as they come.

"If you're so sure," Zack says, "then you won't mind if we come by and take a look, will you?"

He's pushing her too hard. There's no reason Fleur should agree to let two strangers, whose only legitimacy is that they've been on TV, search her house.

"Sure," Fleur says to Cat's bewilderment. "You can come by Thursday morning at ten and look around. Just don't expect to find anything."

"Thank you!" Cat exclaims.

"Just a moment—let me check my calendar," Zack says, opening the app on his phone.

Cat does the same, even though she knows she doesn't have any appointments on Thursday morning.

Zack moves his mouth from side to side as he mulls over something, before shooting a questioning look at Cat. "Does it work for you?"

"Yes."

"We can do it," he says into the phone. "See you Thursday morning!"

"You have the address?" Fleur inquiries.

"We do," Cat replies.

Please don't ask how we found it!

"Oh, and bring some photo ID," Fleur throws in.

"Of course," Zack says. "Thank you again, Madame Hanriot! You've been incredibly helpful."

They hang up.

As Cat and Zack give the rest of the book the blow-dry treatment just to be thorough, they discuss their chances of hitting pay dirt on Thursday. Assuming the goods were ever stashed in the house, Stratte or Guetta must've cleaned them out before Fleur's return. Or, if Fleur is in on it, she'll use tomorrow and Wednesday to relocate whatever's left in the house.

"Fleur's right," Cat says. "We shouldn't expect to find anything."

"Do we have any better leads at the moment?" Zack turns the last page and shuts the book.

They didn't find any more invisible notes in it.

Cat shakes her head. "No, we don't."

"Then we follow the one we have." He stands up, avoiding eye contact. "Need a lift?"

He sounds like Perseus offering Medusa a ride, well aware she'll turn him to stone the first chance she gets.

"Thanks," she replies, "but I have some things to finish here before I go home. Good night."

"Good night." He grabs his coat and helmet and practically runs out the door.

CHAPTER 36

It's ten in the morning. Zack steers his scooter up the meandering inclines of Montmartre to the narrow rue Gabrielle, a picturesque, cobbled street with well-kept houses with shutters open to catch the morning light. He parks the scooter in the designated area, and dismounts.

Cat is already there in front of a cozy little house squeezed between two bigger ones. She waves at him, alluring as ever.

Damn! He was supposed to cool off over the last two days. There was so much work to catch up on, he barely had time to eat. At the office, he hardly thought about her. The late evenings at home were a different matter, of course. He filled them with more work. He was moving in the right direction...

Give it time.

He greets Cat in what he hopes is a friendly way, but nothing more. She reacts in a similar manner. No kisses, not even the customary peck on the cheek, just a smile and a polite "good morning."

They ring the bell.

A middle-aged woman with a round face framed by wavy strands of salt-and-pepper hair answers the door.

Cat and Zack present their credentials as she'd requested. Fleur Hanriot studies both sides of each ID, comparing the photos with their faces before ushering them inside.

"My husband was against your visit," she says, taking their coats. "But I insisted."

Zack adjusts the straps of his backpack, wondering why anyone would insist on letting strangers inspect their home.

As if reading his mind, she smiles. "The thought that you would suspect me of being an accomplice to Luc, in possession of stolen masterpieces… I knew I'd lose sleep over that."

"We really appreciate your gesture," Cat offers.

"That's all right." Fleur sweeps a hand at either side of the corridor they pass through. "Nothing here, as you can see."

"Do you mind if we take a closer look?" Zack asks, producing a sleek, handheld device from his backpack.

"What's that?" Fleur asks.

He holds it up briefly to her curious gaze. "It's a wall scanner. It checks for cavities behind the plaster."

"And you just happened to have one at home?" Cat teases.

"No," he admits. "I asked Letitia to research different models yesterday and buy the best one."

He presses the device against the textured wallpaper, watching the small LED screen intently.

Fleur leans in. "Does it really work?"

He nods, focusing on the scanner. It emits a soft beep, and the green lights flicker across the digital display.

"I'm told it's pretty reliable." He slides his thumb over the buttons to toggle between modes.

The scanner continues to beep, a steady rhythm that fills the quiet corridor. No sign of cavities. Zack moves the device along the opposite wall and sweeps just as methodically. *Nada.*

"Just covering all our bases," he says with a mild smile, switching the device off.

"Not to worry," Fleur says. "Do your thing. That's what you're here for."

She leads them into the kitchen, where she opens the pantry, cabinets, and cupboards with neatly arranged dishes and pans. Next, they move through two bedrooms, where she lets them peek inside the closets. A home office follows. It's cluttered, but there are no false walls or hollow spaces.

In the living room with a small Christmas tree on the table, Fleur dramatizes her innocence by inviting Cat and Zack to take random books from the bookshelf and check the wall behind them. Zack uses the wall scanner on every bit of surface that looks remotely suspicious, but the device never deviates from its consistent negative.

After they've covered all the rooms, including the storage area, the broom closet, and the bathrooms, Fleur suggests they tackle the attic next. They head for the stairs when Cat spots a nondescript door.

She stops and points at it. "What's in there?"

"That's the door to the garden," Fleur replies without breaking stride.

Zack stops.

Rolling her eyes, Fleur goes to the door and turns the key. "Oh, you don't believe me?"

And, like she said, it opens to a garden. After she locks up, they climb into the dusty attic. Fleur flicks on the light and waits for Cat and Zack to inspect the cramped space. It's full of the stuff families tend to collect over the years: old toys, magazines, clothes, strollers, cribs… No artwork, stolen or otherwise.

"There's nothing up here but memories," Fleur comments as they head back downstairs. "Want to see the basement?"

By now, Zack is beyond certain they won't find Stratte's treasure in this house. He glances at Cat.

"Might as well be thorough," she says.

Fleur leads them down a narrow staircase into a dimly lit basement. The air is much cooler here. Cat hugs herself. Zack almost puts an arm around her shoulders to keep her warm, but then checks himself.

When Fleur turns on the light, Zack takes in a bare rectangular room filled with a ping-pong table in the middle.

"See?" Fleur says. "No secret hiding places."

Zack picks up the wall scanner again. "Do you mind?"

"I need to get a few things from the market before they close at one," Fleur says, glancing at her watch.

Zack puts the scanner away. "Of course."

She holds out a hand, as if to stop him. "You know what? You're welcome to keep looking while I'm gone."

"Really?" Cat stares at her, eyes wide.

"Sure, why not?" Fleur heads for the stairs. "I'll be back in an hour. Scan to your heart's content!"

Zack opens his mouth to remark that it's unwise to be so trusting nowadays, but he stops himself at the last moment.

Fleur halts at the foot of the staircase and shrugs. "This way, we'll all sleep easy. No regrets or what-ifs."

She leaves them with that.

Zack pulls the scanner from his backpack once again and turns it on in a corner of the basement. The device hums softly in his hand as he moves it along the rough texture of the bare cinder block wall. Cat watches over his shoulder, rubbing her arms.

With methodical patience, Zack sweeps the scanner slowly across the surface of the first wall, then another. Fifteen minutes later, still nothing of interest. The air between Cat and Zack is thick with disappointment when, on the third wall, the scanner's hum changes. Suddenly it emits a higher, more insistent tone.

Zack stops in his tracks. "Here, listen to this!"

They both stare at the device in his hands as he runs it back and forth over the same spot. Sure enough, the tone is different. Together they examine the wall more closely, feeling for anomalies, pressing and tapping each cold cinder block.

After a few tense minutes, a section shifts subtly under

Zack's palms. He applies a little more pressure, and with a soft grind, a segment of the wall swings open, revealing a dark void behind it.

They exchange a look of astonished triumph and push the secret door farther open. The space behind the wall is a long, narrow storage room. Cat activates the flashlight on her phone. Inside the hidden cavity are shelves lined with rolled canvases, framed paintings, and figurines. There are a few sculptures on the floor. Zack spots four briefcases that could hold anything from money to jewelry. Among the treasures is a small ornate object that catches the light, its oval shape sparkling with intricate craftsmanship.

Hell, it could be a Fabergé egg!

Zack squeezes into the cache, his heart pounding with the thrill of the find and the magnitude of what they've just uncovered.

Cat follows close behind. "A real treasure trove!" she gasps.

He laughs. "Move over, Ali Baba!"

She points to the rows of artifacts. "You don't think the Hanriots knew about this, do you?"

"René Guetta must've built a new wall while they were abroad," Zack says. "He was careful to use the same type of cinder block as in the rest of the basement. I'm sure only he and Stratte knew about this place."

"But they both died prematurely and, in a final act of villainy, took their secret to their graves!"

Zack gives her a wink. "I guess they didn't plan on us coming here to look for *Father Christmas*."

CHAPTER 37

Cat shines her flashlight on a small, framed painting. It depicts a woman cradling an infant, not unlike the woman in *Father Christmas*. She's standing in front of a colorful, dreamlike background with a flying donkey in it. The strokes and themes are unmistakable—it's a Chagall.

Suddenly, a chill cuts through the stale air around Cat. For a heartbeat, the dim space seems to brighten as an image materializes before her eyes. It's her mother, Elise, looking as real as she ever did in life. Her eyes, filled with warmth and deep concern, lock onto Cat's.

"Run now, child!" she says without opening her mouth.

The words still ring in Cat's head when the vision melts away. This encounter leaves Cat momentarily rooted to the spot with her breath caught in her throat. The suddenness of it, the clarity of the warning… It's the first vision of her mother she's ever had. It's also the first time they've "spoken" since the fateful day that took Elise's life and awakened her daughters' psychic powers.

With an effort, Cat pulls herself from her reverent stupor. "We need to get out of here, Zack. Now!"

Will he listen?

Can he hear the urgency in her strained voice? Can he see it etched into her features?

He shifts his gaze from the treasures around them to her face. For a split second, he looks like he's about to object, but then he nods and motions her to the opening in the wall.

They climb out of the cache. Treading softly, Cat beelines to the small, grimy basement window and peers out. Four men are walking toward the house with deliberate steps.

She waves to Zack. "Pst, over here!"

He joins her at the window.

Outside, the men pause at the door, scanning the area. They each put on a face mask. One tries the handle before reaching into his pocket for a tool. The others arrange themselves strategically to shield him from view.

"Back door," Zack whispers.

Cat nods and rushes to the wall. "We seal this first!"

They pull and push against the dusty cinder blocks until the opening is camouflaged again and run up the basement stairs. It's too risky to get their coats, so they head straight for the garden door. Two turns of the key and they're out. Zack helps her climb over the weathered picket fence.

"Over there, quick!" he whispers, tugging on her sleeve.

They skirt the block, duck, and peek around the corner.

Zack reaches for his phone. "We need to call the police—"

His words trail off as something down the street catches his eye. Cat follows his gaze to a black car at the curb. A flicker of movement inside it makes her narrow her eyes and focus. A man in the driver's seat lifts a clunky phone—no, a walkie-talkie—to his face. His eyes meet Cat's.

"He's seen us," Zack says. "Change of plans."

He points to his scooter parked just a few meters away. They dash to it. As soon as they're close enough, Zack hops on. Cat follows. The engine roars to life. They have no helmets or coats. But that's the least of Cat's worries right now.

Just as they're peeling away from the curb, the front door of the house bursts open. Three men spill out and sprint toward the black car.

"Hang on!" Zack yells over the hum of the scooter speeding down the street.

Cat wraps her arms around his waist. Behind them, tires squeal on the wet asphalt. Cat risks a glance back. The car lurches forward. Zack accelerates sharply around a tight corner onto a truncated little street, then again onto a longer one. The cobblestones make for a bumpy ride. The quaint galleries and colorful souvenir shops blur into a streaking backdrop to their flight.

An engine growls behind them. Cat glances nervously over her shoulder. The sleek obsidian beast chasing them veers onto the street they're on.

Zack weaves the scooter through a small square full of cafés and portrait artists. *Is this the iconic Place de Tertre?* Cat is too dazed to tell. The artists, their models, and the patrons smoking outside in the drizzle turn their heads. Brushes pause in midair. The scooter startles a flock of pigeons and clips a wicker chair, sending it clattering across the sidewalk. Zack barely slows down.

Cat looks back. A waiter is shaking his fist and yelling profanities at them.

"Sorry!" she cries out.

"Hold on!" Zack warns her.

She clings to him as he steers the scooter down the steps of a pedestrian passageway, one of many in Montmartre. The scooter bumps and shakes beneath them. Cat's heart pounds in her chest. Every jump feels like it will knock her off the bike and send her reeling and bouncing across the stones. The black car hesitates at the top of the steps, then turns to find a way around and disappears.

Finally on level ground, they speed across the base of the hill and up one of the streets.

"Yell if you see a police station," Zack calls over his shoulder.

"OK!"

"And don't be scared, baby! We'll be all right. I'll get us to safety."

Did he just use a term of endearment?

There's no time to think about it. Cat is sore, cold, and drenched—and the bad guys are catching up with them. Unfortunately, there's nothing resembling a police station in sight.

Why hasn't anyone called the cops on them yet? With all the traffic rules they've broken, shouldn't the police be hot on their heels by now?

Where are they when you need them?

Zack turns sharply onto another street, swerving to avoid a delivery truck. Ahead of them looms the dome of the Sacré-Coeur, white and majestic. They skirt its base. Mercifully, the site is less crowded than usual on this cold and wet midweek morning. The scooter's engine whines with effort as Zack plunges back into the maze of narrow one-way streets.

As they race down the long rue de Clignancourt, Cat hears the terrifying roar of a powerful engine behind her again. Zack's grip on the handlebars tightens. He begins to lean to the left, clearly preparing to duck into a smaller street with a greater chance of steps or bollards.

"Don't! Keep going straight!" Cat shouts over the wind.

Up ahead, she's just spotted what they've been looking out for. A concrete-and-glass building stands out against the historic façades before and after it. There's a good chance it's a *commissariat*. Zack straightens the scooter.

The black car is like a relentless predator gaining ground behind them. Cat's heart hammers against her ribs. Adrenaline floods her system. They're now near enough that she can make out a blue sign with the word *Police* on it, marking the entrance.

We're almost there!

She glances in the rearview mirror. The front of the car is now closer to her derriere than the scooter is to the police station. In a desperate maneuver, Zack swings the scooter onto the sidewalk. The sudden jolt sends a shock wave through Cat's body.

"Get ready to run!" he yells seconds before slamming to a stop.

With adrenaline pumping through her veins, Cat doesn't hesitate. She jumps off the scooter and races toward the police station. Three officers, alerted by either the commotion or the surveillance cameras, rush out the doors. They sprint toward her, hands on their holstered weapons, eyes assessing the threat.

Right behind her, Zack grips her shoulder to halt her panicked run.

"Hands up! Turn around slowly!" barks one of the officers.

"Cat, stop!" he gasps. "Put your hands up!"

They both freeze, hands high in surrender. The officers close in. More orders, more compliance. In a matter of seconds, cold handcuffs click around Cat's wrists. From the corner of her eye, she glimpses the black car. It slows, hesitates, and then accelerates away.

Cat's breaths come shallow as the cops pat her and Zack down before leading them into the station.

"Listen, you need to send someone to rue Gabrielle now!" Cat pleads with the cops.

Zack stands beside her, his face flushed from the chase, as he too tries to convey the urgency of the situation. "We were being chased, OK? By masked, armed men."

"Why?" an officer asks.

Zack's eyes dart to him. "They're after something we found."

"What did you find?"

"Stolen art," Cat replies. "Not just any art, but masterpieces by Marc Chagall and others, stolen in the nineties."

An officer with fancy shoulder straps on her jacket holds up her hand. "Slow down, please! Start from the beginning."

"There's no time!" Cat screams in frustration. "You have to get there before those thugs!"

"Fleur Hanriot," Zack adds, "the owner of the house on rue Gabrielle, has no idea what's hidden in her basement. She went out and let us search."

The officer turns to him. "Street number, please?"

Zack gives it to her, and she scribbles the full address down on a page in her notepad.

Cat holds her handcuffed hands in prayer. "Please! The moment Fleur walks back in, her life will be in danger. If those men went back to look for the treasure, they might kill her!"

The officer rips the page out and hands it to a younger colleague. "Go check this address, on the off chance they're not making this up!"

"I saw the car that was chasing them," he says, taking the note from her. "Black BMW. It took off when we showed up."

The policewoman turns back to her team, "I want two units there, armed. Secure the house."

"The artifacts are in the basement behind a false wall!" Zack shouts after the rushing officers.

Officer Shoulder Straps motions Cat and Zack toward a hallway. "You two, with me! You're going to tell me everything in detail and in order."

Cat shoots Zack a quick, tense look before they're led down the hallway. He meets her eyes. His expression is reassuring and… something else. Cat doesn't know how to describe it.

Maybe it's the ebbing adrenaline that gives him that dazed air.

I probably look the same.

The most important thing is that they're safe now, and there's hope that they've averted disaster for Fleur. And if the cops get to her house before the criminals, then Cat and Zack can brag that they uncovered one of the biggest art hauls in history.

CHAPTER 38

Cat stirs and opens her eyes a crack. Gradually, the room sharpens into focus. This isn't her bedroom.

What the what?

Her eyelids flutter open wide. This place looks familiar… *It's Zack's!* She's in his apartment, in his bed, her head pounding, and her mouth dry. She could drink a lake right now.

I'm hungover.

And, she's fully dressed, which is both a relief and a mystery. Slowly, she turns her aching head to the right. The other side of the bed is empty, but it was slept in.

Where is Zack?

Last night's events flicker through her memory. They were at the police station, telling their story to Capitaine Daloz, the officer with the three stripes. They got to the part about Stratte's secret ledger when Daloz received a call with an excited report.

The cops had beaten the thugs to the treasure.

Whether it was from divine intervention or bad city planning, the BMW got stuck in a monstrous traffic jam. That allowed the police to get to the Hanriots' house first. A few minutes later, Fleur returned from the market. When the criminals showed up a quarter of an hour later, there was a welcome party waiting for them.

Fleur and her husband were shocked to discover the cache in their basement. The police photographed, registered, and secured everything, including the cash. The next step, Zack and Cat were told, will be to bring in art experts who will authenticate and appraise every item. After that the process of restitution for the rightful owners or their heirs will begin.

Damien Wiet's involvement is still a shadow over Cat and Zack's victory. Did he orchestrate the entire hunt to uncover Stratte's hoard? Will the thugs he sent to the Hanriots' house talk to the cops? That remains to be seen.

Yesterday at the police station, Daloz wrote down all Cat and Zack's suspicions with an inscrutable face. It was impossible to tell if she found them convincing and if she would investigate Wiet.

With all the interruptions and checks, it was after seven when Cat and Zack could finally go home, exhausted and famished. Zack said they should celebrate the spectacular conclusion of their treasure hunt.

"We need a proper feast!" he insisted.

Against her better judgment, Cat let herself be swept away to "the best restaurant in Paris," which happened to be in his neighborhood. The food was delicious. The wine flowed freely. The conversation meandered from their adventure to lighter, more personal matters.

After dinner, they ended up in his apartment.

Cat rubs her temples, trying to recall what exactly they talked about and, more importantly, what they did. They crashed on his couch, debriefed and relaxed… Zack seemed a little out of it. Cat remembers laughing and lying down as the room began to spin.

Did I fall asleep on the couch?

She sits up, her head pounding in protest.

I need aspirin.

And a shower.

And a toothbrush.

And coffee—lots of coffee.

Her gaze lands on a note on the bedside table, scrawled in a hasty script:

Gone to get croissants from the baker.

Be back soon.

Zack

Cat exhales with a mix of confusion and relief. She swings her legs over the edge of the bed. As she stands, the room tilts, and she braces herself against the wall. She staggers to the bathroom and splashes some water on her face and finger combs her hair. Feeling marginally better, she heads to the kitchen—straight to the sink. She pours herself a glass of water, gulps it down, then fills it again. The cool liquid is a balm for her parched throat.

Zack's footsteps echo in the hallway. She turns as he enters with a bakery bag in hand.

He flashes her a smile. "How are you feeling?"

"Like I got run over by that BMW." She sizes him up, all fresh and yummy. "You?"

"Never better!"

"Clearly, you handle alcohol better than I do." She points both index fingers at her face. "Look at the state of me!"

He grins. "A little disheveled and puffy, but still adorable."

Adorable?

That's such an unlikely thing for Zack to say that she doesn't know what to make of it.

So, she mumbles, "I need a shower," and scurries to the bathroom.

Cat slips into the kitchen, still feeling the warmth of the shower on her skin. The aroma of fresh coffee draws an appreciative smile from her.

At the stove, Zack is frying eggs. "One side or both?"

"Just one, please."

"Excellent choice!" He turns off the heat. "I have to be at work before noon, but I'm free tonight and all weekend."

Was that an invitation?

It certainly sounded like one, but Cat has her doubts. His behavior this morning is such a contrast to how he acted in the same context barely a week ago that she feels she can't trust herself to read his cues. Hadn't he made it abundantly clear that their night together was a one-off and that they weren't going to be an item?

If you want to see me again, you'll have to ask.

The salad bowl with fresh croissants and other treats from the baker makes her mouth water.

He sets a plate in front of her and another across the table. "Enjoy!"

She picks up her knife and fork. "You too! This is the perfect fix after all the drinking last night."

"And after everything we've been through."

She looks up from her plate. "We really did it, didn't we?"

"You mean, found a bunch of stolen masterpieces, got chased through Montmartre by a squad of hitmen, almost crashed into a police station, got arrested, and lived to tell the tale?"

"Oh, boy." She shakes her head, hand on her collarbone.

"Come on, that was fun! We should do it again sometime."

Her eyes widen in mock horror. "Not in a million years! This psychic can take only so much drama."

"I hear you." He makes a sympathetic face. "Back to the humdrum of crystal balls and visions, then?"

"Exactly!"

He takes the seat across from her, and they dig into their fried eggs. For the next few minutes, they eat in silence.

"During yesterday's hot pursuit," he begins, his face serious, "there was a moment when I panicked and nearly lost it."

"Me, I was scared stiff the entire time!" she exclaims. "Those thugs were going to run us over."

"I was pretty confident I wasn't going to let that happen."

She cocks her head. "Then what made you panic?"

"The realization that if Wiet's henchmen had guns, which was likely, and if they started shooting at us… You were behind me, exposed. That's what freaked me out."

Is that when you called me baby*?*

His eyes are darker than usual, intense, as he stares at her. "Can I see you tonight?"

"Yes."

Oops—did I answer too quickly?

"Great!" He pours her some coffee. "How about this weekend? We could go somewhere."

"Where?"

"I could book a night at a chateau on the Loire." He sits back down. "Which one would you like to see, or revisit?"

She leans back in her chair and eyes him. "Who are you, and what have you done to Zachary Rigaud?"

He doesn't smile. Instead, he studies her face in all seriousness. A few minutes later, he opens his mouth to speak, but instead bites the side of his bottom lip. In the intense two weeks they've known each other, Cat has never seen him so hesitant.

The tense silence is broken by the sudden ringing of Zack's phone, followed closely by Cat's. Her first thought is that it's Wiet with new directions for the scavenger hunt. She exchanges a look with Zack as both their phones vibrate on the kitchen table.

She picks up her phone. "Hello?"

Turns out her caller isn't Wiet but Capitaine Daloz. Cat glances at Zack again.

"Yes, I'm with her right now," he's saying into his phone. "We can both talk to you." He turns on the speakerphone.

Cat relays that to Daloz, who says she'll join Commissaire Giordano in his office and hangs up.

A few seconds later, a male voice, deep and official, booms through Zack's speakerphone. "We are conducting a discreet investigation into Damien Wiet to determine if he was behind the attack on you yesterday. And we cleared the Hanriots, in case you were wondering."

"We never suspected them," Zack admits.

"It's imperative," Giordano continues, "that you keep your suspicions about Damien Wiet to yourselves for now. We don't want to alert him."

"It's really important that this doesn't leak," Daloz chimes in. "No talking to family, friends, colleagues, other contestants and, especially, journalists."

Cat frowns. "Journalists?"

"They'll be all over this soon enough."

"Understood," Cat says.

Zack moves closer to the phone. "Did Wiet's henchmen have guns on them?"

"No," Giordano replies. "We found other items that could've been used as weapons, but no guns. They were being careful."

The conversation wraps up soon after that. A silence stretches out.

Cat is torn between wanting to rehash the call with Zack and longing to put it all behind her.

"So," Zack speaks, "should Letitia book us into a chateau for the weekend?"

God, it's tempting to say yes!

Cat would love a weekend getaway with Zack to explore the architectural and gastronomic gems of the Loire Valley.

But as appealing as the idea sounds, her fear is stronger. She can't afford to get her hopes up too high.

The higher you soar, the harder you fall.

She drains her coffee cup before answering, "Isn't this the weekend of your condo's Christmas party?"

"Is it?" He reaches for his phone and checks his calendar. "It is! I'd forgotten all about it."

"Did the Christmas Planning Committee find an alternative venue?"

"I don't think so… Let me check." He opens something else on his phone, probably his inbox. "Ajay sent me an update yesterday, while we were a tad busy."

"What does it say?"

He scans the message. "They're desperate. All the community spaces and private rooms in the wider neighborhood are booked."

"I think you should offer your place," she says with a determined nod.

He gives her a puzzled look. "And let them disfigure my island of pristine serenity with garish decorations? Not to mention the risk of the neighbors' kids turning everything upside down? Why should I agree to that?"

"Because it's the right thing to do."

"Says who?"

"Me." She shrugs. "Besides, I don't feel like leaving Paris this weekend."

He blinks. Shifts his gaze to his plate. Forks the last bite into his mouth. Chews it slowly.

Finally, he looks up at her. "Will you come to the party if I host it?"

"Yes," she replies, much too quickly again.

CHAPTER 39

Cat glances around Zack's living room. The transformation from bachelor pad to festive haven for tomorrow's party is underway. The concierge, Monica, and her boys are setting up the Christmas tree on loan from her place. The tree is lush and green and already decorated, which is a nice bonus. Cat puts down a bag of garlands she picked up from her apartment and the Tuileries snow globe from her office. She hadn't planned to bring the globe, but grabbed it at the last moment on a whim.

"Zack, where do you want these?" Ajay asks, untangling a string of fairy lights.

Emerging from the kitchen, Zack surveys the room. "Just drape them along the top of the bookcase and... wherever you want."

Ajay nods.

Zack goes to the coffee table and opens a box full of assorted party supplies—paper plates, cups, napkins, and plastic cutlery—all shimmering with gold trims and festive motifs.

Lucile arrives and apologizes for her tardiness. Crouching by the Christmas tree, she opens the box she brought, unpacks her Nativity scene, complete with figurines of the Holy Family and the Three Wise Men, and begins to arrange them.

"This was a great idea, Lucile!" Monica cheers as the older woman positions the last of the Magi Kings.

Lucile smiles. "I checked with Zack first, just to be sure."

"It's a beautiful Christmas crèche," Zack says. "But—and don't take this the wrong way—it could use a cow."

Cat shoots a glance at Ajay who's frozen up.

Lucile tilts her head to one side, surveying her arrangement. "You think?"

"Oh, yes," Zack says.

"Hmm," Lucile intones.

Did she just stifle a smile?

Monica's boys scurry around, hanging the last of the ornaments. Finally, everything seems to be in place.

Lucile steps back with her hands on her hips. "Looks like we're all set for tomorrow then?"

Monica nods. "Tree and decorations are up, crèche is set, supplies are ready." Abruptly, she turns to her oldest. "Tiago, what about the music?"

"The playlist is done," he reports proudly.

"All the greatest hits for old people," his brother Paulo boasts. "You're all going to love it!"

Zack strokes his chin. "Anything from this millennium?"

"Um…" Tiago squints at him. "Whitney Houston?"

Cat claps her hands. "Love her!"

Tiago grins. "There you go."

"What about the drinks?" Ajay asks.

"Covered," Zack confirms. "We'll have enough to start our own bar."

"The boys and I are going to pick up some snacks from the supermarket tomorrow morning," Monica says.

"Gosh, I'm so glad we're not having a potluck!" Lucile admits with a chuckle.

"Why?" Cat asks. "Just curious."

"Oh, you know, after thirty years of being tied to the stove, catering to an old-school husband, I've embraced a noncooking lifestyle."

Cat raises her eyebrows. "You don't like to cook?"

Lucile tut-tuts. "Aren't you from a generation that's not supposed to think women are born with a spatula in their hand?"

"We don't think that way," Cat defends herself. "It's just that I don't mind cooking, even if I don't love it. I guess I project that attitude onto others."

"I like to cook," Zack offers.

Monica nods. "Cooking is fun."

"Both my daughters would agree with you," Lucile says with a conciliatory smile.

Ajay remains silent throughout the exchange.

"Anyway, I stand by my choices," Lucile declares. "These days I only eat out or order in. No more culinary duty for me!"

A short time later, Zack's neighbors say their goodbyes and go back to their apartments. Lucile is the last to step out onto the landing.

On impulse, Cat whispers to Zack, "I'll be back," and runs downstairs after Lucile.

She catches up with her on the second floor, outside her apartment. "Lucile, wait! Can I talk to you for a minute?"

"Of course, dear." Lucile opens her door. "Come in, come in."

They sit down on the sofa, surrounded by soft cushions and the subtle scent of potpourri.

Lucile's curious gaze meets Cat's apprehensive one. "Does this have anything to do with our conversation on the bench a couple of weeks ago?"

"Yes."

Lucile smiles gently. "I thought it might."

"Remember I mentioned my neediness?"

Lucile nods and leans back, her posture open.

"I could use some advice, and with your background in psychology…" Cat's voice trails off. "Unless, of course, you're as fed up with therapy as you are with cooking."

"I'll be happy to help, if I can," Lucile says. "Talk to me."

Cat struggles to phrase her question in a way that doesn't reflect badly on Zack, but still makes sense to Lucile.

Mercifully, Lucile speaks first, "How does your so-called neediness manifest itself? Do you call or text your boyfriend several times a day even when you know he's busy?"

"No, I'm disciplined enough not to do that."

"Then what *do* you do?"

"Um… For example, I like to spend the evenings, weekends, and holidays together."

"Go on."

"I expect to see him often, if not daily," Cat says. "After a year with my previous boyfriend, I started talking about moving in together."

"How did he react?"

"He dumped me."

"Good."

Cat's head jerks back. "Good?"

"You'll understand in a moment, but please, go on."

"What else? I like to hold hands when we walk, cuddle when we watch TV…" Cat lifts her shoulders. "All that silly, clingy stuff."

"It isn't silly or clingy and you aren't needy," Lucile claims. "There's absolutely nothing wrong with you."

Cat blinks. "But all the self-help books—"

"Obviously, you haven't been reading the right ones."

The women stare at each other for a moment before Lucile adds, "Humans are social animals. We're hardwired to seek out partners, so we won't be alone. Aloneness is not a natural human condition."

"But you're alone, and you seem happy."

"My husband lives on in my memories," Lucile counters.

"I have my daughters, and my first grandkid is due in three months. I have my friends. It's not the same—"

She stops herself. There's a troubled look on her face, as if something distressing just occurred to her.

"Anyway," she says with a tiny shake of her head, "we're talking about you."

"Yes, of course. Sorry."

"It's perfectly normal to look for a partner with whom you can build something lasting."

Cat narrows her eyes. "If it were normal, why would it scare off every man I go out with?"

"How many men would that be, if I may ask?"

"Three, not counting Zack."

Lucile settles deeper into the sofa. "Psychologists have identified three main attachment styles. The first is secure attachment. About fifty percent of people are comfortable with intimacy and closeness."

"Half of the population? Same for men and women?"

"Yes."

Cat lifts a skeptical eyebrow. "Apart from my father, I've never met a man like that."

"Based on a sample of how many, remind me?" Lucile teases her.

"Yes, well, I was being careful, protecting myself."

Lucile pats her hand. "You should've dated more men, dear."

Really? "What are the other types?"

"There's anxious attachment, roughly a quarter of all people," Lucile replies. "It's when you crave closeness, tend to be sensitive to any sign of rejection, and worry your partner will leave you."

"Sounds like me!"

Lucile nods. "Could be."

"What about the remaining quarter?"

"That's avoidant attachment. They shun closeness and equate intimacy with losing their independence. They have a challenging time forming relationships and if they do, they tend to be emotionally unavailable to their partners."

Cat curls her lips into a smirk. "Sums up every guy I've been with."

"I'm not ruling out that your three boyfriends all had an avoidant style."

"Are you saying the problem wasn't with *me*, but with our mismatched attachment styles?" Cat asks.

"You nailed it!"

Cat stares at her. "Is there a way to tell if a man is an avoidant before I'm head over heels in love?"

"Yes," Lucile replies. "However, keep in mind that people can change their attachment styles. According to some studies, they do so about twenty-five percent of the time."

Cat snaps her fingers. "Just like that?"

"Believe it or not, yes."

Cat processes those words.

Lucile carries on, "A person may have different attachment styles with different partners. For example, an anxious person can switch to secure in a flash when dating a secure type."

"Can an avoidant switch to secure?"

"It's less common, but not unheard of." Lucile smiles. "By the way, I don't think Zack is an avoidant."

Oh, I'd love to believe that! But what about his behavior after their first night together?

"I could be wrong," Lucile prefaces, "but I think he has an anxious style, like you. People with this style tend to engage in protest behaviors."

"Can you explain that?"

Lucile folds her hands in her lap. "For example, they may act out or withdraw when they feel insecure. But they're not really withdrawing—they're just trying to get a reaction and increase the closeness."

Cat listens intently.

"A protest behavior reflects a need for reassurance rather

than emotional unavailability," Lucile adds. "It can be driven by a deep-seated fear of not being loved and eventually being abandoned."

"You think Zack might be afraid of abandonment?" Cat frowns in disbelief. "But he's so in control, so together..."

"I don't know his personal circumstances, but in the five years since he moved in, I've never seen his parents visit him."

"He lost his mother a long time ago."

"I see. What about his father?"

"He's alive, but they may be estranged."

Lucile tilts her head slightly as if to say, "There you go."

Cat scoots to the edge of her seat. "When someone withdraws, is there a way to tell if it's protest or genuine avoidance?"

"One clue is that protest behaviors don't last long."

It didn't last long in Zack's case, did it?

"Also, when the attachment style changes, it tends to happen quickly." Lucile goes to her bookshelf and returns with a volume that she hands to Cat. "Here, this will help you see more clearly."

"Thank you!" Cat rises to her feet.

Lucile walks her to the door. "Now, here's the advice you asked for. Give him a chance. Give both of you a chance."

CHAPTER 40

Zack's apartment is full of his neighbors. For the last half hour, he's been introducing them to Cat, who's been trying to memorize who's who. Good thing she's already met the Unholy Trinity!

There are four other people here that she knows: her friends Dalila and Christelle, accompanied by their teammates Cedric and Edgar. Zack invited them for Cat's sake, but also as a nod to the crazy adventure that brought them all together. The fact that Edgar is Zack's favorite teacher is pretty neat, too.

The Christmas tree, courtesy of Monica, stands proudly in the corner of the spacious living room. Its branches sag under the weight of colorful baubles and twinkling lights. Beneath it lies an assortment of small gifts for the Secret Santa part of the evening. Lucile's Nativity takes pride of place under the tree, arranged on a cushioned footstool. It draws curious looks from Edgar, who never knew Zack to be a traditionalist.

"What's the deal with the manger?" Edgar finally asks Zack.

"People change," Zack replies.

For some strange reason, he's unwilling to explain to his

teacher that the crèche is here on loan, just like the Christmas tree.

As a matter of fact, people do change.

Zack, for example, isn't quite the same person he was at the beginning of the month. Nothing radical has happened. He hasn't had any revelations or epiphanies. He still doesn't believe in God, psychic phenomena, or Santa Claus. His ambitions are the same, as are his philosophy of life and his political views.

Yet here he is, hosting this noisy Christmas party for his neighbors—and enjoying himself. Although he does look forward to the moment when everyone leaves and he's alone with Cat.

I blame Marc Chagall for this.

Zack looks at the flying lovers in the framed Chagall poster he bought this morning. His gaze moves from the poster to the long buffet table beneath it. Covered in a festive red cloth, it holds an abundance of drinks and a decent number of junky snacks. All in all, it's not bad for a last-minute party. Glasses clink around the table as the guests exchange toasts and Merry Christmas wishes.

Edgar reaches out to refill his glass when a kid of five or six tugs on his sleeve. His eyes wide with wonder, he asks, "Monsieur, are you Santa?"

Around them, a group of people, including the child's mother, Naima, burst into laughter. They all look at Edgar expectantly. Zack wonders if his teacher will play along again as he did at the Galeries Lafayette.

Edgar kneels at eye level and strokes his white beard. "It's true, I look a bit like him, don't I?"

"You look a lot like him!" the kid retorts, pointing at the man's round belly.

A few giggles break out among the onlookers.

"You're right," Edgar concedes. "But I'm not Santa. I'm Edgar. Santa is very busy right now, as you can imagine, packing all those Christmas gifts. Do you think he has time to hang out at a party?"

The boy gives it some thought. "No."

"Correct." Edgar heaves himself up.

Christelle turns to Zack and Cat. "Speaking of Santas, may I ask if you guys think you're close to finding *Father Christmas*?"

"No, *Father Christmas* keeps eluding us," Zack replies without even having to lie.

"Damien Wiet has been deafeningly silent the last few days, hasn't he?" Cat comments.

Edgar nods. "He's gone completely hands-off. It's like we're playing a different game now."

"You have no idea!" Cat blurts out.

Christelle narrows her eyes. "Is there something you guys know that we don't?"

Cat and Zack shake their heads.

"We're just baffled by his change in style," Cat says.

"So are we," Christelle agrees. "Anyway, we keep looking."

"In fact, we just stumbled onto a promising lead," Edgar boasts.

"In Belgium?" Cat asks.

"Yes," he confirms. "What about you? Are you going to just sit on your hands hoping he'll send you a new cryptogram to solve?"

Cat studies her feet, no doubt afraid her face will give her away. Zack shares her pain. He's never had so much trouble keeping a secret.

"We followed a lead last week," he says. "It led us to some exciting places."

"But not to *Father Christmas,*" Cat adds quickly.

Well, that much is true.

The doorbell rings again. Someone opens, and Ajay enters, rolling a bar cart. It's loaded with three large trays of aromatic Indian specialties. Samosas, mini nans, chapatis, onion rings, and tandoori skewers are just a few Zack can name.

Ajay's offerings draw oohs and aahs from the crowd and become an instant hit.

"These are amazing!" Lucile says to Ajay, after tasting a few of the delicacies. "Where did you order them? I need to know!"

With a sheepish smile, he replies, "I made them myself."

"Really?" Lucile stares at him.

"Cooking is my passion," he says. "Even now that I'm all by myself, I cook at least one hot meal a day—and not just Indian. You should try my onion soup and my mille-feuille!"

"I had no idea," Lucile mutters.

He grins. "It's not unheard of for men to cook these days."

"Of course, it's just..." She blushes. "I guess I didn't expect you to be one of those men."

"India isn't as patriarchal as it used to be," he points out. "Besides, my wife died when the kids were young. I had to learn to cook, and once I did, I found I loved it."

Monica claps her hands to get everyone's attention. "It's time for the Secret Santa gifts!"

The guests gather around the Christmas tree. One by one, each person pulls out a gift with their name on it. As the wrapping paper flies and whatnots are revealed, the room buzzes with more or less accurate guesses about the identities of their Secret Santas.

Amid the excitement, Cat gives Zack's arm a gentle nudge. He follows her gaze. Across the room, Lucile is ogling Ajay who's talking to Edgar. Lucile's eyes sparkle with a newfound admiration. Tucking a strand of hair behind her ear, the president of the HOA board approaches her vice president. Cat maneuvers closer to them. Zack sidles up beside her.

"Your cooking is winning all the hearts tonight," Lucile says to Ajay with all the subtlety of a charging rhino.

He meets her gaze. "It gives me joy to share my world with you… um, I mean, with the condo."

She points toward her Christmas crèche under the tree. "Remember you once asked if a cow would be a good addition?"

"Yes." He peers at her.

"I didn't think so at the time, but now I believe it might be a very welcome one, indeed."

Without missing a beat, he reaches into his pocket and pulls out a miniature brass figurine.

"This is the Kamadhenu cow with her calf," he says, handing it to her. "In Hindu culture, it's a symbol of abundance and the fulfillment of wishes."

She accepts the figurine. "It's gorgeous."

"And very auspicious!" he insists with a uniquely Indian head wobble.

Lucile walks over to the Christmas tree and places the figurine next to the baby Jesus. The styles and materials are a total mismatch, but somehow it works. When she steps back to admire the new addition, Ajay watches her, visibly moved.

Lucile turns to him, beaming. "Even if this cow didn't have any magical powers, it makes my Nativity scene one of a kind!"

CHAPTER 41

Cat shuts the door after her last client of the day—her last of this year, in fact—and begins to tidy up the séance room. It's quiet in the shop except for the street noise seeping in through the window. Dalila's side is empty. She's already gone, preparing for the Christmas celebrations that are a huge deal in her family.

Today is the winter solstice. Tomorrow, Cat and her dad leave for Provence to spend the holiday at Grandma's house, where the entire family will congregate. But tonight, like every night since last Thursday, she'll be with Zack. They fell into this daily rhythm without drama or fanfare or any of the awkwardness Cat had braced herself for. It just happened.

On Sunday, the day after Zack's Christmas party, they went to the movies and then to his apartment. On Monday, she was at the shop, expecting to go home after work. They hadn't made plans. Then he called and plans were made. Something similar happened on Tuesday. Yesterday, they both acted like it was understood that they'd spend the night together. She left some toiletries at his place.

This morning as she and Zack were on their way out, Commissaire Giordano called with an update, which was nice of him. The experts hadn't finished appraising everything yet, but the current low estimate of the haul's value was 700 million. Giordano hinted there might be a reward for Cat and Zack.

Hopefully not just symbolic!

Wiet had been questioned by the OCBC officers. His henchmen hadn't snitched on him. He denied everything. Unfortunately, the police had no proof that he'd had Cat and Zack followed, or that he'd tried to have them killed to grab Stratte's treasure. They'd found nothing tangible to link him to the henchmen. The bastard walked out of the OCBC office a free man.

Giordano warned Cat and Zack that if they shared their suspicions about Wiet's involvement, the mogul could sue them for libel.

Tonight, Wiet is holding an event to announce the winners. Cat received an invitation by messenger around noon. She's not going, and neither is Zack. What's the point? They already know who will get the prize. Cat had called Christelle as soon as she'd closed the door behind the courier. The older seer and her teammate Edgar had found *Father Christmas* yesterday in a dusty attic in Néchin.

During this morning's call with Giordano, the commissaire also told them that Wiet's henchmen were facing a wide range of charges, but not attempted murder. All four had stuck to their original story, claiming they'd read André Dafoe's blog and found his theory credible. Cat has no doubt it had been Damien Wiet, and not one of those thugs, who'd read the blog.

The problem is, as with everything else involving Wiet, there's no evidence to back it up.

The thugs told the police that when they heard about the scavenger hunt to find Chagall's painting, they immediately signed up. But since they were neither psychics nor mathematicians, they didn't pass the preselection. Instead, they followed the progress of the hunt online.

After the Pompidou Center, they kept an eye on both Team Catherine and Team Christelle. It was the former that led them to Stratte's cache. They insisted they had no murderous intentions. They just wanted to take everything for themselves and scare Cat and Zack into keeping their mouths shut.

As if anyone would believe them!

Oh, right—the justice system does. And given the sorry state of it, the thugs will be out in no time. That is, if they ever go to jail. Luc Stratte never did, and he was the original thief.

On impulse, Cat picks up the phone. She finds a number online and dials it.

"This is Madame Jacqueline's office," a secretary replies at the other end. "If you're calling for an appointment, Madame Jacqueline is booked through the end of March, just so you know."

No surprise there, seeing as Jacqueline is the real deal, the absolute best out there.

"I'm not calling for a séance," Cat says. "It's to discuss something else."

"I'm sorry but Madame Jacqueline is not available for anything else."

"My name is Catherine Cavallo," Cat plows on, undeterred. "I'm a fellow psychic and a participant in the Looking for *Father Christmas* scavenger hunt. Could you please relay this information to Madame Jacqueline?"

"Hold the line, please."

Cat grips her phone tighter and waits.

The hold music cuts off abruptly, replaced by a gravelly, seasoned voice. "Madame Jacqueline speaking. How can I assist you?"

Not wanting to waste Jacqueline's precious time, Cat cuts to the chase. "*Bonsoir, madame*. I know that Damien Wiet consulted you about the stolen Chagalls. You helped him track down *Father Christmas*. I'm curious why you didn't lead him to the rest of Luc Stratte's haul."

"Because it was in a different location," Jacqueline says. "And that location eluded me, no matter how deeply I probed the ether. It simply wasn't mine to see."

"But what did you see?" Cat presses.

"My vision was clear in its ambiguity," Jacqueline replies with a small laugh. "I saw an odd pair composed of a psychic and a mathematician guiding Damien to the treasure."

"Did you make out their faces?"

"No," Jacqueline says. "They were obscured by the mists of potentiality. Their identities were indistinct, and their forms were constantly shifting like smoke."

Cat's pulse quickens. "And the scavenger hunt?"

"A brainchild of Damien's ingenuity and his passion for solving puzzles," Jacqueline explains. "He hoped to draw the right individuals to him."

"Seriously?"

"Oh, yes. He orchestrated the whole thing, including the extensive media coverage, TV spots, and billboards all over town. The idea was to let fate bring the right pair to the forefront."

Cat absorbs this, her mind racing as the pieces click together. "Would you repeat to the police what you just told me?"

The line goes silent. Cat expects a dry "no" any second now.

"Have you lost your mind?" Jacqueline screams. "I can't believe you just suggested I break faith with a client, and one who hasn't done anything wrong!"

He almost got Zack and me killed.

But Cat can't say that. If she'd been allowed to share her suspicions, Jacqueline might have been more receptive to her plea. On the other hand, she referred to Wiet as *Damien*. He must be a longtime client of hers.

"This conversation never happened, understand?" Jacqueline hisses. "If you tell anyone, I'll destroy your professional reputation, and your career with it. Are we clear?"

"Yes."

"Good." She hangs up.

Cat finishes organizing her office, locks up, and takes the métro to Zack's.

CHAPTER 42

The clock strikes nine. Cat tucks her feet under her and snuggles closer to Zack on the sofa. With a press of the remote, he turns on the TV and tunes in to a special live broadcast from the Petits-Augustins chapel. No doubt Wiet thought it would be neat to wrap up the scavenger hunt where it all began.

On the screen, elegantly dressed contestants mingle under shimmering chandeliers. Cat spots a few TV celebrities. Wiet is among them, chatting. They laugh at something he says.

Cat pretends to throw up. "Such a charming man!"

Wiet steps up to the lectern and draws the focus of all the cameras in the room. "Good evening, everyone," he begins, his voice smooth. "What a journey it's been! This scavenger hunt Looking for *Father Christmas* has been not only a test of wit and perseverance, but a spectacular adventure through the hidden treasures of art history."

Cat looks at Zack. "Seriously, I'm going to puke."

"He's not worth it," Zack says.

"And now," Wiet continues on the screen, "the moment we've all been waiting for. The winners of this extraordinary hunt are…"

A drumroll from hidden speakers fills the air.

"Christelle Djossou and Edgar Jaume!" Wiet cries out.

Applause erupts from those in the chapel.

Cat turns to Zack. "At least, the winners deserve the prize. Especially Christelle."

"For holding out until the end?"

"Yes."

And because she was cool about swapping places with me at the paring ceremony.

On the screen, Christelle and Edgar step up to receive their oversized checks, their faces radiant with pride. The camera pans back to Wiet, who congratulates them and then blows his own trumpet by talking about the money he'll be donating to the Chagall Museum, the Louvre, and the Ministry of Education.

Zack turns off the TV.

Within minutes, Cat's phone begins to buzz relentlessly. One by one, her family members call. Each offers words of consolation for her near miss in the scavenger hunt. They learned of Cat's participation a few days ago, but not from Dad, who'd kept his promise. They found out on their own. It would have been odd if they hadn't, since Julie is the amateur sleuth of Provence and Grandma is taking an online course to become a private investigator.

To each caller, Cat responds, "Yeah, I'm bummed. We were so close!"

Zack isn't spared the barrage of attention, either. He responds to text messages and takes calls from friends, neighbors, and colleagues. Amid the hustle and bustle, one particular call comes in that he sends to voicemail.

Was that his dad?

Cat decides not to pry. But then she realizes how out of character her reaction was. With her ex—with all her exes—she would've assumed the call was from a woman. And she would've definitely pried.

After the last call, Cat breathes a sigh of relief and sinks deeper into the sofa.

Zack settles down next to her. "I'm really happy for Edgar and Christelle, but I hate that Wiet will get away with sending gangsters after us."

"His plan all along was to use us to fulfill Jacqueline's vision, and then get rid of us."

"Yeah, I don't know about a vision..." Zack grimaces slightly, voice trailing off.

It's no secret to Cat that he rejects the possibility of psychic abilities, even after her intuitions helped them get closer to the stolen treasure. Changing one's belief system is hard. Take Julie, for example. She spent half her life in denial of both Cat's and her own gifts until she finally gave in.

Some things just take time.

She gives Zack a playful smile. "Well, that'll teach us to improvise! If we'd just stayed in line, kept looking for *Father Christmas*, and beaten Christelle and Edgar to it, we'd be splitting the two hundred grand Wiet dangled."

"He dangled more than that in my case," Zack grits out. "He hooked me with the promise of a five million investment in QuantumTech Cybernetics."

She lets out an impressed whistle. "Wow, that's not just a carrot—that's the whole vegetable garden!"

"I can't believe I fell for that crap."

She strokes his arm. "Hey, look on the bright side. Everybody gets duped sooner or later. Now you've paid your dues."

"The bright side is that I met you," he corrects her.

She stares at him, feeling ridiculously happy. "How can you deliver such a romantic line in such a low-key way?"

"You wanted it with a flourish?" He pulls her closer and kisses her hard. "Better?"

"Much better!"

He nods smugly. "Is this a good time to exchange our Christmas gifts?"

"OK, sure." A little apprehensive, she pulls a wrapped package from her tote bag on the floor. "I have to warn you, though, I'm notoriously bad at this, even when I've thought it through."

"Bring it on!"

She hands him the package. "Merry Christmas!"

He unwraps the present and unfolds a garishly patterned sweater. "A Christmas sweater!"

"It's supposed to be ugly by definition, right?" She smiles nervously. "So, I told myself, the worst thing that could happen is that you'd think it looks great."

He examines the riot of colors and reindeer designs. "Rest assured, I don't."

"Yay!"

He reaches for his own gift for Cat, a neatly wrapped package that suggests something pricey. "I'm not good with personal gifts either."

"Welcome to the club!"

"I asked Letitia to pick something fashionable," he admits. "She assured me that any woman with taste would love this."

Cat unwraps an exquisite purse. "*Oh là là,* it's as beautiful as that sweater is ugly!" she exclaims. "I do love it."

"Phew." He wipes imaginary sweat from his forehead with the back of his hand. "It's even prettier on the inside. Open it."

She peers into the purse. While not exactly prettier, the interior is flawless and functional. She runs her fingers over the satiny, subtly embossed lining and opens the various zippered compartments. Inside one of them, her fingers brush against something—a set of keys. She holds them up and gives Zack a quizzical look.

He meets her eyes. "That's a spare set of keys to my apartment," he explains. "This way, you won't have to wait around when I'm working late. You can come and go as you please."

She stares at the keys gleaming in her hand, then at Zack, dumbfounded.

"Or you can move in," he adds.

Cat's mind struggles to process the import of his words. "You want me to move in with you?"

"Damn!" He scrunches up his face in panic. "Was that too soon? Please bear with me. I have no experience with real relationships."

"Are we in a relationship?" she asks cautiously.

"I sure hope so!" He searches her face. "Are we?"

She nods.

He lets out a slow breath. "Oh, good."

There's an awkward little silence, during which she puts the keys back in the zippered pocket of her new purse.

He speaks again, "So, how long are you staying in Provence?"

Before she can answer, a text pops up on his phone sitting on the coffee table. She glances at the sender's name, "Francis." *His dad's name?* She averts her eyes. He ignores the message.

"I'll stay a week," she says. "Enough time to catch up with everyone—especially my grandma and my niece, who I don't see nearly enough."

"Why not?"

"My oldest sister lives all the way in Canada," she answers. "What about you? What are your plans for Christmas Eve?"

He smiles a little too brightly. "I'll be at the office, enjoying the quiet and getting a ton of work done while everyone else is stuffing themselves into oblivion."

"What about your dad?"

His expression hardens. "He's been bugging me to spend this Christmas Eve together, but I don't see why I should."

"Why not? He's your family, your only parent."

"A parent who didn't hesitate to send me away when I was only eight," he says, mouth twisting with resentment.

"I understand." She puts a comforting hand on his arm. "But here's the thing. Christmas is about more than stuffing your face. As corny as it sounds, it's about love. It's an opportunity to come together and forgive the hurts of the past."

"I'm not ready to forgive him."

"Then don't." She shrugs. "Just go, spend an hour at his place and give him a chance to unburden himself, if that's what he needs."

Zack slumps on the sofa. "You make it sound so easy…"

"Trust me, it won't be that hard. You won't be committing to anything—just hearing him out."

"Assuming I go," he says, "I wouldn't even know what gift to bring. It would be rude to show up empty-handed on Christmas Eve, wouldn't it?"

"Let's brainstorm! What genres does he enjoy reading?"

"I don't know," he replies with a helpless gesture.

"Does he like classical music? Theater?"

"I'm not sure."

"You could give him a gift card," she suggests. "Or is that considered rude? God, I'm bad at this!"

Her eyes drift to her snow globe on the shelf above the TV. It's been there since the Christmas party.

"You could give him a snow globe," she tries again, half-joking.

"Or a Chagall poster," Zack retorts, nodding toward the framed reproduction of *Over the City* hanging on the wall.

"That's an excellent idea!"

He leans back against the cushions. "Speaking of Chagall, when I was researching his life for the scavenger hunt, it struck me how deeply he loved the women he was with—especially, Bella, and then, at the twilight of his life, Vava."

"He was a desperate romantic," she says. "My sister Flo calls him the anti-Picasso of art in how he treated the women in his life."

Zack gazes at the poster and then at Cat. "Chagall often painted a couple hovering over a city."

"Yes, he did."

"I never thought I'd say this, but I think it's very cool."

She squints at him. "You want us to go paragliding?"

"You're funny." He leans in and kisses her. "I love that about you."

She keeps her tone light. "What else do you love about me?"

"Everything," he replies at once, his expression earnest.

She wraps her hands around his neck and kisses him, dizzy with the rush of affection. Her eyelids begin to flutter down when something jerks them up again. Stuff is happening inside the snow globe on the shelf.

She draws back a little and peers at it.

The snow-covered house, the Christmas tree, and the Eiffel Tower fade away, just as they had when she first saw the globe at the Tuileries market. And just like then, Zack appears. Only now he's wearing the ugly Christmas sweater instead of the turtleneck, and he's holding hands with a woman.

That woman is Cat.

EPILOGUE

Zack pulls up to a building in the 14th arrondissement. He enters the lobby and climbs the stairs to the third floor, inhaling the smell of old wood, fresh wax, and his early childhood.

He rings the doorbell on his left. Dad opens the door. Zack hadn't seen him in how long? Three years? More?

Dad's hair is a little thinner and a lot grayer than it was the last time. In fact, it's almost all white now. He has more wrinkles. New glasses. Not much else has changed.

"It's so good to see you, son!" Dad says, stepping aside. "Come on in."

Zack follows him into the apartment that feels frozen in time. The hallway still has the same wallpaper. Some of the pieces Zack remembers from his childhood—the dining table, the bookshelves, the coffee table. The couch and chairs are new. The oddly shaped ceiling fixture that's been there forever bathes the room in a cold, white light.

Zack sniffs the air. "A roast?"

"It should be ready in fifteen minutes," Dad says, adding quickly, "I know you can't stay long."

Zack hands him a wrapped book. "Merry Christmas."

Dad begins to peel off the glossy wrapping paper. "What is it?"

"An art book with paintings by Marc Chagall." Zack wrinkles his nose. "I hope you like his work."

"Very much! Wait!"

He brings out a small, neatly wrapped package and holds it out to Zack. "And Merry Christmas to you!"

Zack unwraps the package to find a book of puzzles, ciphers, and cryptograms.

"Seeing as you did the Christmas scavenger hunt, I thought you might like this," Dad says. "Also, you loved riddles as a kid."

Zack flips through the pages. "It's perfect. Thanks!"

They sit across from each other in armchairs flanking the long coffee table, one side of which is cluttered with stacked binders and manila folders.

Dad pours an apéritif. "You made it to the finals of that cool treasure hunt, huh? Sorry you didn't win."

"Don't be!" Zack accepts the drink. "Cat and I are actually quite pleased with how it all turned out."

Dad raises an eyebrow. "Cat?"

"She was my partner during the hunt."

"Ah, I see."

Zack smiles. "She's more than that to me now."

Him sharing something private for the first time since middle school causes a subtle shift. There's a softening in Dad's eyes, a flicker of emotion. It's obvious he's dying to know more about Cat. If he asks, Zack will tell him. *After all, why not?*

Dad puts his glass down, fidgets, and finally says, "Zack, I've decided to go against your mother's wishes. I want you to know the truth."

Zack frowns. *What truth?*

Dad pushes the pile of binders in front of Zack. "Her death wasn't an accident. She took her own life."

Zack stares, trying to process this revelation.

"There's a good reason the truck driver who hit her was never charged," Dad carries on. "And I never blamed him. There was nothing he could've done in that situation."

"Why... why did she kill herself?"

"Your mother had been battling a severe mental illness for years," Dad says. "It became too much for her."

Zack stands up and begins to pace the room, trying to understand, to match this information with his memories, his image of his mother. She used to be so sunny and loving, and then suddenly she didn't want him around anymore.

Dad opens the binder on top. "Come, take a look."

Zack returns to his seat and flips through medical papers, diagnoses, and prescriptions. All very specialized and full of Latin terms. All for Mom. After a while, they become a blur on his lap.

With shaking hands, Dad places another document in front of Zack. It is Mom's suicide note. All the inner misery that drove her to do the irreparable is condensed into three pages of tight, hurried handwriting. Zack finds himself unable to read it all, so he focuses on the sentences she underlined:

...I hope you forgive me.

...Zack cannot know.

...I want him to remember me as I was before.

She underlined "Zack cannot know" twice.

Dad watches him with a mixture of sadness and relief. "She didn't want her illness to color your memories of her."

Zack puts the note back in the file. "I don't blame you for keeping this from me. My problem is... Why did you send me away? I was only eight, years before Mom died."

"You may not remember, but her illness made her very unstable," Dad says, his voice thick. "Our home environment was becoming unsafe for you. So, I had two choices: institutionalize her or…"

"Ship me off to boarding school," Zack finishes for him.

"Yes."

Zack takes a long moment before he speaks again, "You should've told me all this before, Dad."

"I respected your mother's wishes."

"Except, she was dead, and I was alive—and desperate for a sign that you cared about me."

"Oh, Zack!" Dad's voice cracks. "If only I could turn back time and do things differently! I should've considered your feelings and tried harder. Maybe I could've convinced your mom…"

Zack picks up his glass. "I doubt it. It seems her vanity was stronger than her love for me."

"Please, son, don't judge her so harshly," Dad pleads. "She was so very sick, so miserable!"

Zack says nothing, just stares across the table at Dad.

"It was so hard to be a helpless witness to her decline," Dad says, eyes welling up. "What saved me was knowing that her illness wasn't genetic, that you wouldn't suffer a similar fate."

Zack finishes his apéritif.

Dad jumps to his feet. "The roast must be ready!" Sniffling, he flees into the kitchen busies himself.

While Dad is occupied, a small miracle happens in the living room. The resentment that had become part of Zack's identity for so long dissipates. Though no blinding revelations or heavenly bliss pours into his heart, it simply jettisons the ballast that's been holding Zack down.

Dad returns with the roast. He sets it down on the dining table and pulls out a chair. "Come on, I'm not letting you go without a bite."

Zack gets up from the armchair, but instead of sitting at the table, he puts his arms around Dad for the first time since he was a little boy. It's just a quick hug, to show the old man how he feels now, and to spare himself from uttering words far too sentimental for his constitution. Dad hugs him back, just as briefly and clumsily.

They eat in silence. Zack compliments Dad on his cooking. Dad thanks him.

When they've finished eating, Zack stands. "I'm going to need some time to process all this."

"Take all the time you need," Dad assures him, rising to his feet. "I'll be here when you're ready to talk."

Zack walks to the door.

Dad shuffles after him, hesitation in his step. "I feel bad, Zack, like a coward who blamed a dead woman for his own failures. I was a terrible father."

Zack pauses, his hand still on the door, and turns around. "I'm not going to lie, you weren't great."

Dad smiles through tears.

"But it's not too late to try again," Zack says, surprising even himself.

"You think so?"

"Absolutely, Dad."

"You think you can forgive me?" Dad searches Zack's face.

"There's this psychic I'm seeing," Zack begins, before interrupting himself, "Not professionally—she's my girlfriend."

"Cat?"

"Yeah," he confirms. "She says Christmas is the time to forgive old wrongs."

Dad's eyes light up.

Zack grins. "As far as I'm concerned, it's a done deal. Are you ready for a reboot?"

"I've been ready for years!"

Zack opens the door, still smiling. "See you soon, Dad!"

AFTERWORD

Are you curious to find out what's fact and what's fiction in this novel?
Here we go!

Father Christmas
The *Father Christmas* painting in the book is based on an actual canvas painted in 1952. Its last recorded sale appears to have been in 2005, at the Galerie Kornfeld in Bern.

Damien Wiet's claim in the book that Chagall painted many Santas is also based on fact. The painter seems to have been particularly fond of that subject matter in the 1950s, often depicting Father Christmas in the presence of a mother and child (see, for instance, his better-known *Motherhood and Father Christmas*, 1954).

Luc Stratte
Luc Stratte's character is based on a real-life con artist named Jean-Luc Verstraete, alias Yann. In 1988, the flamboyant and wildly charismatic high school dropout, who was working as a mole catcher in northern France, saw a TV story about Marc

Chagall's estate. It was then that he hatched a plan to steal from Chagall's widow, Valentina "Vava" Brodsky, who lived alone in Saint-Paul-de-Vence and had all these works stored in her big house.

Incredible as it may sound, he pulled it off.

Well, for a time. In 1994, Verstraete got caught. And once again, though improbable but true, the real Jean-Luc Verstraete served no jail time, just like the fictional Luc Stratte. His only punishment was a tax adjustment. The cunning weasel could thank the statute of limitations—only three years for art theft at the time—and the absurd diagnosis of mental retardation pronounced by the court's experts.

For the next twenty-three years, Verstraete laid low. Sort of. Although he owed millions to the French tax authorities, he lived like a nabob. He continued to deal in works of art and juggled multiple foreign bank accounts, including an offshore trust in the Virgin Islands called Aberlady Holdings Ltd. that opened through the notorious Panamanian law firm Mossack Fonseca. According to the Panama Papers leak, Aberlady Holdings Ltd. ceased operations in 2013 and was definitively dissolved in 2014.

Verstraete died in 2017, at the age of sixty, after years of alcohol abuse and untreatable cirrhosis, compounded by an injury he suffered in a helicopter accident.

The Chagall Affair

In the book, I changed all the names and many minor details, but the case I described remains very close to the real-life Chagall affair.

The deception perpetrated by Verstraete and Vava's housekeeper Irène Menskoï, might never have come to light.

But Irène decided to leave her husband in 1990, and he murdered her in a fit of jealous rage. The investigation into her death, coupled with an anonymous tip to OCBC, led to some surprising discoveries.

Some twenty-five paintings were recovered. How many weren't? The figure five hundred cited in the book is based on the estimate of art historian and journalist Adrian Darmon (mentioned in the novel as André Dafoe). In fact, Darmon believed that Jean-Luc Verstraete and his accomplices had stolen about one hundred paintings and five hundred lithographs from Vava Chagall.

The Palais Garnier

Everything you've read about the mythical Paris Opera house is fact, including the Chagall ceiling, the bees (see paragraph below) and the Phantom (trust me on this one).

Five beehives were installed on the roof of the Palais Garnier decades ago. They produce fifteen hundred jars of delicious, pesticide-free honey a year.

Blaise Cendrars

Cendrars (1887–1961) was a Swiss-born French poet, novelist and journalist, and a close friend of Marc Chagall, whom he began to frequent during Chagall's first stay in France in the early 1910s.

The two poems quoted in this novel are from Cendrars's collection titled *Nineteen Elastic Poems* or *Dix-neuf poèmes élastiques* in French. Both are about Marc Chagall. The first one focuses on the painter himself, and the second on Chagall's studio in The Beehive.

The Beehive (La Ruche)

The Beehive is a real place at 2 Passage Danzig, not far from

Montparnasse. It's an artists' colony founded in 1903 by the sculptor Alfred Boucher. Wealthy, Boucher bought a plot of land and recycled leftovers from the 1900 Universal Exhibition (aka Paris Exposition, aka World's Fair) to create his Beehive. These recycled bits and pieces included the structure of the Bordeaux Wine Pavilion, designed by Gustave Eiffel for the fair, and the wrought iron entrance gate from the Women's Pavilion. Boucher's goal was to provide penniless artists with a place to live and work.

Among the artists who stayed at La Ruche at one time, or another were Marc Chagall, Amedeo Modigliani, Pablo Picasso, Henri Matisse, Fernand Léger, Chaïm Soutine, Robert Delaunay, Guillaume Apollinaire, Henri Rousseau (Le Douanier Rousseau), stylist Jeanne Lanvin, and many others.

Almost everything you've read about The Beehive in the novel is authentic, including Chagall's studio and the fact that The Beehive is still an active artists' colony.

The only detail I made up is the photograph of Madame Boucher on the billboard in the lobby. At the time of my visit, there were only two photographs on that billboard, both of Alfred Boucher.

Bakery in Chartres

The bakery and the conversation about ancient grains were inspired by a real-life encounter with a lovely couple who run a family bakery in the delightful town of Mougins. It's called "La Mouginoise des Pains."

Attachment Theory

The attachment styles that Lucile tells Cat about were first theorized in the 1960s in relation to children. In the 1980s, psychologists realized that the theory also applied to adult relationships, especially romantic ones. A great deal of research has been done since then, resulting in a robust framework used by a growing number of psychologists.

The results of adult attachment research have been popularized in several books. I highly recommend *Attached: The Science of Adult Attachment and How It Can Help You Find and Keep Love* by Amir Levine and Rachel Heller, Penguin, 2010.

PS:
If you ever find Jean-Luc Verstraete's treasure trove, I hope you do the right thing and wire me 10 percent.

Just kidding! I hope you turn everything over to the French authorities.

I hope you enjoyed "The Snow Globe Affair"! Please consider **leaving a review** on Amazon, Goodreads or social media to encourage me to write more of what you enjoy and to help others discover my work.

If you'd like to prolong the festive mood, check out **"The Twelve Suspects of Christmas"**! In that novel, Cat's grandmother and another granny investigate a cold case that leads them to the most unexpected places (both figuratively and geographically).

Here is a sneak peek:

Grannies, gangsters, murders—and a rollicking journey across France!

It's January 4, 1961, and Marseilles housemaid Annie Malian is in love. It's also the day her fiancé René takes his life under peculiar circumstances.

Many decades later, an old Christmas postcard addressed to Annie arrives, and all her doubts come flooding back.
At 84, there's no time to waste!
Annie enlists the help of Rose Tassy, an eccentric retired teacher and amateur sleuth.
Thus begins an unforgettable journey from Provence to a quaint village in Picardie and then on to the sparkling Riviera, with a detour through wintry Paris.

Amid yuletide festivities, Annie and Rose navigate perilous terrain. Their list of suspects quickly grows. Was it Rene's older brother? Maybe the ex-gangster turned chicken farmer? The powerful Monegasque tycoon?
Stumped, Rose begins to question her detective mettle when a new death compounds the plot…

This Christmas, will Annie receive the overdue truth as a gift?

Get your copy now!

If you haven't read any of the Julie Cavallo mysteries yet, here's a preview of Book 1, **"The Murderous Macaron"** (Chanticleer MYSTERY & MAYHEM Book Awards winner).

Julie has her freedom,
a dream job as a pastry chef,
and a corpse growing cold on her floor...

Welcome to Beldoc, a small town in the heart of Provence, imbued with lavender and fresh baked bread! You can idle around, or you can puzzle out a murder mystery.

When a man dies on her watch in her pâtisserie, newly divorced chef Julie Cavallo is dismayed.
It isn't that she's a suspect.
The local gendarmerie captain signs off the death as a natural event. A heart attack.
But for a reason she won't discuss, Julie suspects Maurice Sauve was poisoned.
What's a girl to do?
She'll ignore the risk and seek justice for Maurice on her own!

Well, not quite on her own. Julie's eccentric grandmother, her snarky sister and her geeky sous chef are keen to help.
The team's amateurism is a challenge.
But there's also the pesky matter of no evidence, no clues, and soon, no body.
The murder—if it was a murder—was planned and executed flawlessly.

Can a small-town baker solve the perfect crime?

You can get The Murderous Macaron as an individual book or at a reduced price in a set of Books 1 - 3.

Or you can turn the page to read an excerpt.

EXCERPT FROM "THE MURDEROUS MACARON"

JULIE CAVALLO INVESTIGATES, BOOK 1

"People drop dead on strangers all the time." Flo gives me an emphatic look. "Stop sulking, it's bad for business. Life goes on, Julie!"

At that, she waves and exits the shop.

Heeding my younger sister's questionable pep talk, I pick up a box of pistachio macarons and begin to gift wrap it.

The front door chimes, announcing a new customer.

I force the corners of my mouth upward in what I hope resembles a professional smile. But my face lengthens again when I realize who's entering the shop. The man in the doorway isn't a customer. He's a cop, Capitaine Gabriel Adinian of the Beldoc Gendarmerie. The one who's looking into the death of Maurice Sauve.

I hug myself, as a sudden shiver runs through my body on this balmy June afternoon.

That poor man!

To go so quickly and irreversibly, and at the worst possible time! Not just from my perspective, even though I can't deny I'd rather he suffered his heart attack before or after my macaron-making class. On a less selfish note, the timing was unfortunate for Maurice himself. When I asked everyone at the beginning of the workshop to tell the class about themselves, he said he'd been through a prolonged midlife crisis and had finally glimpsed the light at the end of the tunnel.

He said he'd embarked on a quest for a purpose to his life after realizing two years back that sorting mail at the post office wasn't it. A year of volunteering with the Red Cross in Southeast Asia convinced him that charity work wasn't it either. Back in Beldoc, he dipped a toe into all sorts of things from music to stock trading. Recently, he discovered baking.

I remember him gushing as he concluded his introduction: "I have a really good feeling about this!"

Twenty minutes later, he grimaced, collapsed to the floor, and died.

I shudder and rub my arms.

As Capitaine Adinian draws nearer, I train my gaze on his face. His features are highly irregular. In theory, no woman would find him handsome unless she'd been studying iguanas on a deserted island for a year.

In actuality, the matter of his attractiveness is less straightforward.

The overall structure of his face makes up for the flaws of his individual features. His prominent nose and mouth match the angular firmness of his jawline, which his three-day-old stubble cannot hide. His dark brown eyes reel you in. He gives off an aura of effortless, natural virility.

Chill out, Julie.

It's just a visceral reaction of a thirty-year-old woman to a guy she finds hot. It'll pass in a moment. Besides, I don't find him hot. And, recalling his attitude during our first encounter last night, I don't even like him.

Capitaine Adinian halts across the counter from me.

A thought crosses my mind. What if this isn't about Maurice Sauve? What if he's come here with the aim of purchasing an assortment of my confections?

Ha-ha. That was the most ridiculous of all the ridiculous ideas I've ever had. And, trust me, I've had many.

Adinian surveys me, muttering something unintelligible under his breath.

I choose to interpret it as "Good morning, Madame Cavallo" and not "You didn't think I was done with you, eh".

The latter option is more likely though. I'm sure Flo would agree. My little sis likes to say that if you keep mentally photoshopping the ugly truth out of people, you'll surround yourself with friends you can always rely on to backstab you. At twenty-two, she's full of acerbic wisdom, aka snark, that she dishes out to all and sundry.

"Julie's Gluten-Free Delights," Adinian says, quoting the sign above the entrance. "But here in Beldoc, we like our gluten."

Is that his idea of a friendly icebreaker? The butterflies in my stomach calm down, as he confirms that he's exactly who I think he is. A discourteous hick.

"I may have lived in Paris half my life"—I look him directly in the eye—"but I'm a Beldocian like you. You'd be surprised how many residents are gluten-intolerant or gluten-sensitive."

Personally, I'm neither. But for the sake of coherence, I stopped consuming wheat-based food the moment I decided to launch a gluten-free bakery.

"Of course," Adinian deadpans.

And then he looks left and right, as if trying to figure out where all those gluten-free buffs might be hiding in my empty shop.

The cheek of him!

I wish Rose was here this morning! She'd flip back her perfect silver bob and arch a masterfully shaped eyebrow. "What happened to good manners, young man?" she'd say in her most la-di-da tone of voice while staring him down. My grandma might even tell him to step out and reenact his entry, politely this time.

And you know what? He just might do it. There's something about Rose that compels people, pets, and potted plants to indulge her.

Eric steps out of the kitchen. "The vanilla macaron shells are ready, Chef. Want to check before I stick them in the oven?"

"No, that's fine, go ahead," I say to my sous chef before turning back to Capitaine Adinian.

"We're going to conclude natural death," Adinian says, skipping any form of transition.

I give him a small nod.

"Monsieur Sauve's family said he'd been under a lot of stress over the last two years," he adds. "Too much beer, too little exercise. They had feared he'd end up with a heart attack."

"His *family*?" I was under the impression Maurice Sauve was single. Then again, he never said as much.

Adinian puts his elbow on the counter. "He had a cousin living on the same street."

"I see."

He half-turns toward the door, then scratches the back of his head, and turns toward me again. "Can you recount last evening's events again, everything you remember?"

"Er… again? Why?" The prospect of reliving those moments doesn't appeal to me at all. "Didn't you just say there wasn't any foul play involved?"

"It's just formality. I'm finishing my report, and I want to make sure I have all the details right."

My shoulders slump. "OK."

He heads toward the sitting area, plonks himself down into a vintage bistro chair, and points to another chair. "Have a seat."

Making ourselves at home, are we?

Trying not to show my irritation, I sit down across a round table from him and begin my sad tale of yesterday's macaron-making workshop that didn't go as planned.

He listens, barely taking any notes.

When I get to the part where I asked my students to mix the ingredients I'd prepared for them, Capitaine Adinian leans forward. "Who prepared and laid out the ingredients?"

"I did."

"When?"

"Shortly before the class began."

"Did you leave the shop, even for a brief time, after you had everything ready for the class?" he asks.

"No."

He scribbles something in his little notebook. "Please continue."

"Most participants struggled to get their batter to stiffen," I say. "Some gave up, claiming it was impossible without an electric mixer."

"Did Maurice Sauve give up?"

"Quite the contrary. He whisked unrelentingly, switching hands but never pausing. He was the first to complete the task."

Capitaine Adinian writes that down.

"I gave him one of these." I show Adinian the remaining badges that Flo had made for the workshop.

"Great Baking Potential," he reads aloud.

"Then I went around with his bowl and had everyone admire the perfect consistency of the batter."

"Did anything stand out or seem unusual at that point?"

I gaze up at the ceiling, picturing the scene of me praising Maurice Sauve's firm, satiny batter, students giving him their thumbs-up, and him smiling, visibly stoked. But he isn't just smiling, he's also… Panic squeezing my throat, I zero in on his face. He's panting.

Oh. My. God.

I clap my hand over my mouth. "What if he'd whisked too hard? What if that exertion caused his heart attack?"

"Only an intense workout, especially at freezing temperatures, can trigger a heart attack," Adinian says.

"He whisked intensely."

"Madame Cavallo, I've never heard of anyone whisking themselves to an early grave."

End of Excerpt

You can get The Murderous Macaron separately or in a set of Books 1 - 3, at a reduced price.

ALSO BY ANA T. DREW

THE JULIE CAVALLO INVESTIGATES SERIES

The Murderous Macaron

Pastry chef Julie Cavallo has her freedom, her shop, and a corpse growing cold on her floor.

The Killer Karma

Julie unmasked a killer. Life is good once again… until her sous chef becomes a murder suspect.

The Sinister Superyacht

When a luxury cruise turns deadly, the caterer and her breezy gran must figure out which guest is the killer.

The Shady Chateau

Three unlikely culprits plead guilty for a baron's death at a Napoleonic re-enactment. Who's lying? And why? And who really killed the baron?

The Perils of Paris

When someone tries to kill her sister, it's time for Julie Cavallo to don her sleuthing cap.

The Bloodthirsty Bee

It's springtime in Provence! Trees are in bloom and critters are abuzz — including a murderer or two.

The Deadly Donut

As bodies pile up at the secluded hotel Villa Grare, Julie has precious little time to find the killer!

The Ruthless Rice (coming soon)

When an influential food critic turns up face down in the Rhône River, the gendarmes call it an accident. But Julie disagrees.

CHRISTMAS SPECIALS

The Canceled Christmas (novella, free with signup)

Mayor Victor Jacquet receives a mystifying note. And then his small town mounts a rebellion…

An (un)Orthodox Christmas (novella)

While in Cassis with Gabriel's rowdy relatives, Julie and Gabriel investigate a thorny family situation—and a murder!

The Twelve Suspects of Christmas (full-length novel)

A cold case meets new mayhem in two quirky grandmas' rollicking journey from Provence to Picardie.

The Snow Globe Affair

As Christmas cheer spreads across Paris, a psychic and a mathematician compete in a scavenger hunt — and get entangled in the heist of the century!

Printed in Great Britain
by Amazon

53491259R00158